I0685672

THE
EXEMPLAR

JOSH CHETWYND

Snog Dog Publishing, Denver, Colorado

ISBN (print) 979-8-9992987-0-6
ISBN (ebook) 979-8-9992987-1-3

Cover design by Stefan Prodanovic
Interior design by Emmanuel Okpeniku

For Jennifer, Miller and Becca

Table of Contents

CHAPTER ONE

Will Herndon woke up feeling groggy and uncharacteristically nervous. He was certain something wasn't quite right as he strained to focus his eyes. But when he could finally see his surroundings, everything appeared to be in its proper place.

His sophomore dorm room at Harvard featured all the posters he and his roommate Cooper Fielding had carefully placed on the walls. "It's a bit overkill on the baseball," he thought as he looked at infielder Nolan Arenado wearing the uniform of his hometown team, the Colorado Rockies.

Arenado didn't even play for the Rockies by the time the roommates had put up the poster, but they picked the vintage picture because it reminded them of when Arenado was a superstar at Coors Field and Will and Cooper were kids starting their baseball journey. The boys often talked about how they missed Denver and seeing the mountains. Colorado was a point of pride for both of them. That meant that when many of their Harvard classmates slowly and resentfully became Boston Red Sox fans to fit in with their surroundings, Will and Coop remained true to the Rockies – even when the team was terrible. It was one of the many things that kept the two 19-year-olds so close.

Will's eyes began to shed their bleariness, but his mind continued to feel off-balance. A wave of lightheadedness washed over him as he sat up. He instinctively looked over at Cooper's bed, which was neatly made. The sight puzzled him, though he didn't quite know why. Will fumbled for his phone, foggily recalling his numeric password. He unlocked it to find a photo of his mom, brother, and grandfather. He exhaled and smiled. It was the first calming moment of the morning.

Maybe a look at the news could help him clear his muddied thoughts. But as he tried to connect to the Internet, he found he had no service.

"That's odd," he muttered, remembering his WiFi was usually very reliable. Those two words – that's odd – were the first he'd uttered that day. But, again, it didn't feel right. He had to force them out of his throat and the noise he made was abnormally muted.

That unsettled him again. He was still trying to pinpoint the source of his jitters when there was a knock at the door. Will got up, but his legs were feeling a little heavier than normal. As a result, he walked a bit slower than usual, ambling a bit awkwardly to the front of the room.

"Who is it?" he asked.

There was silence. Will furrowed his brow. "What's going on?"

"Sorry," came a familiar, yet slightly off-pitch, voice. "It's your grandpa."

Will froze. What was he doing all the way in Cambridge? Was someone ill? Had somebody gotten hurt? Deacon Herndon often boasted he'd never traveled east of the Mississippi—not even to watch his beloved grandson play ball. If that was true, it made no sense he'd be at Eliot House on the campus of Harvard University.

He hastily opened the door.

With only a glance of the tall muscular man, Will yelled, "Grandpa!", and launched himself into Deacon's arms. Considering how much this morning was making Will so uncomfortable, seeing his grandpa, who had effectively been his father, filled his heart with joy.

When Will completed his extended hug, he swiveled, and with Deacon to his back, he said, "Come in, have a seat!" Generally speaking, Will was the type of person who would get straight to the point. Under normal circumstances, he'd immediately ask the most logical question – "What are you doing here?" But he was so out of sorts that he suppressed that desire. First, he wanted to enjoy Deacon's presence for at least a moment.

Will sank onto the long sofa that was nestled against the wall across from the two dorm room beds. While Harvard prided itself on its academic reputation, the role that Will and Cooper played in turning the school into a national baseball power had not gone unrewarded. Their room was larger than most – even if the décor proclaimed both were still teenagers.

Deacon was – and had always been – elegantly handsome. The two looked a lot alike. Will and Deacon both stood 6'2" with light-brown skin and dark, distinguished eyes. They each possessed a purposeful approach that made them naturally charismatic. The big difference was that Deacon was bald and had been bald for as long as Will could remember. But even with that feature, Deacon's smooth and easy movements always counteracted any assumption that he was older than his age. A great athlete in his own right, he'd never played anything in college. In fact, he'd never gone to college. Instead, he went straight to work after high school in the construction trade and could proudly say that he'd put his daughter, Will's mom Anya, through a local college in Denver called Metro State.

Will met his grandfather's gaze, finding a heightened, almost unnerving, intensity in his eyes. This didn't necessarily surprise him. Deacon was serious nearly all the time. It was that commitment to discipline that had inspired Will to travel down from his central Denver home in the historically poorer Five Points neighborhood to the wealthy south suburbs to work on his chosen craft of baseball and still find time to perform in the classroom.

But despite his grandfather's humorless expression, and Will's general uneasiness, there was something about his grandfather that looked lighter than normal. Deacon appeared a good 20 years younger than the 73 years he'd been on this planet. Deacon's softer skin and bulkier physique distracted Will from all the other issues swirling around his head.

"Grandpa, have you been working out?" Will blurted, unable to ignore his appearance.

"No more than usual Willie," he responded, averting eye contact. He then sat down and intently turned his head toward his grandson. Staring at Will for the first time, Deacon smiled.

His perfectly white and angular teeth sparkled in the muted morning light that was obscured by the drawn blinds in the room. Will sighed and returned the smile. As much as his grandpa's grin reassured him, Will knew he was only delaying the inevitable. He needed to find out why Deacon was there. His heart began to pound fast as he thought about his mom and his little brother, Royce.

"Is someone sick? Did someone get hurt?" Will said, practically swallowing his words as he quickly tried to ask the questions that he assumed had answers he didn't want to hear.

"No Willie," Deacon said slowly, his gaze drifting. "This isn't about the family." He paused to consider what he just said. "Well, it may be about family but not in the way you would think or would be worried about."

While Will's mind continued to feel adrift at sea, the waves did seem to be calming a bit. He was reassured his grandfather wasn't there to unload a full crate of bad news.

"Then are you here to see me play some ball?" Will asked, hoping his sense of foreboding was misplaced. But as the words left his mouth, a strange certainty hit him: he wasn't sure what time of year it was. In fact, the more he tried to pull facts from his brain, the more he began to realize that there were blind spots in his memory. Will wasn't a drinker, but he must have done something crazy the night before. When he concentrated on trying to remember what it might've been, it was a blank. His heart began to race.

He looked at Coop's bed again and couldn't remember the last time he'd seen him. Coop was his indispensable partner in moments of uncertainty. Where could he be? He was happy to see his grandpa, who he loved so much. But every time Will tried to come up with an additional positive thought it felt off pitch. Will possessed great intuitive senses and everything here pointed in the wrong direction. "Where's Coop?" he thought to himself, getting all-the-more uneasy.

Deacon sensed Will's struggle to process what was going on. He wasn't a man who liked to show emotion, and it took all his strength to avoid crying at the sight of his grandson. He saw much of himself in this boy who had accomplished so much and worked so hard. *Harvard.* His grandson had achieved a spot at the pinnacle of academic excellence. And, not only that, but he'd also already made his mark. As a freshman, he and his best friend Cooper had carried Harvard all the way to the College World Series.

Playing on ESPN, Will shined so brightly that if it hadn't been for the fact that Major League Baseball prohibited players from coming out of college until after their junior year, Will would already have been penciled in as a first-round draft pick. Nevertheless, Will intended to get his degree before embarking on what was sure to be a glorious baseball career. And Cooper, who was a standout player in his own right, would surely go with him every step of the way.

Deacon had to catch himself. He was fantasizing about a past that had already been determined, and the fact that he'd let himself do it at such an important moment left him angry. "I can't get nostalgic," he thought to himself. It was a path that he knew would be very, very destructive if he continued to follow it.

So, he swallowed hard. He saw his grandson's deep unease and accepted he couldn't wait any longer to explain why – or at least partially why – he was here. It would be an awkward and difficult conversation, but he wouldn't let anyone else have it with Will.

CHAPTER TWO

Will never liked to show weakness to his grandfather. Beyond being a father figure, Deacon did so much for him. Deacon never missed a day of work as a construction foreman. He also never failed to take Will to baseball practice. No matter the traffic on University Blvd. or I-25, he made sure Will was on time and looked just like the wealthier players that inevitably made up his team.

By 2015, when Will started coming up, baseball had long morphed into a suburban white boy sport. Inner-city kids like him didn't have the equipment or the infrastructure to compete in America's Pastime. For all the hand wringing and speckling of urban baseball academies across the United States, the primary way to compete in baseball was to enter wealthy, or at least upper middle class, areas and practice with the kids who could afford batting cages in their backyards, private coaches and elite teams that jetted off around the country. Cooper Fielding, who became Will's best friend from the moment they both joined the same travel ball squads as 9-year-olds, was one of those kids.

Despite Cooper's privileged background, he was just as relentlessly hard-working as Will. Even more important than that, despite being a member of one of Denver's blue blood families, he lacked any pretension. While his cousins played golf at the fancy Cherry Hills Country Club, Coop, as Will always called him, was working on blocking balls pitched in the dirt in the hope of becoming a first-rate catcher. He brought some athleticism to the table – though not nearly as much as Will. Still, his dedication and natural leadership qualities were as much of the reason Harvard reached college baseball's highest peaks as Will's all-around natural talent at bat and in centerfield.

"Grandpa, why are you here?" Will asked somberly. "Something just isn't right."

Deacon pursed his lips. "That feeling. It's the right one."

"What do you mean?" Will said, playing over his grandfather's promise that his brother and mom weren't the reason for his visit.

The two locked eyes.

"This is not what it looks like," Deacon said.

"What do you mean?" Will responded with a half-hearted laugh. "My grades are good. I'm following all the rules. Is something up with my academic scholarship?"

"I wish…" Deacon stopped for a moment in order to control his emotions. "I wish it was that simple."

He took a piece of paper from his jacket pocket, unfolded it, read it over for a moment, then neatly folded it back up and carefully placed it back in his pocket. He'd been in this very conversation once before. Only then, it was a bit different.

"Willie," he said, looking directly at his grandson. "If I were to ask you what day it is or what you had for dinner last night, could you tell me?"

Will, already so uncomfortable, stared at the ceiling. Just moments before he'd tried to remember the date and what he'd done the previous evening and he failed. When he tried again, his mind was like a bottomless, black hole. He could remember specific at-bats from when he was 12-years-old. He could recount in great detail getting the call from his college coach telling him he'd been accepted. But yesterday, forget it. In fact, there were clearly many spaces in his mind that were empty.

"Did I get a concussion? I don't remember it happening, but it must be…" Will half-heartedly said before trailing off.

"No Willie, I assure you that you're in perfect health. It's just that…" Deacon also drifted.

"It's just WHAT?" Will exclaimed, losing his patience. Both knew this was totally out of character. Will never questioned his grandfather and, even with his patchy memory, he was well aware that Deacon Herndon did not tolerate talking back. It was the only time Deacon would shoot dagger eyes at his beloved grandson. But eerily, Deacon broke eye contact. It was a sign of fragility the man never showed.

"Will, you are not who or where you think you are," Deacon said in the firmest manner he could assemble in order to leave no doubt in Will's mind that he was not joking.

"I'm not…? I don't get it," Will responded weakly.

Deacon stood up and looked around the room. He'd never seen Will's dorm room, but was sure this was exactly the way it looked.

"All of this, Willie, is just a model. This has been created so your first moments *back* would offer some comfort before somebody served up the reality."

The statement was so outlandish that Will had nothing to say. He waited for his grandfather to continue and start filling in the pieces of what was such an incomplete puzzle. The few moments of quiet gave Deacon the momentum he needed to begin the heavy lifting.

"You, Will Herndon, have been designated an Exemplar," Deacon said. "When you pull up the shades from your window, you won't see a quad in

Cambridge, Massachusetts. You will be somewhere very different. It also won't be 2025. It will be 2090. All in all, you'll recognize things from your time and place. But it's different and so are you. In fact, you aren't quite you. Willie, you are what we call an OHF – an Organic Human Facsimile."

If Will's mind had been navigating high tides before, it was now in a full-fledged tsunami. He was trying to keep up. He wasn't Will Herndon? Or was he? He sure felt like Will Herndon. That said, whatever he was, he understood his grandfather well enough to recognize when he was serious and when he was having some fun. This was definitely not the latter.

He stood up and looked at the drawn blind – unsure whether he wanted to open them.

"What's an OHF?"

"Well back in the day, we'd probably call it a clone. But technology has come a long way. You have close to the identical genetic makeup that you had in 2025. You're a new version – but still the same wonderful and special kid you always were.

Will appreciated his grandpa calling him special. Deacon knew how to meticulously and judiciously offer words of support. They were always well-earned and, as such, were all-the-more appreciated when they arrived.

Will took a couple more steps toward the window. The light at its corners was growing increasingly more intense and Will could feel the warmth. He thought it must be summer or late spring with that kind of early morning sun. He tried to snap his brain back to this strange and traumatic news. Doing the math, some things just didn't add up.

"Grandpa, if it's 2090, you'd be like 140 years old. Even my supposed clone head can tell you are looking way too good for that age."

Deacon chuckled. Even as an OHF, Will was still as sharp as ever.

"You're right about that and it's something worth explaining. Just not at the moment. All I can say is I'm the last of the Herndons, and if there was ever a competition that mattered, you're in it now. That's what being an Exemplar is all about."

Deacon stood up as straight as he could and said: "You are the best of the best that we, as a family, ever produced. Only the best becomes the Exemplar. And if the Herndon bloodline is to survive, it'll be up to you."

An *Exemplar*. Will was familiar with the word and knew what it meant: A person or thing serving as an ideal model. But it didn't quite make sense in this context, Will thought. It was too much to comprehend.

Deacon appreciated that as much as anybody. For precisely that reason, he'd insisted he be the one to introduce Will to this world. He'd hoped that dangling the idea of competition would properly focus his grandson's mind. Willie, at least the Willie that Deacon knew in his mind's eye, loved the idea of competing.

Still standing straight and dignified, Deacon watched as his grandson rolled his shoulders back and strode to the window. He pulled on the drawstring, letting the light rush into the room. He squinted. What he saw was a large circular courtyard surrounded by what looked like twenty floors of windowed white offices that amplified the sunlight streaming down from the sky.

He was definitely not at college.

CHAPTER THREE

B attling the mental overload of it all, Will followed Deacon out of his fake dorm room. He shuffled a bit, zombie-like, numb to all the completely unusual elements bombarding him. Instead of his dorm hallway, they were in a long, white, curving passageway.

He noticed everyone was dressed in white or light pastel colors and struggled to figure out what it meant. After walking silently together for about five minutes, they reached a door. Deacon touched a hand pad. When he removed his hand, a light blue sketch of his palm and fingers remained and after about a second the outline turned green. An elevator opened and they entered. Neither had spoken since leaving the dorm room. Will just didn't know what to say, while Deacon was afraid of what he might say. The elevator whizzed up, and almost instantly, they were at the very top level, above the atrium.

"Willie," Deacon finally said hesitantly. "Inside is an administrator. He'll give you some more information about all this."

"Aren't you coming in with me?" Will responded confused. If ever there was a time when he needed some moral support, now was it. To say Will was feeling vulnerable would be an understatement.

"I wish I could," Deacon said, looking at the ground. "I've already pushed so many rules just to be here. Talk to the man. And, the good news is when you're done, we'll be travelling immediately back to Denver!" Deacon attempted to infuse some enthusiasm, though it felt more like false pep.

"Okay," Will said with a deflated exhale.

Deacon touched a hand pad similar to the one that opened the elevator and the doors opened. Will stepped out into a large white room. Unlike the small window in Will's fake dorm that offered just a snapshot of the internal courtyard, this skybox had a picture-perfect view that gave a better sense of the scope of the complex. It was immense. The white walls appeared to be made of some sort of plastic-like material, and all the windows had a heavy tint. They looked a little like see-through solar panels. At the top of the ring, he could see the bright sun pouring down.

Will was so taken by the view that he didn't notice the person at the white desk until he spoke.

"Mr. Herndon," the slightly overweight man said, offering his hand. "It's a pleasure. My name is Milo Swenson, and I'm the U.S. Administrator here in Eden. Please have a seat."

Despite being a bit heavy, Milo boasted a distinguished appearance. He was about 45 and had a tightly cropped beard and goatee that was brown but speckled with gray. His clothes were a bit tight based on his size, but he wore a sash that obscured his slightly bulging tummy. His demeanor was serious but not cold. There was an air of reliability around him, and Will believed he could trust him.

Will shook his hand and then sat on a white cube located in front of the desk. As soon as he put his weight on the object, it made a noise and then reconfigured into a full chair that conformed perfectly to Will's size. It was the most comfortable seat he'd ever experienced.

"I must say," the man continued, "it's very unusual for OHFs to experience their re-integration here. With the exception of a few Exemplars from local districts, I don't think we've ever had a situation like this. But you are no ordinary OHF."

Milo trailed off and looked closely at Will, before starting again.

"I'm sure you have many questions, but if you'll indulge me, I'd like to fill you in on the big picture. Normally, what I'm about to tell you is provided by your Counselor when you arrive in your district. There was some discussion about whether you'd have any sort of advantage by receiving this information a little early. But as I'm the U.S. Administrator, I do have some latitude to bend the rules, and I believe the background information I have to offer won't impact the competition."

Will nodded his head. He still didn't understand what was going on and, without the comfort of his grandfather's familiar face, he chose to keep quiet.

"Good," Milo responded. "Let's start with where you are and how we got here. In truth, it's one of humanity's pivotal stories."

Milo stood up and gestured grandly toward the window.

"This is the Yukon in Canada and you're at an installation known as Eden."

Milo chose his words carefully. If he were to add that this is where Will was cultivated from genetic fabric, then farmed, with the help of AI, in a series of advanced machines that Will couldn't even comprehend, and finally brought back "online" at his current age, Will might pass out. Such stark explanations were used in the early days of the Exemplars and drove some of them insane. Those mistakes were no longer made.

"Your last memories are from the fall of 2025, right?" Milo asked, as if needing to be reassured Will's memory horizon didn't stretch any deeper into the future.

Will gave a faint head gesture to acknowledge "yes".

"Well, not long after that, the world began changing faster than anyone anticipated. Temperatures climbed higher and higher, faster and faster, every year," Milo continued. "That old story about the frog who gets in the warm pot and doesn't realize the water is slowly boiling him as the temperature rises? Well, that's where we were going. Everyone realized it was getting hotter and, of course, politicians argued over the causes and who or what was to blame. But the wheels just kept spinning, until, eventually, seeing 127 degrees on the thermometer was common on a late spring day."

Milo sat back down to emphasize the seriousness the world was facing.

"Nobody expected the climate to heat up so quickly. All those stories you heard about a future full of rising water levels and famine taking over? They were coming true by 2038. Death tolls were shocking – and not just in Africa. You know hot and bothered? Well, the leaders of the world were at a boiling point. I'd say most people thought that we, as a species, were short on time. This was called the *pre-apocalypse* period. The carnage was so great that people weren't sure whether humanity's day of reckoning had come."

"So, how'd we make it?" Will asked. Discussing the world broadly was easier than going over his situation. After all, the fact that he existed served as a walking, breathing spoiler alert.

"Hard choices," Milo replied.

Milo explained how it came down to a difficult realization that there were simply too many people populating the planet. With the famines – and various outbreaks of civil war (including a short one in the USA) – populations plunged. And, to a certain degree, fewer people meant less fighting over limited resources. Nevertheless, a more controlled strategy was necessary. China introduced a plan that was simply one step beyond a program they'd once had. That country once insisted on a one-child-per-family rule for nearly 40 years. That wasn't going to get numbers in line, so the governments of the world agreed to allow bloodlines to die out.

"As heartless as it might seem in the mind of a person from 2025, it was considered humane compared to what people were going through," Milo said. "Scientists and public policy folks came to an ideal, stable population number and each country was given an allocation. Everybody, the U.S., Russia, Thailand, you name it, recognized how many people they could have and they all figured out plans to determine which families could continue to have kids, and which were at the end of the line. There just wasn't enough food, and energy consumption had to be cut drastically."

"How'd they choose who got to continue?" Will asked, now completely intrigued by the course of history.

"At first, it was like a military draft – if your name got called – your family was prohibited from having any more children. But much like the draft in the United States during the Vietnam War, the rich and powerful families generally figured out ways to sidestep getting the call. In some countries, there was rioting. In the U.S., civil liberties organizations fought a legal battle but lost in the Supreme Court. That was in 2045. The law is often a balancing act between individual rights and what's perceived as the greater good. In this case, our wisest believed the right to have children was less important than national – and world – security. It was amazing, but within less than 20 years the worldwide population had stabilized. Then, a new crisis, one of unintended consequences, cropped up. Population *decline*. Now world leaders had to deal with a birth rate *below* our optimal population numbers. That's when The Crucible was created."

"The Crucible?" Will said, wondering out loud more than really asking a question.

"It gave families the opportunity to revive their bloodlines," Milo said, not skipping a beat. "This offered the combined value of increasing numbers while creating more genetic diversity. I know it didn't seem like it was possible in 2025, but we were closer than we thought to being able to clone people. You know, in the past, in times of sorrow and mass destruction, religion would see a big boost. People would turn to religion to explain the why and how of horrible things and use it to find consolation in the belief that if their time was coming, there was something waiting for them. The leadership response to the pre-apocalypse was deeply troubling for people of faith. First, there was the idea of stopping procreation, and churches fought. But when faced with the prospect of extinction, the human trait of practicality won out. And then came the suggestion of using OHFs to normalize our population level. Predictably, it was also met with resistance as well. But the pushback was surprisingly less than you would have expected. The result was the Crucible."

"What did The Crucible do?" Will asked.

Milo straightened up in his seat. He wanted to navigate this part just right. He needed to thread the needle.

"What *does* The Crucible do?" he corrected. "It's still in existence. It's why you're here."

As Milo added more details to his explanation, he wasn't sure a softening of words could paint an accurate picture. This wasn't the Hunger Games with people dying left and right, but he understood that downplaying it undersold what was at stake.

A group called the WU, short for Worldwide Unity, was responsible for setting acceptable population totals down to the district (Milo was not only the Crucible's U.S. Administrator, but also its representative to the WU). The Crucible, then, was the generic term for a competition that existed in equally apportioned districts around the world. When a given area's population was about to dip below its allotment, a Crucible would be called.

This would be a competition between families who were on the verge of going out of existence. Each family that had *a final remainder* – in other words, just one person who was left in a bloodline – could apply. Four final remainder families were chosen by lottery to compete for *re-initiation*. In the U.S., districts were given considerable leeway in how these contests were organized. For Will, who would return to Denver, the details of his Crucible would be created by the Colorado district.

"But what kind of competition could be created for the final remainders? After all, aren't most of them probably old people?"

"Exactly," Milo responded, pleased by both Will's engagement and perceptiveness. "There needed to be an equal playing field, and it was decided each family should have the best of the best representing them. Enter the Exemplar."

Will had heard that term from his grandfather. *He was his family's Exemplar.*

"The ability to create OHFs meant that with enough biological material, any ancestor to the final remainder could be brought back to champion his or her family," Milo said. "The last remainders, who win the lottery, comb their history for candidates to be their Exemplars. Then a genetic screen is done for the remains of the best candidates and, based on DNA markers, the ideal example of a bloodline is brought back."

Milo paused for a moment to allow Will to connect the dots. The administrator didn't want to have to do it for him. After a moment, he pressed on.

"So, that brings us back to where you are now," Milo said, waving his hands around the room. "When temperatures began to rise globally and resources thinned, Canada became one of the last bastions of strength. Their acreage of tillable farmland rose in their northern reaches and, while they experienced land loss from the rising oceans – like every coastal country – their population per square mile was manageable. When the world started going into a population deficit and the idea of reanimating bloodlines caught on, the biggest fear was that the technology to create Organic Human Facsimiles could be used for evil purposes."

Will's mind quickly filled with images of Stormtroopers in the Star Wars movies. Sure, he thought, clones could be used for galactic conquest.

"No matter how often civilization might come close to ruining Earth, the thirst for power always remains a reoccurring human characteristic," Milo observed. "Like nuclear weapons, the worry was OHFs would become a technology that could be used as a sword. This meant that the handful of scientists who had perfected the cloning secret sauce agreed to move here to the Yukon, which, incidentally, has become quite a nice place to live thanks to climate change, and set up shop in this fortress of a town that was named Eden. As a member of the team, it's a great honor, and commitment, to be included in this essential human endeavor."

Will listened carefully to every word, but it would take time for him to take in the magnitude of what he was being told. It was so much that his mind was like a dam. All the questions were sitting behind an impenetrable wall. He needed to start picking at that cement structure one question at a time to allow the water to flow through.

"Why is it that I remember so much but not everything?" was Will's first effort to break down the wall.

"Primarily, it comes from a memory chip. It was inserted by a referee from your district. It is a carefully produced piece of technology that allows OHF's to remember large amounts of their previous iteration's life. But there are also echoes as well."

"Echoes?"

"Yes, scientists still can't explain it. But, in biological terms, you are basically the same Will Herndon. And, amazingly, with the same building blocks as you had back in 2025, Exemplars sometimes possess memories that don't come from the chip. They were somehow ingrained in the OHF's very fiber. For religious types, this was deeply reassuring. To them, the only explanation was that God's signature was in each of us. For a time, there were various religious leaders who argued it was the Lord's providence and cloning should be restricted to the faithful. But they were in the minority and their effort failed."

Milo halted. He feared he was threatening to over-inform Will. Of course, he knew that Will's memory chip wouldn't be complete even with echoes of the past. He tried to steady himself with a forced smile, but it looked more like a smirk.

"And that's where my story ends," Milo said softly. "You and your grandfather will board a train to Denver. That is your home district and where you will compete in the Crucible."

Milo stood up with the intention of leading him to the door, but Will, who was beginning to build strength in this foreign environment, wasn't done.

"Mr. Swenson," he said. "You said that I was unique. Why is that?"

Milo stopped walking. Standing still and staring out toward the door, he pursed his lips. He'd forgotten to deliver one important directive and was disappointed in himself.

"Normally, OHFs return, so to speak, in their district. We try to give as little time as possible between the reawakening and the start of the Crucible. It cuts down on distractions. But your grandfather made an impassioned plea to give you a bit more time, which brings me to a very important final point."

Milo turned to Will, who was still sitting, and squatted down so that he was eye-to-eye with him.

"As an Exemplar, you represent your bloodline first and yourself second. This means that equally as important as what you know about your past is what you *don't* know. Your mind has been scrubbed of all of your most traumatic experiences. Even Exemplars have traumatic backstories, especially those from troubled eras, and the global Crucible code decrees such events shall not be included in an OHF's memories. Those who created the process wanted to prevent unfair disadvantages to individuals with particularly harrowing memories. It was determined that forcing them to confront those demons led to an uneven playing field. It is an essential aspect of the Crucible's code."

For the first time, Milo looked menacing.

"While in the Crucible, you are strictly prohibited from seeking out any personal information about your past beyond what is provided to you in your chip. Do you understand?" he said.

Will's first reaction was how unfair this was, but he was in no position to argue.

"I do."

"Your grandfather, as is the case with all last remainders, has signed an agreement that he will not dispense any additional information," Milo added. "Obtaining such information can, at the discretion of the chief referee in your district, lead to expulsion from the Crucible."

Milo said locking eyes directly with Will. "Do you understand?" He'd already asked the question, but wanted to reinforce the point, pausing between each word.

"Yes, sir," Will said, reaffirming the only answer that would end the awkward moment.

"Good," Milo responded with a smile.

CHAPTER FOUR

The porter was working hard to make sure Will stayed close to him as they navigated the crowd on the train platform. It was orderly but busy, and the older man, who wasn't accustomed to ferrying someone without luggage onto the long white train, was hell-bent on getting Will to his proper carriage.

"Sorry for all the excitement," the short fellow said, evading hovering luggage carts carrying bags of all shapes and sizes. "The train comes here only once a week. Came in late last night and goes out in 30 minutes and then we don't see it again until next Thursday."

The porter was nervous. Although the man had worked at Eden as the head porter for nearly 15 years, he'd never met an OHF before. He wanted to do everything by-the-book and was careful not to stare at Will – even though he desperately wanted to marvel at him.

Will gazed in awe at what he saw. The long white machine looked more like a vast chain of small bullet trains rather than a series of connected carriages. The large majority of the vehicles had their own nose – although a few appeared to have a second or a third normal carriage. Each mini-train looked like it was lightly touching the one in front of it.

After a few moments of hustling, the two men reached a car with a nose, and the porter touched the side of the vehicle. Just like with his grandfather, a blue outline of his hand appeared, then turned green and a door opened.

Away from the bustle of the other passengers, the porter smiled and said proudly, "Welcome to the Maglev 2068!"

Will walked into a surprisingly spacious car. There was a bed, a table and some seats near each window. The glass was heavily tinted like the windows in Milo Swenson's office. In a few locations, there were what looked like ultra-thin flat screen TVs laid horizontally like tables. The porter walked over to one of them and touched it. Immediately, an image that was unlike anything Will had ever seen before appeared. It was a perfect hologram of the globe. Will was sure that if he reached out and palmed the orb, he'd be able to pick it up and throw it in the air. The porter touched it and it flattened out into a map with the words Eden and Denver on them.

"This isn't like any train I've seen before," Will blurted out.

The porter realized he'd fallen short on his manners. He should have figured that an OHF was likely not from this time and wouldn't know what he was on.

"I'm so sorry," he said. "I'd forgotten your kind might not be familiar with this old lady."

Will physically cringed at the statement, "your kind". He was an African-American kid who had spent extensive time in white neighborhoods playing baseball and knew when someone was trying to use language to minimize him. In this instance, though, Will intuitively recognized that the man's comment had nothing to do with Will's skin tone and everything to do with his OHF status.

He chose to say nothing because he simply wasn't sure how to react. Anyway, the porter didn't notice Will's reaction and jumped into an explanation of the train.

"When the pre-apocalypse began, air travel was one of the first things to be rationed," the man said. "Scientists realized that planes were causing so much damage to the environment. We already had magnetized coil Maglev trains, but engineers had to up their game to make a fast and dependable form of transportation that could replace going by air. Those guys really kept at it. And slowly but surely, they got there. This one has a top speed of 500 mph, which isn't that much slower than old jetliners."

The porter looked out the window trying to crane his neck to see the tracks.

"You can't see it, but the train nearly floats," he said with pride. "Anyway, the hard part was getting the infrastructure in place. North America was the first continent to go full Maglev. This train is actually a collection of different trains. At certain points on your journey, you'll hear a *pop*, and part of the train will break off to its destination. Now, normally a town as small as Watson Lake, Yukon, which is where we are here in Eden, wouldn't be a junction for a Maglev 2068 and you'd have to travel to your closest junction before getting on one of these babies. But because of Eden, you're lucky. You won't have to connect anywhere to get to Denver. You're going to a one-car stop as you and your grandfather are the only two passengers heading to your destination. This means you'll be able to go at top speed for a large part of your journey. It should take you just a little over six hours to get there. Your estimated time of arrival is 4:15 p.m. Denver time."

Will surveyed the car as he listened and walked over to a panel near the window. The porter smiled because Will was touching his favorite element of the Maglev.

"That's the Era Simulator," the porter said with a smile. "As you're travelling, press the green arrow and then toggle to the date you want to see outside. You'll get a sense of that era's weather, the landscape, everything!"

Will looked up at him and smiled back. The porter clearly loved his job, and his enthusiasm was heartening.

"When will my grandpa be coming along?" Will asked longing to see the only familiar face he knew.

"I was told he'd be just a couple of minutes behind us. He came in on the night train so I'm sure he'll find his way just fine. Drinks and food can be ordered by touching this pad. Otherwise, I'll leave you to get settled. I wish you a safe and smooth journey."

The porter turned to leave the cabin, but stopped just short of the door. He didn't know if he'd ever meet an OHF face-to-face again and couldn't help himself. He turned back to Will and asked in almost a whisper.

"What's it like?"

The porter was like a child – compelled to ask, but embarrassed to do so.

At first, Will wasn't completely sure what the man was getting at. But he had a sense and didn't like it. He tried to control his emotions, but he spoke with some edge in his voice.

"What is *what* like?"

The porter could tell he'd made a mistake but figured he was in too deep.

"What's it like to be an OHF?"

Will thought for a moment. He had been an OHF for about one hour and was befuddled every step he took.

"What's it like to be you?" Will responded defiantly.

"I dunno. Normal, I guess," the porter responded.

"Well, that's what it's like for me."

Just as Will said those words, Deacon entered the compartment. The porter looked at him and hurried off the train.

Deacon could sense that he'd entered into an uncomfortable situation, but chose to ignore it because he was well-aware it would be the first of many.

A warm *ding dong* chimed, telling passengers the Maglev was about to get underway.

"You ready to go home?" Deacon offered Will with a smile. "I've got your new passport, birth certificate and all other documents. So, we're good to go."

Barely jerking, the train got underway effortlessly and Will eased into one of the seats by the window. He was silent in the hopes that Deacon would initiate conversation and begin unraveling more of this foreign world to him.

He was immediately disappointed when Deacon headed to the bed on the other side of the room.

"Willie, I've been up for 36 hours straight. I took the train in this morning and didn't sleep at all coming out. I need just a bit of rest. Are you going to be okay?"

Deacon feared he was being a bit harsh in the request. It was more abrupt than he wanted, but he was so tired and knew he wouldn't be able to think straight without some rest.

"Sure," Will said. He was not okay and needed his grandfather now. But he always respected the man, and he intended to be the person he'd always been – or at least was.

"Can I ask you just one question?" Will reflexively added before Deacon could lie down.

Deacon's heart skipped a beat. No matter what, he was not going to mess this up for his grandson or his bloodline. Each answer would be carefully vetted in his mind. At the same time, he didn't want to show any fear on his part, so he calmed himself and answered smoothly, "Sure, Willie."

"What day is it?"

Deacon laughed. He assumed every question would be a test. He chided himself for being so uptight.

"November 23, 2090. Now, I'm going to bed!"

Deacon put his head down and within moments was asleep. Will looked out the window to see the large walled fortress Eden quickly disappearing in the background. In his mind, he was still born in Denver, but logically, he grasped that like all OHFs, he was actually made in Canada.

The train was now whisking through green and lush prairie. Will manipulated the large flat tablet and a weather report popped up in front of him. It was 61 degrees with a 40 percent chance of light rain. He then followed the porter's instructions and toggled to 2025. Will's mouth immediately became slack as he looked out the window to see what looked just as real to him as the prairie he'd just been viewing. But instead of verdant grassland, the landscape was now harsh and icy, the sky far darker, and snow was falling.

The panel now said *24 degrees Fahrenheit, snow accumulation: four inches.* For hours, he watched what 2025 looked like, toggling back to the present every once in a while. It was so absorbing, and scary, to see the difference. Slowly, as the train quietly moved south (the only loud noise was a periodic *pop* when a part of the Maglev broke off for a different destination), Will watched the green change to a brown. The transition was gradual but noticeable, and the only aspect of the view that seemed to show up again and again were these vast fields of small white buildings with black turbines in the center. Each time one of these compounds zoomed by there were hundreds of these small structures. When he was in high school, Will once played in a baseball tournament in Tucson, Arizona. These perfectly organized buildings reminded him of seeing airplane graveyards with neat rows of old decaying aircrafts – vast and strangely mesmerizing.

While he was intrigued by the turbine farms, the farther they went, the drier the world became and the less he looked at the actual world, preferring to move to the November 2025 setting instead.

"What am I doing?" Will thought to himself.

There was so much he wanted to know. Why was he so special that his grandfather had picked him up in the Yukon? And, more importantly, what happened to the people most important to him: his mom, his brother Royce, and his best friend Coop. He could run those questions in his head all day, but that wouldn't yield answers. He needed to set a plan for himself. Will was conditioned to set goals and meet – or, more often than not, exceed – them. He was painstaking in constructing a roadmap to success. What did he need to eat? How much did he need to sleep? What exercises were required to get him in optimal shape?

The only problem was that he currently understood so few of the variables he was facing. He would be entering something called the Crucible, and his family's bloodline was at stake. He got that. But he lacked so much of the important background about himself that could help him tailor a plan. Surely, there were scattered memories from before his 19th year, which is all he could currently remember. Would that help him in this competition?

Recognizing his limitations, he decided he needed a shorter horizon for his goals. First up was suppressing all the anxiety that was welling up just below the surface. He'd been chosen as an Exemplar for a reason. He'd always trusted in the system. Every obstacle that Will faced in his life – sports, school, limited financial means – was overcome with hard work and commitment. This wouldn't have to be any different. There was no room for fear.

Second, forget what Milo Swenson said about his past. He would get Deacon to tell him why he couldn't remember more. From the time Will was a small boy, they'd always been able to communicate well. He could count on him to share the hard truths. More than ever, he needed those answers to figure out a way to perform his best.

Though he possessed no specific memory that told him otherwise, there was more to his life than waking up in his dorm room. So much more had happened. It was the one fact he was certain was correct and he could feel it. For a moment, he allowed himself to wonder whether he and Coop had led Harvard to its first NCAA baseball championship in the spring of 2026. The team was going to be good and ... then he caught himself. There was unquestionably a long list of more important things he needed to know both to succeed in this world and to keep his sanity.

CHAPTER FIVE

Originally opened in 1881, Denver's Union Station had been renovated many times in its 200-plus-year history. Most of the past versions would have appeared familiar to Will, but the way it looked now did not. This was surprising, since recognizable pieces of the past were usually embedded in any present. Will was now six decades into the future and clearly the intervening years had been traumatic because, in order to make it to the current time, this version of the old train terminal was fundamentally changed in so many key ways to keep the landmark running.

While the main part of the station was big and busy, just as he'd remembered it, the grand ceilings were gone. The large concourse area was now broken into more compact rooms with underground tunnels leading to and from all the platforms. It wasn't just that the walls were white – like so much in this world – but they were also made of a different material than the stucco or concrete Will might expect. It was a plastic-like substance, similar to the stuff used to make the massive building in the Yukon, where he'd woken up. When Will came closer, he could see small holes peppering the sides of the building. He felt a cool air and thought it was like a wall-to-wall air hockey table.

As Deacon led Will to the exit, he kept reminding himself of the rules. He could give a broad overview of the world to his grandson, and the basic overlay of his own life. But he was barred from discussing the tremendously traumatic elements of Will's own life. One exception Deacon fought hard for was he could tell Will about what happened to his mom and brother. The trauma of that information was ruled "extraneous" and was, therefore, permissible. Deacon thought it was insulting to call what happened to Anya and Royce extraneous, but he took the win.

"Mavis, please come get us on Wynkoop St.," Deacon said to a thin band on his wrist as they walked out into the 85-degree late afternoon.

"I will be there in 2 minutes, 25 seconds," said a voice that sounded like the cousin of Siri from the iPhones that were popular in Will's day.

It was too hot to be November, Will thought. Because of the altitude, the direct sunlight always felt more powerful than anywhere else he'd been. But this still felt like an 85-degree summer day.

"Dang, grandpa, it's unseasonably warm."

"Nah, Willie, it's the new normal."

Will already got that, but had momentarily forgotten because he was distracted by a lower downtown Denver that looked so very different from what he knew. In Will's lifetime, "LoDo" reflected a continuity of architecture that tied the area to the early 20th century. The neighborhood's old buildings, which were cleaned up in the 1990s after decades of disrepair, were grand concrete monuments to Denver's longstanding history as the Rocky Mountains' preeminent city.

But no more. With very few exceptions, there were hardly any buildings more than two stories high, all of them made of that white material. Will did the math. This was almost exactly 65 years since his last memory. If he were going to go back 65 years from 2025, it would be 1960. Sure, the world would be different, but he didn't think it would be this different.

Deacon noticed Will staring at the buildings. "Yeah, you'll see some old buildings. I still live in our old Denver Square home in Five Points. But they cost so much to cool. That white plastic-like polymer is called Millinex. It changed everything – a wonder creation. It has cooling properties that helped humans survive even in constant 130-degree weather. Shelter, after all, was the first thing needed when faced with an unpredictable environment."

"Sounds great," Will said, looking around and only paying half-attention.

"It is great," Deacon said with authority, in the hope of getting his grandson's attention. "It's how your grandpa makes a living. Homes have changed completely. You'll now see the Ratzenberger design everywhere. They look like two-story igloos, but the majority of these structures are located underground. The shell absorbs solar power. They're cool, durable and constructed with 3D printers. I run a 3D printing crew that builds Ratzenbergers. Ah, Mavis has arrived."

Mavis was his car. It featured a pale peach exterior with a Tiffany blue interior. A honeycomb pattern on the top of the automobile looked like next-generation solar panels. Deacon opened the door to the back of the car for Will. He was slightly taller than the cushioned bench allowed, but the front seat sensed the misalignment and moved up. Seat belts were still the same, and Will buckled his as Deacon went around to the other side and sat in the back next to his grandson. "Mavis, let's go home," he said, peeking at Will out of the corner of his eye.

"Yep, self-driving cars," he added before Will could ask. Because a driver was no longer needed, the shape of the car was very different overall, boxier than those in the early 21st century, which allowed for more passengers. Even so, the corners were still rounded at the edges as the human desire for a little style still existed. There was a front but it was just for additional seating and emergencies if the car malfunctioned.

Deacon sensed where Will's mind was going. Everyone thinks they live in the most interesting times. They believe the end days may be just around the corner. But for centuries, humanity had dodged bullet after bullet. There were great advances like getting to space. But no half-century could compare with the last 50 years. Sure, there were some scary aspects, but Will lived in a world of steady progress. However, not long after his memory ended there had been a huge step back. It was necessary, Deacon thought. Before Earth's most dominant beasts, humans, could begin to take a significant leap forward again, they needed to truly stumble.

Will fell silent. He'd reached information overload. He stared out the window as the car snaked its way through the downtown streets, which was a patchwork of the recognizable and the completely odd. Gas stations were gone, replaced by what looked like electrical stands. Will noticed the nearly silent hum of the electric cars that appeared to have completely replaced automobiles with combustion engines. There was also more open space and fewer vehicles. He still didn't know the day of the week, but Will would have expected more traffic if it was a weekday.

As they left downtown, Will saw more of the Ratzenbergers. They were a completely foreign construction, but what struck him was how homogeneous they were. Nobody had grass lawns and each house was nearly indistinguishable from the next.

"Couldn't they personalize the houses a bit?" Will asked looking out the window.

"The Ratzenbergers are like living breathing organisms. They need to be just right to get the flow of air into the homes on the hottest days. You wouldn't put a tattoo on a beautiful woman, would you?"

Will smiled. While Deacon looked younger than Will ever remembered, his grandpa was showing his age with that comment. For Will's generation you sure would put a tattoo on a beautiful woman. It was a badge of individuality. But Deacon thought such things weren't right. Unlike so many of his friends, Will bought Deacon's perspective and never got one himself. But he wondered if he had a tattoo, whether they would have put it on his OHF self. He figured they wouldn't go that far.

"So is individuality a thing of the past?" Will asked.

"I wouldn't say that," Deacon said. "But after great disasters, people begin looking for ways to increase sameness. They aim to cling to the things that bind them. Whether it's clothes or houses, they want to remind themselves they have more in common than they have different. It becomes reassuring. I can tell you that what the world endured – the famine, the rioting and the death – was enough of a disaster. It was the pre-apocalypse times. I reckon no one thought they needed a unique lawn or a big house to tell them they were special for living through it. The fact they survived already told them that. Then again, it's been a good amount of time since those years, so maybe we're in for a change soon."

Will appreciated the value of sameness. He always believed that the teams he played for that performed the best did so by, metaphorically, all rowing in the same direction at the same speed. Unity through a shared look and approach, he figured, eliminated distractions. Will never wore bling on a baseball diamond and never tried to stand out with anything other than his drive and performance.

Deacon was more fidgety than normal and kept looking at Will as if for a sign. Will sensed his grandpa was uncomfortable, which didn't help his efforts to keep calm. To distract from the moment, Will began to strategize. "Should I jump right into questions or let the situation breathe a bit?" he pondered. He'd hoped that they would have time on the train, but Deacon had slept until just before arriving in Denver. Will decided to wait. He would keep it light for the moment.

"Where are we going?" he asked.

"Home, my boy. Home."

CHAPTER SIX

The house looked almost like he remembered it. Though the block featured a number of the bubble-like Ratzenberger homes, his grandfather's two-story brick structure stood out as a proud artifact to a time even before Will was born. Built in 1903, it was purchased by Deacon in 1985. The transition from a small one-bedroom apartment in a particularly unsafe location just off of Colfax Avenue to this beachhead of relative luxury was a huge achievement for the man. It meant a better life for his wife, Charlotte, and two-year-old daughter, Anya.

It wasn't a perfect transition. The home was in Five Points, Denver's historically African-American neighborhood. In the late 1800s and into the first half of the twentieth century, the area was resolutely middle class. In fact, it was known as the "Harlem of the West" and attracted such jazz greats as Billie Holiday, Count Basie and Dizzy Gillespie to play in clubs on its streets. But by the 1970s, drugs and crime made the area a far more dangerous proposition.

The four-bedroom house admittedly needed work, but that sort of problem was never an obstacle for Deacon. He spent every off-hour and every spare moment fixing pipes, patching walls and re-tiling bathrooms. As for the neighborhood, he kept a watchful eye over his family, working hard to shield his daughter and wife from the problems that surrounded them.

Years later, in 2012, when Anya, Will, and Will's infant brother, Royce, moved to the house after Anya's failed marriage, there was never a question or a criticism from Deacon. In truth, the man was glad to have the company as his beloved Charlotte had passed away from lung cancer just a year earlier. Will never really knew his father, who was rarely around, and Deacon straightforwardly slipped into that role. So much so, that rather than take the last name of his absent dad, he was insistent that he be known as Will *Herndon* rather than Will Jones. The Herndons were *his* family, and he had it legally changed before he was even a teenager.

The house was so meaningful to Deacon, but given the circumstances of world events, Will couldn't believe it had weathered the storm. As he stood in the hot late afternoon of the day admiring it, Deacon put his arm around him.

"Nobody in the family would ever let it go," Deacon said. "It was the greatest compliment I ever had."

The pair walked up the four steps to the porch and the front door. While at first glance the place looked so familiar to Will, he did notice some differences. A thin transparent coat covered all the outside brick and the front door was now white and made of that same plastic-like Millinex polymer as the Ratzenbergers. Deacon put his hand on the door knob, producing an almost immediate unlocking sound.

Inside, as Will could predict by this point, the house was also white – furniture, walls, everything had been gutted. The chairs and sofas were made of a material that looked gel-like and there were cubes that were surely the same as one that morphed into a chair in Milo Swenson's office. Just like Union Station, the walls emitted cool air. He had to admit it was far more comfortable than the outside.

"I was lucky," Deacon said, trying to avoid Will's questions by controlling the conversation and sidestepping the issues he couldn't discuss. "The place had been in pretty bad shape, but between my job and my federal pension, I had enough to whip the old girl into shape. It's a bit muggy in the summers compared to the Ratzenbergers, but it's no bother. This is a place of so many memories."

Will roamed the front room looking at pictures. He even recognized a few very old tattered ones in frames. But most were a form of high-resolution holograms. The clarity was astonishing compared to those see-through versions he could remember seeing in those old sci-fi films. These were thick and complete, like those on the Maglev, and if you didn't touch them, you might not realize that they were less than solid.

He studied one featuring an older woman, who he was sure was his mom. Then there was a hologram of his grandpa sitting on a rocking chair out on the porch. He looked tired and weathered. Will scrutinized the image and took a quick glance at Deacon, who was walking into the kitchen. He peered at the picture again and while the man he was now with was arguably the same as the one he was looking at, the version of his grandpa in the hologram was much, much older.

"Do you want anything to eat?" Deacon asked from the other room. "There was a time when it was hard to get produce. But leave it to scientists, they came up with towers to grow the stuff. People gave up on complaining about GMOs and were just happy to eat something fresh. Meat's a little harder to come by as there are limits on raising cows, pigs and chickens. We're definitely more careful about water use. But you get used to it."

"No thanks," Will said as he continued to assess each image.

"How about a drink then? You used to love grape juice."

Deacon's statement gave Will pause. For a moment, he had to mine the recesses of his mind. It was as if he was asking himself, 'Do I really like grape juice?' His brain slowly whispered the answer, 'yes.' The time it took for that reckoning was demoralizing to Will. It reminded him that, perhaps, he wasn't really fully himself.

But whether he was the "real" Will or not, this strapping version shared the same steely fortitude. He gritted his teeth and brushed aside doubt.

"Yeah, grandpa, that would be great," he declared with resolve. He probably said it with more certainty than he needed for the moment, but he figured he needed a strong statement to reassure himself that he was alive and that he was there for a reason.

Deacon came back in with an opaque white cup.

"Here you go," he said. "I know, everything's white. With the heat, it just became the color of the time and it stuck. I miss more wood and cement, but advanced materials are all produced now to keep things, for the most part, cool. When it comes to fashion, winter quickly became the new summer. And, well, summer became a time to avoid going outdoors."

Deacon chuckled as he handed over the drink. The grape juice was cool and refreshing to Will's throat. He hadn't spoken too much since he'd awakened in what he thought was his college dorm room. But, as far as he knew, this was the first thing this version of Will had eaten or drank and it felt a bit strange, like his body was getting used to it.

After another swig, Will looked around again before asking a question that was burning in his head even more than details on the Crucible or what he was expected to do as an Exemplar. It was time.

"Grandpa," Will said in a questioning voice. "What happened to mama and Royce?

Deacon was happy the conversation had remained light, but he was equally pleased to finally get to this question. He'd anticipated it and had practiced in his mind how he would respond. There were so many difficult answers Deacon was aware Will would have to hear down the road, and this was the only one he was allowed to deliver. In truth, Will's story was too difficult for one man to explain. But when it came to revealing the fate of his mother and brother, he wouldn't cede that responsibility to anybody else.

The hard part of it all was Will's memories of both his mom and brother were of two happy people. Anya was a physician's assistant and Royce was a precocious but sweet 13-year-old when Will had left for college.

"Willie, there are a lot of stories you'll eventually hear about the Herndon clan," Deacon started. "In truth, so much of it will be tough to accept and, maybe, even harder to understand. When it became clear that you'd be our bloodline's Exemplar, I was asked whether the Will I knew could handle those trials. I mean biblical trials. The trials of Job. To be honest, I wasn't sure if any man – or teenager – could. But I said with confidence that if anyone could, it would be my Willie. Whether you were on the ball field, or in the classroom, or picking up your brother when me and your mom were working and then riding two buses to get home, you never complained, and you always kept grinding."

Will lacked any memories to back up Deacon's assertions about his family's hard times, but his grandpa's words didn't surprise him. It was as if his bones recognized he and his family had somehow become forsaken. Each sentence that left Deacon's mouth further reinforced that understanding. Each word was like a brick that could be used to build a wall he would create as protection from everything and anything that would come next. I've worked so hard to be a winner, Will thought to himself, and there would always be obstacles. He would just have to navigate them one at a time.

For a moment, there was silence in the room. Deacon was gathering courage.

"Your mother died in 2034. She got sick quickly and passed just as fast. It was just her time," said Deacon, who usually spoke in a slow rhythm, but offered that news with a sharp pacing.

Will, who was always skilled at reading people, could tell the man was trying to speed through this and he wasn't going to push for more detail on that. Was he there? He tried to access his memory like he did with the grape juice, but there was nothing that drew him past being in the fall of his sophomore year at college.

"And Royce?"

"And Royce..." Deacon said, looking up at the sky with a wry smile. "Man, that boy was mischievous." Deacon's grin slowly transformed into a frown. "Unfortunately, what was cute when he was young was not a good thing when he got older. But I'm afraid that Royce never quite found his place in this world and took his life at age 23."

Silence again. It was easy for him to think of cheerful moments with his brother. His mom's passing, as sad as it might be, didn't compare with this story. How could he have not saved his brother? Royce always listened to him. It felt like the brick wall Will was trying to construct was facing an undeniable and unbeatable pressure.

"Breathe," he said quietly to himself. He looked at the floor. The wood still looked original but had that same coating he saw on the outside of the house.

"Was I there? Why can't I remember any of this?"

"It's complicated," Deacon sighed. Being an OHF came with strings attached, Deacon explained. "As an Exemplar, you are given only foundational memory through the chip planted in your brain."

Will had heard all this. He didn't want or need to hear it again. Frustration was welling up, but he opted to give his grandfather the benefit of the doubt so he continued to listen.

"What is included is carefully determined," Deacon continued, "and it's the role of your Counselor, who is your teacher and overseer in the Crucible, to help you through the rough patches. Over time, there will also be echoes of memories that come back. Sometimes in dreams. Sometimes when you least expect it. Beyond that, you do have your last remainder to offer some broad historical context – but often that person never even knew the Exemplar. That's the basis for your knowledge."

Watching his grandfather speak, he considered a fundamental question about *his* last remainder. It didn't make sense. Deacon looked great but had to be well-more than a century old. Will remembered that his grandfather had told him back in his dorm room that he'd at least explain that fuzzy math.

"Grandpa, how are you my last remainder? I mean, you were born in 1952, and you promised …"

Deacon cut him off. He'd already disclosed the maximum information he was allowed to provide, and now Will was asking a question that he couldn't answer without putting his grandson's position in the Crucible in jeopardy. Deacon was angry at himself for creating this opening and, in his next words, he took it out on Will.

"I *can't* discuss it," he blurted out more loudly than he intended. He tried to reel his emotions back in. "I get your interest in some things that seem weird, but I'm just limited on what I can share while you're in the Crucible."

Will had heard enough. This wasn't fair and, without thinking, impatiently interrupted.

"I know," he interjected with a mocking tone. "When it comes to the bad things, the big powers mandated that anything traumatic must be cut from my basic memory."

"Your role now is as a representative of this family and that's enough of a heavy load," Deacon said, again, trying to ignore Will's exasperation. "Those that govern this process didn't believe they needed to add to that weight by giving you the memories of death and heartache. If you want to learn about those things, it can wait."

Then Deacon paused for dramatic effect and placed his hand on Will's chin to move the teenager's eyes to meet his.

"For now, Willie, don't go looking for the pain. Whether you like it or not, it will eventually find you."

"But grandpa, that's just not enough," Will said testily. He'd reached a boiling point. "I've got to know more. Why did you pick me up in the Yukon if that doesn't normally happen? What does that have to do with my past? If I'm going to be the best version of myself, you've got to tell me more. I need to understand what made me an Exemplar. How can I do that without my memories!"

This response was uncharacteristic. Will always followed the rules. He'd lashed out at his grandfather back in the Yukon and now he was doing it for a second time. Did this mean that Will, version 2.0, was fundamentally different from his former self? Will couldn't know that Deacon had already battled just to give him knowledge on the fate of his mom and brother. Now, he was acting like a spoiled teenager. Deacon hadn't raised him that way. He scowled and Will reflexively recoiled. The teenager knew he'd gone too far. Deacon was angry, but he was also sensitive to everything Will was going through, so he waited a moment before he spoke.

"I've said it nicely, but don't make me say it again – don't look to the past. You have a job to do and there are rules we all have to follow."

Deacon moved his hand to pat Will on the back of the head and offered his best comforting smile. Will didn't want to reciprocate, but he did love his grandpa so he forced a smile back. He could feel the unconditional love and, so, begrudgingly, he offered a "sure, grandpa."

"Good," Deacon said. He'd hoped that this conversation would unburden himself, but it didn't feel that way.

"I need to go to work, but here's your schedule," Deacon said, changing the subject. "You report to the Crucible Compound tomorrow. You'll recognize it. It's what used to be the University of Denver. There's testing and lots more for you to learn. You get about a month before the Crucible starts so the preparation begins immediately. Though, good news, the day after tomorrow is Thanksgiving and, while meat is usually hard to come by, I got a Turkey!"

Deacon got up and walked to the door. He stopped for a moment, turned around and said, "I love you, Willie. I'm happy you're here."

He then walked out into the bright sun.

CHAPTER SEVEN

It was a fairly restful sleep for Will Herndon, considering how much – and how little – he knew. He was an Exemplar, who would fight for his family's bloodline. That was the easy part. He wasn't happy his grandpa had shut down any additional discussion of his past. All he could do for the moment was concentrate on the task of being an Exemplar. But even with Deacon around, he felt so alone in his quest to reach this goal.

At that moment, more than ever to this point in his new life as an OHF, Will wished he could remember beyond the start of his sophomore year. Why did it all stop there? Clearly, there was far more story to be told. Could the rest of his life have been so horrible that it was all cut out? Or were the tough times, like his mom and brother's lives, so intertwined with his that to remind him of any more would be distracting from his pressing mission? Adding up the years, it was possible that an old version of his best friend Cooper Fielding was still around. Despite the age difference, if he was, Will was confident his old friend would help him through this crazy world he'd now entered and the contest to come.

He was thoroughly trained in how to approach competition. But, in the past, he'd always done it as part of a team. Baseball was the perfect sport for him. He loved the camaraderie. He loved the group effort to achieve a winning result. But he also appreciated the individual moments of performance. Your actions could stand out in baseball while still having the safety of your teammates to pick you up when you didn't quite get it done.

In particular, he was grateful for Cooper Fielding. Coop was the ultimate team player. He was a catcher, who had overcome being a good-but-not-great athlete by devoting consistent commitment to his craft. Baseball and catching, in particular, were perfect for that attitude. It was a position that rewarded hard work, and for that reason, it was a spot many, particularly top players, shied away from.

In spite of all that, it would be impossible to say Coop was an overachiever. The Fielding clan was one of the first families in Denver. They were up there with the Bonfils and the Evans. Buildings were named after the Fieldings, and every opportunity was laid before him. His future could have easily been a trust fund to set up any sort of business and a ton of golf outings. His older brother Brandt had already taken that route by the time Coop and Will were in college.

Instead, Coop marshaled his resources to better himself in every element of his life. Elite academics were not a high family priority, but when Coop was struggling in math in high school, he insisted on a tutor. As for baseball, he lucked into the right time and place to embrace the sport. A generation before he would have taken the typical route of simply playing Little League and then going on to high school and American Legion baseball. He would have either been good enough for college and the pros based on innate ability and the quality of the handful of team coaches he came in contact with, or not.

But Coop came of age at a time of specialization. Not only did he have a batting cage in his backyard (which wasn't uncommon in his upscale south suburban Denver neighborhood), but he also had a personal hitting coach and a personal catching coach. Then there were the travel teams, which began when the boys were 9, and by the time they were sophomores in high school, trekking to showcases to prove one's value to college coaches and pro scouts was second nature.

Through all of it, Coop took Will along for the ride. They spent countless afternoons swinging in Coop's cage together. And, while Will didn't have Coop's personal coaches, the Fielding family had paid for his travel ball expenses – and showcase fees – throughout.

No doubt, Will was the better athlete and the better prospect. This meant offers to bigger baseball schools than Harvard and even the enjoyment of being drafted in the 26th round by the Rockies – an offer he knew he wouldn't take over college. Stanford, which was the best of all worlds, was offering an all-expenses-paid opportunity. But when Coop, who had secured his spot at Harvard thanks to both academic and athletic performance, said four simple words, it would shift the balance.

"Let's do it together."

Coop said it with the determination of a leader, and there was no way Will could say no.

So, they did. Both were Freshman All-Americans as they took a team from the Ivy League to the College World Series for the first time since 1974.

The more he thought about Coop, the more he recognized that his friend was always there for him. Will wasn't great with girls, but Coop always found a way to make sure he had a date for big events. Will was always confident in the field, but if the mechanics of his batting swing got a little out of alignment, Coop often recognized it before the coaches and gave him just the right advice – and encouragement – to get him back on track.

A nagging fear started to develop in his stomach. Between his grandfather being distant and Coop not being with him, did he have enough support to handle all of this?

Will took a deep breath, exhaled slowly and then shook his shoulders around.

"There's no room for pity or doubt," he whispered to himself.

He then went into the bathroom. It appeared a lot like the ones he used in his time, though there were certainly some differences. The faucet was a little narrower and the water pressure was not as strong. The toilet also looked a little odd. It wasn't as round below the seat and there wasn't any water at the bottom. It was more like the type he'd seen on airplanes. Both pieces of plumbing had digital displays indicating how much water was used in the month and how much more was allowed. Clearly, water rationing was still a part of life. Will awkwardly learned just how much, when, rather than water, the toilet used some sort of pneumatic sucking process that was wholly uncomfortable if you got too close.

Following his near bathroom catastrophe, he cleaned his hands with a type of sanitary solution (water was apparently too valuable for this activity, too) and steadied himself. He then looked into the mirror. His hair was cropped short and his complexion clear. He was thorough about washing his face and was proud of his perfect skin.

As he looked closely in the mirror, he found the answer to his question from the day before about tattoos. A scar over his left eye was missing. It was a small blemish that he'd gotten when his two-year-old brother smacked him in the head with a wooden bat by mistake. Will didn't even realize the damage until blood started bleeding profusely. He ultimately went to the hospital to get three stitches. He examined the perfect skin above his eyebrow.

"I guess that doesn't rate as being traumatic enough to take away from my memory," he reflected. He thought about his brother. Why couldn't he help him?

He tried to move on from his uneasiness, but even more than his missing scar, what was beginning to bother him was just *how* he retained the memories that they'd allowed him to possess. It was so unnatural. As he grew into his late teens, Will always considered a memory a bit like a printed copy of the original activity. And, each time he summoned that same memory it was like the most recent copy was being copied again. This process made the memory a little more faded each time it was accessed. A memory never totally went away, but when he'd pull up his first home run when he was 9 years old for the 500th time, the picture in his head was just a bit less vivid – not as colorful and a little cloudy.

Now, memories came to Will so differently. In an Exemplar's head, everything was sharp 100 percent of the time.

For instance, if he wanted to think about that home run when he was nine, it was in high definition – which was particularly weird because his mind somehow knew that it should be a faded thought. Over and over again, he pulled up mental pictures of the past, but no matter what else was placed in his mind, those old memories remained pristine.

Will figured this ability was a huge advantage over the general population. After all, it was like crystal-clear photographic memory. But this phenomenon led him to a series of troubling internal questions: First, was this advantage to compensate for the missed memories? If an OHF got to know less about his or her past, was this clarity a way to at least ensure that what they did receive was a better quality? Second, how was any of this possible? How could they plant these exact memories into his mind? He figured it was conceivable that 2090 technology had improved in ways that he never thought possible 60 years earlier. But it was so outlandish to him that it led to a more ominous thought – were these memories manipulated? If the people from Eden weren't there to witness these moments, did they cut corners or artificially create these scenes he could seamlessly recall? Were these memories not exactly what happened but just similar recreations of the past?

"Willie," Deacon yelled from the bottom of the stairs, breaking Will out of his deep thoughts. "It's time to go. You need to be at the Crucible Compound."

Will walked back into the bedroom where a pair of pants and a shirt (of course, both white) were sitting on a dresser. As soon as he put on the perfectly fitting outfit, he was instantly cooled. He slid on his sneakers that seemed to have some form of built-in socks and the shoes immediately conformed to his feet. It was snug but comfortable. Everything he wore was so breathable, and it energized him.

He bounded down the stairs to see his grandpa, dressed in a similar white outfit. Will realized that Deacon had dressed as if he'd been in the past when they first met in his fake dorm room so as not to freak him out.

"I like the clothes," Will said to his grandfather.

"Yeah, lots of nanotechnology. It goes a long way to keeping you cool on even the hottest days. Here's a breakfast sandwich. Why don't you eat it on the way."

Deacon handed Will what looked like a hot pocket. It was room temperature, but when Will bit into it and began to chew, it was fantastic. It was like that gum in the story of Willy Wonka that combined all the flavors of a meal into one.

"They sure cracked the code on this," Will said, thoroughly enjoying the sandwich as they hopped into the back of the car.

"Mavis, Crucible Compound on University Boulevard," Deacon said and the car was on its way.

If Will wasn't going to get answers from his grandpa, he was committed to keeping the conversation light.

"Grandpa, why'd you name your car Mavis?"

"Come on, the Staple Singers; Mavis Staples?" Deacon said with an incredulous tone.

"So?" Will said, remembering the old soul band that his grandfather loved.

"Well, name their biggest hit?"

Will thought for a moment. Somehow memories of that old band were included in his head and he quickly chuckled. He did love his grandpa's sense of humor. While he was now in on the joke, he played along so that Deacon could enjoy the payoff.

"The name of the song is 'I'll Take You There,'" Will conceded.

"Exactly ... and that's just what my car does every time!"

As much as Deacon loved the levity of the moment, he reluctantly understood he needed to shift the conversation to more pressing matters.

"Will, today is your Exemplar orientation. You'll have a physical, meet your Counselor, the referees and your competitors. You'll also be given the overview of what comes next. You are allowed to stay on the compound, but I asked for you to stay with me, which is permitted. I hope that's okay?"

The question seemed simple, but the answer was important to Deacon. He knew that Will, the previous version, at least, would want to stay with him. But he'd shown a rebellious side the day before. If the OHF Will said otherwise it might be a sign that he wasn't quite the same, which might hurt his chances in the competition.

Even though he was annoyed with Deacon, Will loved his grandpa and figured being close to him was the best opportunity to generate more information.

"Grandpa," Will said. "Of course, it's okay. In fact, it's great. There's no place I'd rather be. It's home."

"Alright," Deacon said as the car pulled into a white parking garage. "I see good things for you, Will Herndon. I truly do."

CHAPTER EIGHT

Deacon wasn't allowed past the door. Instead, he handed Will over to a pretty mid-20s woman who gave Will a quick, but polite, glance and then asked him to follow her. Will drove by the University of Denver hundreds of times on his way to Coop's house. Back in 2025, it was a beautiful campus and a solidly ranked private university. But now the buildings looked different in a number of perceptible ways. For example, he always noticed the copper roof on one of the buildings, which looked like a big shiny penny then, but was now oxidized green like the Statue of Liberty.

The older buildings were also slathered with the same see-through gel that now covered Deacon's home. And, of course, there were some of those white buildings made of Millinex that looked like the Ratzenbergers but only larger. Then there were tunnels that appeared to connect most of the structures. As he followed the woman down a long hallway, curiosity got the better of him and he asked, "What happened to DU? I mean, where did the college go?"

She glanced at him again, but it wasn't quite as polite as the first time.

"When we achieved population stabilization, there wasn't the same need for universities," the woman said matter-of-factly. "Cost of education came down and most private schools weren't able to stay in business. There weren't enough students to go around. The University of Denver, or DU as you call it, closed down for good in 2059 and became this district's Crucible Compound in the first year of the Crucible in 2063."

Will wondered whether his college had made the cut.

"We're here," the woman said as they reached the door. She looked him over one final time and gave a perfunctory "best of luck." She waved at the door as if to say she wasn't going in, but he should. She then turned and walked back down the hall.

Will watched her walk away for a moment and then entered the room. He expected something smaller, but found himself in what appeared to have once been some sort of hockey arena. The boards were still in place, but instead of ice there was a white floor with four chairs located at the near end of the part of the rink in which he'd entered. About fifteen feet away from those seats was a stage with just a few seats.

It seemed like a lot of space for just a few people, Will thought. But he was starting to get used to nothing really making sense. He stepped forward into the expansive arena. The room was empty with the exception of one woman, who seemed about his age. She was sitting in one of the four chairs. The woman was pretty with high cheekbones, a small nose and twinkling brown eyes that hinted at a deep sense of curiosity.

She smiled.

"I think you're supposed to be in one of these seats," she said. "At least, I was told if anybody came in who was dressed like me and looked as confused as I unquestionably am, that's what I was supposed to say."

"Thanks," Will responded as he took a seat next to the woman. "I'm Will Herndon."

Thin but with broad athletic shoulders, she extended her hand, "I'm Amy Pham. At least, I think I'm Amy Pham."

That sense of uncertainty immediately resonated with Will. The combination of self-awareness and humor compelled Will to chuckle a little. She had to be an Exemplar. Will didn't enjoy someone else feeling the way he did, but, admittedly, he was relieved to meet another OHF. Milo Swenson told Will he was unique in having seen Eden, but at this moment he didn't believe that experience gave him any sort of competitive advantage. He decided to tread lightly in talking to Amy.

"This is all surreal, isn't it?" He asked, trying to be vague but chatty.

"Surreal? This is downright crazy," she said.

Amy also kept it short. She had only been re-awakened a couple of hours earlier. From what she could remember, she had always been tough and not easily rattled. And, yet, she threw up within minutes of being told she was an Exemplar. Her handlers explained that such a reaction wasn't uncommon, but it was little consolation. It was embarrassing. Right after, she reassured herself that she'd pull it together and remain upbeat.

There was a pause in their conversation, which created an awkward moment before the door opened. A third person, again around the same age as Will and Amy, entered. While Will was 6'2" and Amy was around 5'10" (both above-average heights), this guy was short and stocky. His face seemed off. It was a study in misalignment, one side a perpetual shrug, as if the world had hit him with an off-center blow and he wasn't able to adjust. This made him somewhat unsettling. He was also different in that he had a scraggly beard, which was the first unkempt facial hair Will had seen.

After having welcomed Will, Amy took it upon herself to do the same again.

"Hi. I'm Amy and this is Will. I believe you're supposed to take one of these seats."

The man grunted and sat down.

Will looked at Amy, sharing a feeling of amusement and just a bit of fear. Neither said a word as the door opened, yet again, and a guy strode in with what could only be described as possessing quarterback good looks. He was the same height as Will, but obviously more muscular. His blue eyes sparkled and, while his blonde hair was parted in the middle, which seemed like an odd choice, it glistened. He had a perfectly symmetrical face, featuring a square jaw and a small-but-distinguished nose. If all that wasn't enough, he flashed a broad and inviting smile that seemed designed to disarm. He may have been daunted by what was going on, but if that was the case, nobody could tell.

Before Amy could fulfill her hostess duties, the man confidently walked up to the other three.

"Pleased to meet you," he said in a rich baritone voice. "I'm Trent Aberforth."

He shook Amy's and then Will's hand, making solid eye contact with each as he went. He then reached out to shake the squatty man's hand, who ignored the offer and sounded like he sneered under his breath. Undeterred, he smiled again.

"I'm Amy, this is Will and, I'm sorry, we didn't get your name," Amy offered, looking at the mysterious runty member of the group.

"Kevin," he said with deep indifference.

"Kevin, it's a pleasure to meet you," Trent said as he took the final empty seat next to the surliest of the group. "It's also a pleasure to meet you, Amy and Will."

Kevin didn't seem to be paying attention, but Trent's level of confidence was off-putting to both Amy and Will. He came off as far too relaxed. While it could have easily been a tactic to intimidate the others, that didn't seem to be the case. No, Will thought, this guy was just naturally comfortable in what was probably the most uncomfortable situation humanly possible.

"So, are you ready for this?" Will asked in Trent's direction, not really knowing what to say, but figuring he wanted to exude a bit of confidence as well.

"To be totally honest, I'm not quite sure what 'this' is," he replied. "All I can say is I'll do the best I can, whatever we're asked to do."

The words resonated with all four people in the room – even Kevin. Will may have known more than most, but the reality was nobody really understood what they were doing there.

After a brief silence, the door opened again and a line of six people walked silently into the room, marching past the four who were seated. All of them kept their heads pointing straight ahead toward the stage, though Will thought he saw one make eye contact with him and wink.

As the three men and three women took the stage, Will noticed that there were five seats on the far-right end of the platform. One-by-one those were taken. As for the sixth person, a woman in her late 50s, she continued to stand. After everyone was set, a sleek white lectern rose from the base of the podium. The woman who had remained standing took a few steps to the microphone. She had sharp features and a short bob haircut that angled into a point just below her jaw. Her hair seemed to carve the air around her. She also possessed a pinpoint small nose and crystal green eyes that pulled attention to the center of her face. She had the aura of unyielding authority. Her thin lips opened.

"Good morning, I am Alexandra Marks, chief referee for the Colorado Crucible District of the United States of America," she said. "You will refer to me as Chief Marks. As is my duty as an elected official, I welcome and congratulate you as Exemplars."

Chief Marks paused for a moment. Knowing she was telling these four newly minted OHFs something completely foreign, she wanted to evaluate each person's reaction. Would it be fear? Excitement? Anguish? She was sizing them up. She had always enjoyed seeing the first reactions of OHFs when they entered the Crucible. Some bloodlines could handle the shock more than others, she always thought. Of course, Will Herndon's inclusion made this event more important than normal. She got that. But despite strong feelings against him, she was confident that a bad Exemplar like Will from an unremarkable bloodline was doomed to failure.

For his part, Will was equally keen to read his fellow Exemplars' reactions. But Chief Marks was staring down the group and he knew if he didn't meet her stare, it would be like failing a test. So, he kept looking intently forward into her eyes. If the woman received any data from Will or the other three, she didn't betray what she'd learned.

"As Exemplars, you have been chosen as the most robust example of your bloodline," Chief Marks continued. "In this role, you carry both a burden and an opportunity. In each of your cases, your lineage has one final living member. That individual, who is known as the last remainder, petitioned the government and won a spot on your behalf to compete in what is known as the Crucible. It is a competition that assesses how you – and by extension those who will come after you – can serve as a vital member of our society. The winner will be permitted to continue their bloodline, and the losers here will not. Remember, each family that enters the Crucible gets *one and only one* chance at this. You are the *one* hope to continue the legacy of your respective families."

Again, Chief Marks took a break, this one even longer as she gazed, one by one, into each Exemplar's eyes. Will started to worry that his mind was playing tricks on him. He was sure that when Chief Marks looked at him she pursed her lips, narrowing her eyes ever so slightly. Will didn't break eye contact and with the exception of what sounded like a cough from Kevin, nobody else made a noise.

"No doubt, you will all have questions," she said.

One more time, the elegant woman paused to read the room. It was getting annoying, but maybe she finally got what she wanted out of each Exemplar because her next words shifted into a more conversational, softer tone.

"Look, I've been telling Congress for years that we need to take a more holistic approach to bringing you all, um, back, so to speak. I'm on *your* side. You all know you are OHFs and you all know you are in a different time and place from whence you came. But to put this pressure on you without any additional information? Well, it's more pressure than I'd want to handle."

Her words would have seemed sympathetic to Will, if not for the fact that Chief Marks appeared to twist her mouth into a mischievous smile. It was as if she wanted to plant additional seeds of doubt in each of the Exemplar's minds.

"In any event, we do have tremendous infrastructure to help you through this process," she said, returning to her official tone. "Each of you has already been assigned a personal Counselor, an individual appointed to serve as your primary contact." She waved to the other people with her. "These colleagues of mine are the best in the business. They have a multi-disciplined background and, with the exception of our newest member, Ms. Kathy Riley, bring nearly 60 years of experience guiding Exemplars through this journey to this podium.

"You will have almost exactly one month before the Crucible officially gets underway. Your Counselors will take you through a rigorous curriculum that encompasses the mental and physical aspects of this process. They will also be your cultural guide, as each of your memory spans reflect a different – and limited – period in the past. You are restricted in what information you will be allowed to consume, but your Counselors are adept at the dos and don'ts."

For the first time, Will took his eyes off Chief Marks. He couldn't help himself. He needed to take a quick glance at the others who clearly came in with less information than him. Will looked to the far end of the row and Kevin just seemed bored. Next to him, Trent was attentive and serene. On his other side, he could see Amy fighting her nerves. Her skin was perfect, but two vertical worry lines above her nose were crinkled.

"Please pay attention," Chief Marks said, startling Will. The other three quickly turned and ascertained the chief was talking to Will, the only Exemplar not looking at the stage. Will wanted to say sorry, but just mustered a half-smile.

"Thank you," she said curtly. "Now before I assign you to your Counselors and send you off for your physicals, I'd like to introduce one other member of the team. Mr. Charles Reed."

She pointed at a man sitting in the chair closest to her. Charles Reed couldn't have been much older than 35 and while everyone else had short haircuts, Reed sported longish curly hair, his big brown eyes behind a pair of circular wire-rimmed vintage glasses. Reed smiled warmly, showing a beautiful set of white teeth, and waved, bowing his head respectfully.

"Mr. Reed is my deputy referee. The competition commences with a ranking competition that will place you from top seed to fourth. It is followed by a semi-final round and culminates with the finals, which feature the top two Exemplars. Mr. Reed will have an oversight role throughout the Crucible and will serve as the primary referee in one of the two semi-final round matches. Now, let's get to assignments."

"Kevin Richard McNabb."

Kevin finally showed a bit of attention. Though it sounded like he grunted again.

"Mr. McNabb, you have been assigned to Mr. Paul Waldman."

A sleek bald man with a tightly cropped white beard stood up. He left the stage, walked to Kevin and shook his hand warmly. For the first time, Kevin's features seemed to soften.

"Mr. McNabb," the Counselor said. "It is a pleasure to work with you. Let's be on our way."

Next came Amy. She was paired with a tall sagely looking African-American woman named Maya Mays who appeared to be about 50. Again, the Counselor had an undeniable calming vibe, and Amy, who'd looked anxious just moments before seemed reassured.

Trent's counselor shared an eerie resemblance to the football coach at Manual High School, where Will had gone to school before his junior year when he joined Coop at a private school called Regis Jesuit, a baseball powerhouse. He was tall with salt-and-pepper hair and a square chin that made him look like his better life's calling would have been as a TV anchorman. The pair looked perfect for each other as they firmly shook hands before heading off.

"And, finally," Chief Marks said. "William Michael Herndon."

Will stood up reflexively. By process of elimination, his Counselor was the youngest looking of the bunch. In fact, she probably was only a handful of years older than Will. Her clothes were awkward and ill-fitting. Her strange octagonal glasses seemed far closer to what Will would expect for the time compared to Charles Reed's retro spectacles, but they kept sliding down her nose ever so slightly, forcing her to constantly realign them. She had dark wavy hair, soft blue eyes and round features that made her appear endearing.

"Mr. Herndon," Chief Marks said with a slight grin. "Your Counselor is Kathy Riley."

Unlike the other Counselors, Kathy jumped up with enthusiasm and hurried down from the stage, almost race-walking to Will.

"Will, can I call you that?" she said not waiting for an answer and shaking his hand quickly. "I'm so excited to work with you, Will! I promise to be a great guide."

Will smiled, but his stomach sank just a little.

CHAPTER NINE

Will entered a room where, for once, white seemed appropriate. The reason: It was a doctor's office. As a kid, Will had never been a fan of checkups. Although he was generally optimistic when he was young, Will just didn't see an upside to getting prodded and questioned by medical personnel. The best-case scenario from a visit was that he was simply in the shape he thought he was in before walking in the door. On the flip side, he could end up getting shots or there was always the possibility that something was unexpectedly wrong. Even though he was always told he was perfectly healthy, Will consistently worried that a bad result was looming.

Now he was an OHF and, if he was being logical, his expectations for a clean bill of health were high. After all, he was specially grown to be an Exemplar. If they'd developed the technology to clone him and make him feel like he was the same person he always was, even eliminating the scar over his eye, they must have figured out how to bring him back fit. A less-than-perfect Exemplar, Will thought, wouldn't be an Exemplar at all.

Still, he felt uneasy about being in a doctor's office. It might have been irrational, but it was ingrained in his psyche.

"Mr. William Michael Herndon?" asked the man in a white coat. "I'm Dr. Wilson."

The examiner looked straight out of central casting. He was balding and with glasses, just in that age sweet spot where he appeared knowledgeable and experienced but not so old that you wondered whether he had forgotten some important pieces of information.

Will nodded – although Dr. Wilson didn't wait to get his response. He carried what looked like a strange stethoscope around his neck. While it had a flat circular metallic head and a tube running from it into two other slender tubes, there were no earbuds for listening. Instead, one tube was connected to what looked like an iPad and the other to a small silver box. The box must have been light because Dr. Wilson let it dangle, using one hand to cradle the iPad and the other to press the dial against different parts of Will's body.

When the cool head of the instrument touched Will's skin, he felt a small pinprick. Will winced not so much because it hurt but because he was surprised.

"What time are you from?" The doctor asked as he dutifully pressed the instrument in various places.

"I, er…" Will halted and started again. "The original version of me, at least, was born in 2006."

"Ahh, you've never seen this doo-dad before have you?" Dr. Wilson smiled.

"It has a small needle in the center," he said as he offered it to Will for investigation. "It will take tiny pieces of genetic material that will be analyzed in real time in that little box and then sent to my handheld." He lifted up his iPad-looking computer. "Shouldn't take more than a moment more."

After a bit more prodding, he walked over to a small desk and sat down with his back to Will. He placed his handheld down flat and up popped what appeared to be a hologram, much like the pictures in his grandpa's house or the images on the Maglev. Will craned his neck to see what emerged. It wasn't like a traditional screen but a series of objects that could be moved around at the touch. Each icon looked so real.

"All right," Dr. Wilson said to nobody in particular. "6'2", 185 pounds. Blood pressure, good. Body mass index, excellent. Joints solid though some laxity in the right shoulder. Chip implant online and working at maximum functionality. Now the important number – DNA Match Percentage…"

Dr. Wilson began to hum to pass the time as the little silver box did its thing. It was a bit unnerving considering whatever the DNA Match Percentage represented was clearly important to the doctor.

Losing concentration for a moment, Will nearly jumped when Dr. Wilson let out a resounding "Wow!"

"What is it?" Will asked nervously.

The doctor swiveled his chair around with a smile.

"The DNA Match Percentage is a formula that reflects just how exact your OHF configuration aligns with the original. The closer to 100 percent an Exemplar scores, the better. It means you reflect a greater amount of the physiological – and as far as research has shown, psychological – elements of, well, your former self. You see, the thing with the cloning process is there's an inevitable degree of – and I hate to use this term – degradation. Back in your time you might have remembered how GMOs didn't have quite the same protein as naturally grown fruits and vegetables or how cloned sheep weren't quite identical to the original? There's no such thing as a perfect carbon copy."

Dr. Wilson coughed. He could see in Will's eyes he was going down a path that no OHF would like to hear, so he pivoted.

"Well, anyway, a solid score is typically around 85 percent, but you've come in at 96 percent. It's one of the highest scores I've seen for an Exemplar." He slapped Will's knee as he turned around. "It should put you in a good position for the Crucible."

Dr. Wilson went back to manipulating figures on his computer, while Will tried to process this. He was a GMO? What was lost by that 4 percent? He wasn't him. He got that. But what was the fundamental difference? The philosophical debate in his mind was stopped cold by another Dr. Wilson outburst.

"Oh, you'll also be happy to know you're fertile. That's the one characteristic that if you failed to have, you'd be out of the Crucible. Remember, you are competing for bloodlines … wait a minute," he then said abruptly. "This can't be right." He was now furiously moving around the numbers that hovered over his handheld. Enlarging some and pulling up graphs. "This just can't be right."

The doctor stood up and as he walked to a corner of the room he said, "Phone. This is Dr. Wilson calling Chief Marks."

Almost instantaneously, a woman's voice came from a speaker. "Yes, Dr. Wilson?"

"Chief Marks, I'm so sorry to bother you, but we have a significant abnormality with one of the Exemplars."

"Which one?

Dr. Marks swung his head back to look at his handheld before saying "William Michael Herndon."

"I'll be right there," Chief Marks said in that short tone that was already beginning to grate on Will.

As soon as she appeared to be off the phone, Will tried to cut the obvious tension.

"I was just born," he said with air quotes around "born". "Am I already dying?"

"No, no, no," Dr. Wilson said, avoiding eye contact. "You're perfectly healthy and with that DNA match percentage, you'll almost undoubtedly lead as long a natural life as you were intended in your first iteration."

The door opened and Chief Marks walked in. She avoided eye contact with Will and beckoned Dr. Wilson to the far corner of the room. It wasn't a big space, but Will was struggling to make out what they were saying while not appearing to be grasping for any words he couldn't make out. Luckily for him, Chief Marks quickly lost her temper.

"This is WILLIAM HERNDON, Dr. Wilson!" She said incredulously. "Do you not know who he is?"

Chief Marks' decision to raise her voice left Dr. Wilson completely off-balanced, but did make him comfortable enough to talk in full pitch.

"But Chief Marks, he's 19."

"There is a reason for that," Chief Marks said as she picked up the handheld and began moving objects around. The woman certainly commanded attention. While everyone seemed to wear white, Will noticed her outfit was a pale pink. When she found what she wanted, she shoved the handheld into Dr. Wilson's hands. Will tried to decipher what was being projected, but the angle made it impossible.

"Oh my gosh, oh my gosh," Dr. Wilson said, returning to a hushed tone. "Of course, I'm so sorry. Oh my gosh."

"Dr. Wilson, you need to be better prepared. You play a vital role in the Exemplar procedures," Chief Marks chastised. "If you cannot adequately handle its responsibilities – as such an oversight as this suggests – we should talk about your value moving forward."

The doctor continued to look at the holograms. What could he say? He just remained silent. Chief Marks turned for the door and opened it halfway before stopping.

"What was his DNA Match Percentage?" she said while still looking toward the hallway. It took a moment for Dr. Wilson to process that she was talking to him and he furiously moved figures around before meekly saying, "96 percent."

She turned her head and looked at Will for the first time, sizing him up and down more seriously than at the introduction. The value of a good percentage is useless if you're a rotten representative of your bloodline, she thought, trying to convince herself the number didn't matter. Will could see Chief Marks was grinding her teeth. She didn't like him. It was clear-cut to Will.

She made an audible "hmmmph" and then stormed out of the room, slamming the door.

Will turned back to Dr. Wilson, who laid the handheld back on the desk and stared at the floor, crestfallen.

He may have been 19, but Will felt sympathy for the doctor and rather than ignore what just happened, he asked in a soft tone, "Are you okay?"

"What was I thinking…of course," he mumbled to himself.

"Are you okay?" Will offered again.

"Yes, of course, I'm okay," Dr. Wilson said in a defensive tone. If there was one thing Will knew it was that frustration always rolled down hill, and, right now, Will was standing at the base of this mountain.

"You're done here," said the now testy doctor. "Be sure to let your Counselor know your DNA Match Percentage. Don't forget. Please let…" he looked at the handheld again, "… Ms. Riley know that all the other vitals for both you and the other Exemplars will be sent to her promptly tomorrow morning. Can you do that?"

Will was put off by Dr. Wilson's suddenly aggressive manner, but he figured there was no value in rising to the bait. The doctor was clearly not angry at him.

"Absolutely," Will said with a sincere look.

Dr. Wilson caught his breath, realizing he was not handling the situation properly.

"Thanks," he said, returning to a calmer demeanor. "I'll step out now. Please get changed and then close the door behind you." The doctor scooped up his stethoscope-like device and the handheld and scurried out of the room.

Will's mind began to race. Was being 19 a good thing or a bad thing? Will it help me? Surely, my 96 percent is a good thing.

He walked into a waiting room that was empty with the exception of his Counselor, Kathy Riley. She was noticeably fidgeting like an expectant father.

"So, how'd it go?" she asked, speaking so fast that she swallowed her words, making them almost incomprehensible.

There was a clear warmth to Kathy, but the nervous energy added more stress to the situation than was necessary. Instinctively, Will talked a bit slower than normal. He hoped she'd catch on and the maneuver would calm her down.

"The doctor told me that I was supposed to give you my DNA Match Percentage and that you'd get all the vitals for me and the other Exemplars tomorrow morning."

"What was your DNA score?" Kathy said nearly cutting Will off.

"I got a 96 percent," he said, sticking with his cool approach despite the fact that Kathy's initial response offered no sign that it was working.

"Bywary!" Kathy shrieked, then clapped a hand over her mouth, a slight, embarrassed giggle escaping. "That's fantastic news, Will! It's really good news."

The rest of the day was a blur. The pair spent it in a study room visibly designed to make Will feel he was back in his time. In fact, he was sure it was similar to one of the professor's offices at Harvard. He lamented that the chairs and sofas in the spacious area were not nearly as comfortable as the modern-day furniture that perfectly contoured to his body.

Kathy talked quickly, which paradoxically meant it took her a long time to explain anything. The orientation of sorts laid out what was in front of Will. He would have a month to prepare for the preliminary phase of the Crucible. This included learning a vast array of skills from modern coding to the newest welding techniques. There would also be math and science refreshers. (She promised that nothing would be above a level he would be expected to know).

The first round, which ranked the four Exemplars from top to bottom, featured a written test followed by a practical examination. Then the top-ranked Exemplar would square off against number four, while two and three would compete in the semi-finals, which also had a practical and a written component. In both rounds, the subject matter varied from Crucible to Crucible. But in the U.S., at least, the final was always the same: a single event called the Gauntlet – a comprehensive challenge that was part obstacle course, part problem-solving spectacle. It was also a local extravaganza, held at the city's old Ball Arena and open to the public.

Throughout the tutorial, Kathy kept offering reassuring words like, "you're such a good athlete, you'll do fine on the physical part" and "bywary, you were so smart I'm sure you'll do great throughout."

The assurances didn't deliver their intended results, since every time Kathy told him how great he had been, he wondered whether his version of Will Herndon could or would perform at that level. Kathy dominated the discussion in narrative form, leaving Will with little to say throughout most of the day.

He looked out the west-facing window as the sun began to disappear behind the mountains. He was tired, but reminded himself that he'd need stamina to handle both the tasks ahead – and Kathy. Still, he was getting his sea legs. He now had enough information about his new world to keep firmly focused on specific tasks. He remembered how a coach once said that if you're having trouble with your swing don't try to fix it all at once. Break it down into parts and methodically work at mastering each element. He could do that here.

"Well, that's about it for today," she said. She had not lost a bit of her emotional velocity and was still talking and acting as if she was in fast forward. "I know you must have lots of questions, but I need to set some ground rules."

For the first time, Will noticed a slight change of tone when Kathy said "ground rules." He perked up but didn't say anything.

"My primary role is to guide you through all elements of this competition – and help you navigate any issues that arise. But…" she said abruptly. "Protocol dictates that I cannot assist you in delving into your past life if your memory does not already include details of a particular moment. To make it fully clear, I cannot help you fill the gaps. It's a strong public policy determination that your role is as an Exemplar, and if there are unseemly moments in your past that the referees have chosen to edit, it's for a reason."

Will didn't like that answer. His grandfather was already withholding information, but Kathy's job as his Counselor was to prepare him. Why would she be doing the same thing? Will thoroughly respected rules – unless they were counterproductive. And he was positive this was the case here. But just as with Deacon, he could tell this was one area she was unlikely to budge on, so he shifted the subject.

"What does bywary, mean?" Will asked truly curious about the odd word.

"Bywary?" Kathy repeated. She seemed stunned Will hadn't pushed back, but kept her composure. "It's an exclamation that became popular after your time. It's something like 'oh my gosh'. Does that make sense?" Kathy asked, showing a neediness to be reassured that she was doing this right.

"Absolutely," Will said with a nod.

"Great," Kathy smiled back. "Well, we're done for today. Tomorrow is Thanksgiving. Yay! You're off, but we'll be right back at it on Friday. Other than holidays, this is a seven-day-a-week endeavor. Will, I know you'll do great."

Will nodded and sighed.

CHAPTER TEN

It was night. The first thing Will saw was the light reflecting off the smoke of a fire and then embers crackling indiscriminately into the air. He looked down into the warmth of the flame and then across from where he was seated. There, on the other side of the fire, was a woman standing and laughing. She was so naturally beautiful, he thought. His heart started to beat faster at that thought. She looked around 18 and was so striking she must be a model. Blonde with blue eyes, her athletic build was obvious. Muscular and tan, she continued to laugh and then made eye contact with Will. Although it didn't seem possible for his heart to race faster, it did. She stopped laughing for a moment, giving him a shy come-hither glance. Will felt paralyzed and then, suddenly, she began to laugh again. Dejected, he looked down at the fire again.

Shaking, Will opened his eyes to see the white ceiling in his grandfather's house. It had been a dream, but the realness of the vision left him wondering for a moment whether it had actually happened. He took a few seconds to revisit the images in his head. "It was a dream," he reassured himself. But even so, it aroused emotions in him – from elation to anger – that he couldn't easily wave off.

He rolled his head and got out of bed. What *was* real was that today was Thanksgiving. It was a holiday he always loved. Cooler temperatures and lots of food. Although today was supposed to be a new normal holiday average of 87 degrees, at least there would be a lot to eat. Will never failed to chow down everything he could. He fought for every bit of muscle he put on, and if he wasn't constantly packing on the calories, he'd nearly waste away. His mom was a great cook so that was no problem. When he first got to college, he received the nickname "cafeteria" because he took his time in the meal hall very seriously. Of course, as soon as he got on the baseball field, a teasing nickname like "cafeteria" quickly fell by the wayside. His abilities commanded too much respect for such a silly moniker.

Will and his grandfather didn't say anything to each other when Will returned home after his first day at the Crucible. Deacon had sent Mavis to pick him up and there was just a short hologram message when he arrived from his grandpa saying he still needed to catch up on sleep and had gone to bed early. Will was dejected by this. He had been excited to talk about the day and break it down with his only family. When he was a kid the two of them would break down every game – the good and the bad. Later on, when the baseball got more advanced, he had Coop to mull over the nuances of a performance.

Always certain of himself, Will started to wonder whether he could do this on his own. Was his past success a reflection of his own abilities, ambition and desires? Or was he really only as good as the people around him. Between the dream that had left him unsteady and his diminishing confidence, he felt deflated.

Internally, he didn't have enough of his bearings to give himself a pep talk. But he resolved that he would not ruin Thanksgiving with self-pity.

It was 10:30 a.m., and Will could already smell the buttered mashed potatoes, yams and turkey downstairs. He changed quickly and bounded all the way into the kitchen. Deacon was hard at work. The reason Will's mom had been so good in the kitchen was undoubtedly a genetic thing, because Deacon was every bit the master chef himself.

"Not too early to start cooking?" Will asked, mustering his most upbeat tone to mildly poke fun at his grandfather.

"Come on now! It's never too early to begin the festivities!" He looked up only briefly before returning to the gravy simmering on the stove. "This is your one day off – other than Christmas – through this whole thing. I figure I better make sure your stomach is full for the duration."

Will was surprised that ovens still existed – though they were all-electric. For all the improvements, the stove, while a bit fancier looking, seemed to broil, bake and generally cook like the ones they had back in the early 2000s. Despite the stove being a recognizable appliance, for all his talents, Will stayed clear of it. Ability in the kitchen had surely skipped his generation. He was never good in there and knew better than to offer his help. He remembered whenever he volunteered – Will never wanted to feel like he was shirking a responsibility – he'd get shut down almost immediately. He'd begin cutting cucumbers or kneading dough, until, invariably, his grandpa or mom would grow frustrated and, rather than try to explain the correct way to do it, would step in and finish the job. By the time he was 15, he decided he was a back-room guy. He could clear the table, wash dishes and take out the trash, but he'd never have a glory job.

Instead, he sat down at the table and watched in wonder how his grandfather, so much sprier than even he remembered him, jumped from one task to another as if he was a short order cook in a busy diner. After a couple of moments, he glanced at the table, which, amazingly, his grandpa had also prepared. There were three place settings.

"Grandpa, who's the third person eating with us?

"A friend," his grandpa replied simply.

Will tried so hard not to be angry at his grandpa, who seemed unwilling to share nearly anything. But every instance in which Deacon held back, it increased Will's irritation and confusion. He couldn't figure out why the people who were meant to be so close to him – his grandfather, his Counselor – were the most tight-lipped. Despite the promise to himself not to mess with the joy of Thanksgiving, he was teetering.

"Really? That's all I get? Come on, I've had so few answers to so many things. This one can't be too hard," Will said in a friendly tone. Even though he was riled up, Will attempted to show discipline. Keep it light and maybe I'll get answers, he told himself. He needed a win, even if it was a small one.

Deacon took a kitchen towel hanging over a chair and turned to Will.

"Fine. His name is Charlie Reed," Deacon said. "I'm a pretty solitary old man, but Charlie has been there for me. Helped me through many important moments. He's single and doesn't have a family so having him over is, without a doubt, the neighborly thing to do."

The name sounded familiar to Will, but he knew practically no one from this time and place. He gave a quick thought about whether Coop might be around somewhere, he could sure use him right now. But Will didn't want to get shot down with another unanswerable question. So, instead, he offered up small talk.

"I had a pretty vivid dream last night," Will said nonchalantly, trying to hide how much the vision affected him. "There was this pretty girl and we were around a campfire…"

"What?" Deacon asked sharply. Will was trying to balance a handle of a knife on his two forefingers while talking, and the unexpected reaction led to him losing balance and the knife falling to the ground. Deacon immediately regretted his startled response and tried to reclaim the moment.

"Sorry," he said, retreating to the stove. "Wasn't you, I just realized I'd left the burner on too high for the gravy. I don't want to burn it. No pretty girls come to me in my dreams. Gotta say, I'm pretty jealous."

"This one would have kept your attention grandpa," said Will, picking up the knife. Unlike most dreams that tend to fade quickly, he could still see her vividly in his mind. It felt more like one of his OHF memories than something you'd see in your sleep. "She wasn't just pretty. She had a charisma; a magnetism. I can't really explain. It felt like a love-at-first-sight sort of thing. But it also felt uncomfortable. You know I was never great with the ladies."

"Hmmm," Deacon said. He had little he wanted to add to the conversation and opted to shift the subject. "Well, I do have some bad news. The NFL folded about thirty-five years ago. First colleges stopped playing the sport after a number of lawsuits, and then as things started getting worse with all the real-world problems, football just faded. By the time the league closed down nobody seemed surprised. So, no Thanksgiving games."

Will wasn't too bothered. He was never so much a fan of sports as he was a person who liked playing them. He'd dabbled in football his freshman year, but decided it wasn't for him and focused on baseball the rest of the way in high school.

"Do people still play baseball?" Will reflexively asked.

"Yep, that old nag has stuck around," Deacon said with a smirk. "Mind you, seasons are shorter and it's now a winter game that's played only at night. For a good game, you'll get 5,000 folks. Nothing like when you were coming up. Basketball was the one sport that's sort of survived the way you might remember it. It was just better positioned than the other big games. Indoors. With water rationing, ice hockey seemed a bit excessive. They created artificial rinks but it wasn't the same thing."

"Isn't there just some regular TV?" Will asked.

"You can watch some stuff, but people mostly play virtual reality games," Deacon explained while preparing some cooked carrots. "They enjoy the interactivity. All the big networks and streaming services – NBC, Fox, ESPN, Netflix – they went away. But the executives who ran those companies sure had a hard time giving up both control and the money that came with it. They still wanted a piece of the entertainment pie."

Deacon explained that Congress got co-opted by big companies to create this thing called the Product. It was a government organization made up of the same people who used to run the networks and streaming services. They'd decide what was good viewing and what wasn't. It wasn't censorship, mind you. You didn't need that organization's support. But if a program got certified as Product then it got more online bandwidth. If not, it was hard to get attention – or download speeds – to properly view it.

"As I'm sure you can guess," Deacon continued, "the powerful friends of those on the Congressional panel owned most of the Product. People just got tired of it, so there isn't much worth watching out there. This all means that you're stuck talking to me instead of sitting in front of some fancy holograms."

Even accounting for Will's frustration, small talk came easy. The two never suffered any difficulty when it came to chatting. Deacon was a natural storyteller and launched into an explanation of how he built Ratzenbergers – those strange white houses. Amazingly, it was a job that only took seven workers and could be finished in about a week. The 3D equipment, as long as it didn't break down, was fast. The hardest part of the work for Deacon and his team was tearing down the old Denver Square-style houses, which like the Herndon home, were sturdy and roomy two-story brick homes built around the start of the 1900s. They were popular in the city but were basically so expensive and inefficient to maintain that they had to go.

"So why didn't you build a Ratzenberger for yourself?" Will asked.

Deacon, who was at the open oven checking the turkey, looked around. "Too many memories," he said. "It anchors me to the past. I'm afraid to say it, but, while I get along okay with my crew, I spend way too much time looking back. Both the good and the bad. It isn't healthy, but some things are just hardwired."

It was 3 p.m. when the doorbell rang. Will moved to get up and answer the door, but Deacon was faster.

"I'll get it," he said hustling into the other room. "You stay here."

The door opened and the unfamiliar voice said, "Big D, how are you, my brother?" Will could hear Deacon whispering something back, to which his friend said, "It's not a problem. I thought he might be here. There are no regulations against it and, remember, I'm arms-length. To be honest, I'm kind of excited to spend a little time with him."

Whispers again from Deacon and then a laugh from the stranger. "Deacon, you are such a rule follower," the man said. "It will be fine. Trust me, I know."

With that the two men walked into the room and, to Will's great surprise, it was a familiar face. He'd seen him the day before at the introduction in the old hockey arena. This man was on the stage with Chief Marks. Again, a wave of frustration hit Will. His grandfather sure left out a big fact when telling him about the guest.

"Will," he said, looking like he was coming in for a hug. "It's so good to see you." Although a couple inches shorter than Will, the bespectacled man did offer an embrace. Uncertain how to respond, Will politely reciprocated, but his effort was not as emphatic as the man's. Will's response was a signal to the guest that he was not acting properly.

"Whoops, where are my manners," the guest said. "I'm Charlie Reed. I've known your grandfather for about a decade, isn't that right Big D? And you probably recognize me from yesterday."

"Uh-huh" was all Will could manage.

"Well, I'm an attorney by trade, but I'm also the deputy referee for the U.S. Crucible District of Colorado. I'd heard that you might not be staying on the Crucible Compound, which isn't typical for an Exemplar, but I've assured your rule-following granddad that this won't have any impact on your competition. And, if some things slip, well, I won't tell anybody."

Charlie winked and slapped him on the arm.

"Let's sit down and eat," said Deacon, who was increasingly thinking Charlie's presence was a mistake. He was a good friend, but Deacon didn't want to jeopardize anything for Will. Charlie didn't diminish that concern any when he said: "We should do a bit of drinking too. I've got some whiskey – although none for you Will."

It was clear that Charlie had been here before. He had a familiarity with the house and knew exactly where to find the glasses to pour himself and Deacon a drink. They clinked glasses and Charlie took a swig then sat down next to Will with glass in hand.

"96 percent," he said.

"Excuse me?" Will responded.

"You got a 96 percent on the DNA Match Percentage. That's just fantastic. Heck, I only got a 93 percent when I was in the Crucible. My boy, a 96 percent is a truly worthy score."

"You're an OHF?"

"Why yes. In fact, you could call me an OHF activist. I bet you've already figured out that I can be a bit loud and demonstrative. A big part of the 93 percent that came from my original iteration was tenacity for the things I believe in. Chief Marks may have been elected, but the deputy referee is appointed. You can be sure no OHF would be elected by the general populace – but I would not be denied. Somebody has to uphold the integrity of this circus."

"What exactly *is* an OHF activist?" Will asked. He was intrigued.

"My boy, we OHFs are a tremendous minority in this world. Even with Crucibles being held across the globe, most people rarely meet an OHF. And, as is so often the case, if you don't know a person from a group, you tend to think the worst and start stereotyping."

Charlie wasn't joking. When he said he liked to talk, he meant it. He spoke with great rhythm and pacing and his magnetism was so inviting that he could probably tell a story about nothing and make it interesting.

"The problem really started with the Crucible itself," Charlie continued. "Some argued the opportunity to basically reboot a bloodline should be based on merit. This line of thinking went that each bloodline should be tested and then only the greatest should be allowed to return. In America, some believed this was the essence of a meritocracy – if you're the best bloodline, you get a second chance. But, in truth, there was nothing meritorious about it. After all, just being born to the right bloodline doesn't mean you'll live right. No, the lottery gave every family a chance. It presented the Exemplar – through tangible action, rather than a bloodline history – the opportunity to assure his or her family's right to continue."

"And I bet Chief Marks doesn't think I merit this opportunity," Will blurted out. He'd already gotten the feeling from the chief that he was a marked man, and Charlie's warmth made him comfortable to admit it.

Charlie stopped cold. He looked up at Deacon, who was in the middle of scooping up some mashed potatoes. Deacon raised his eyes, looked at Will, and then shifted his gaze to Charlie and shook his head ever so slightly.

Charlie sighed and began to talk again.

"You might be ..." he said before Deacon cut him off with a "NO!"

Charlie sighed a second time.

Though he assumed far too much familiarity, at least Charlie was willing to dish, Will thought. But again, Deacon put up a roadblock. Charlie knew not to try to blast through it. Instead, he transitioned into telling *his* story for the next two hours. The original version of him – or as he called it "the mold" – was born in 1964 in Denver. He came from a well-respected Colorado Springs family of doctors and lawyers. A bloodline, as he put it, of "unassailable quality." After attending Princeton as an undergraduate and Yale for law school, he returned to serve as a prosecutor in the Denver suburbs of Jefferson County. He did this for most of his life before ultimately moving back East in his later years.

"When I returned as an OHF, I did some research on my family and was so humbled and honored that I'd been chosen the Exemplar," Charlie said. "In your first go around, you just don't give those things much thought. But the research proved extraordinary. It spurred me to victory in the Crucible and in the 12 years since, I've aimed to make my mark in a way that exceeds anything I did in the past. I'd like to say that at 33, I did more than the 75 years my 'mold' did when he lived on this planet. Now I just need to find a partner and start having kids before I get too old!"

By this point, Deacon was clearing the table. The food was fantastic with Will filing his plate twice. Neither he nor his grandfather had said more than a handful of words during Charlie's monologue. Following his shut down of the Chief Marks discussion, Deacon listened with passing interest as he'd heard it all before. On the other hand, Will hung on every word.

"So, what does it take to win in the Crucible?" Will asked at the first plausible pause from Charlie.

The deputy chief smiled. The boy was asking the only question that mattered, he thought. He took a swig from his whiskey glass before answering,

"Some things you can control and others you cannot. I was lucky. My opposing Exemplars didn't have the same DNA match and were simply shadows of their former selves. Your 96 percent puts you in a strong position. Although..."

Charlie looked at the bottom of the empty glass, then reached for the half empty bottle and poured himself another drink before continuing.

"Although, Trent Aberforth did score a 94 percent. It's also an astonishing score. But Amy Pham is 84 percent and Kevin McNabb is an appalling 62 percent. I'd like to face him in the semis."

"Charlie!"

It was the first thing Deacon had said in some time, and the other two looked up at him. After a handful of drinks, Charlie moved a little slower and was having a bit of difficulty making direct eye contact as Deacon tried to catch his attention.

"What?" he said defensively. "This is all the information that your grandson will get, probably as soon as tomorrow."

"Don't put him – or me – in a bad position," Deacon responded. "You know you can't talk about that outside the compound." Will could tell his grandpa was getting irritated. But Charlie was offended by such a suggestion.

"After all I've done?" he said indignantly. "After all I've done? You should know better. I've recused myself as far as Will's involvement is concerned and you should be grateful for giving *you* a second chance."

Those words hit Deacon hard. This statement was too much for Will *not* to enter the discussion.

"Grandpa, how is this a second chance?"

"Come on Deacon, he deserves a little more detail doesn't he?" Charlie's anger had not subsided yet, but Will was grateful to finally have a partner in his fact-finding mission.

"This isn't something we should be talking about," Deacon offered. But he didn't say it with conviction. Maybe it was the whiskey or some unspoken guilt.

"Deacon," Charlie said with a bit more sympathy. "This is now his world, too, and while I understand there's a bright-line prohibition for discussing some events, it's good for both of you."

Will's head was on a swivel looking back and forth between the two older men.

With that, Deacon made some calculations in his mind, took in a deep breath and then let it out. He looked at his grandson.

"Willie, I was an Exemplar just like you."

The moments that followed his grandfather's statement left Will dizzy. Of all the revelations to date, this one was the biggest. Subconsciously, Will knew it made sense. It turned out that *this* Deacon was just 48 years old. Heck, Will wasn't even alive when his grandfather was that age the first time around, and, all of a sudden, Deacon actually seemed really old for his age.

Will couldn't help it. His anger finally reached critical mass. It had only been a couple of days, but he really could have used somebody who understood his plight. And who could grasp the disorienting world of an OHF better than someone who had gone through it? How could sharing that information be traumatic? To know they had that in common would surely be the opposite of traumatic. It would be comforting. Negative thoughts continued to flood Will's mind, until he came to the dark conclusion: If his grandfather was holding out on him about this, what else was there?

What made matters worse is Deacon wouldn't have any of it and wouldn't offer any more information. Will wanted to know why Chief Marks had insisted that each bloodline had only one chance and, yet, here the Herndons were with a second opportunity. Deacon may have been silent, but Charlie tried to explain that the law of the Crucible was more flexible than Will could understand.

Caring deeply about Deacon, Charlie had put on his lawyer's hat and represented the Herndons in court. It had taken years and led to Charlie even arguing for Will's opportunity in front of the U.S. Supreme Court. And he'd won this unique second chance on behalf of Deacon, Will and all their ancestors.

As Charlie added more details, Deacon regretted ever opening his mouth. Each additional scrap of information would inevitably lead to another question. This was a dangerous path and he was utterly angry with his friend. Charlie got it, but he wanted to give Will at least a base of information. When he reached a certain point, he said no more and found a quick excuse to leave.

"Willie, I believe in rules, and I'm just trying so hard to make sure we follow them," Deacon said once Charlie left. It was the best he could offer. Will, who was dutifully cleaning the dishes, wanted to accept that answer. He loved his grandfather, even if he was an OHF who was keeping him in the dark on so much. But Will was coming to an undeniable conclusion. He needed some information quickly. Otherwise, if he spent any more time with Deacon, who was withholding so much, he'd end up resenting his grandfather beyond the point of repair.

"Grandpa, this is hard enough as it is," Will said through clenched teeth. "There's got to be a difference between the letter of the law and the spirit of the law. I don't really know who I am, but each step, I'm feeling more and more different. I'm an OHF. There's something weird about me being 19. I seem to be the only second-string Exemplar…ever. You've got to give me more."

Will continued to clean. Deacon sat in a chair looking out the window. He was done with this conversation. To speak would be to further break promises he'd made to those that ran the Crucible. Deacon did not break commitments, no matter how difficult the situation – especially when it could ruin Will's chances. But if he was done, so was Will – at least for the time being. Will determined at that moment it would be best for the both of them if he left this house full of a Swiss cheese set of memories.

"I'm going to be staying at the Crucible Compound," Will said, hoping that maybe it would jar his grandfather's resolve a bit.

But the only response he received was the sound of the newly cleaned dishes he was now stacking.

CHAPTER ELEVEN

avis the car drove Will to the Crucible Compound without Deacon. The eerie silence of the electric vehicles quietly navigating the road left Will with little distraction from his thoughts.

He felt deep pangs of doubt about his decision to leave his grandfather's home. A voice in his mind told him that he surely over-reacted. He should trust that his grandpa was well-intentioned and, if he was withholding, it was for Will's own good. But he couldn't shake the nagging question: why didn't he tell him about the fact that they were both OHFs? No doubt, if Will had given it enough thought, he would have realized that the only explanation for Deacon's youthful appearance was that he was also a clone.

It was obvious. Will wondered whether maybe his grandfather thought he was so dumb that he wouldn't figure it out. And, if Deacon couldn't even tell him the obvious stuff, what other vital nuggets of information was he refusing to share? Not only that, but Deacon had to also know that Will *needed* answers. Anyone who loved him would have to sense Will's deep desire, at his core, for at least some information.

More than that, without Coop and his grandfather, his insecurities were growing. Could he do this alone? He began to wonder if he'd ever accomplished anything without real team support.

Will pushed his lips together hard before taking in a deep breath and exhaling. He could continue to agonize over this all day. It would do him no good. He couldn't deny he was angry at his grandpa. Whether that was right or wrong, he'd acted on that emotion. Ironically, Deacon's words were rattling in his head to explain how to handle his next steps.

"There's no room for regret in this world," his grandpa once said. "You make a choice and you just have to make it work as best you can even if it isn't the best choice."

The advice made sense to Will here and he decided that, for the time being, he'd drop all the drama and do his best to suppress his personal doubts.

"Mavis," he said a little self-consciously because he was talking to a car. "Play some popular music."

If there's one thing that changes from generation to generation, it's popular music. Will was about two generations removed from what he thought was cool, so he let out an audible laugh when he heard what passed for fashionable in 2090. It was a combination of a clarinet, cello and some sort of keyboard synthesizer. He'd remembered Deacon telling him that clarinets were really trendy in the 1940s. That band leaders like Benny Goodman and Artie Shaw were rock stars in their time.

"I guess what goes around, comes around," Will thought, beginning to enjoy the foreign melody of the song.

When he arrived at the Crucible Compound, he was greeted by the same pretty twentysomething woman who met him at the door on his first day. She was no nonsense and with nothing more than a "come with me" began walking at a brisk pace.

One major difference between the current campus and when it housed the University of Denver during Will's first life was that now there was so little outdoor space and so many hallways. Actually, they weren't so much hallways as they were tunnels that looked a little like the rounded and see-through ones hamsters ran through. The only difference was they were heavily tinted, presumably to keep the heat out during the day.

As they walked, Will peered outside at what appeared to be a strange grass lawn. The blades were shaped like grass but they were a red brick color instead of green. The woman noticed his amazement.

"It's called grass-AGE," she said off-handedly. "It's that color because it keeps better in the extreme heat. It's real and genetically engineered so that it needs less water than old green grass. Also, if you step on it during a scorching summer day, it will be somewhat cool on your feet. Very expensive. You can't find it in many places."

Will wondered how long it took people to accept grass that wasn't green. There are so many things that he took for granted, he thought, and green grass was one of them.

After a five-minute of briskly striding through various tunnels, the woman led Will to a more traditional hallway. Two doors down on the right, she pointed to a room.

"This is yours for the duration of the Crucible," the woman said. "It requires your biometric signature. You need to place your hand on the door knob to unlock it."

Will touched the cool white nob and heard a click. He turned the handle and walked into the room. It was pretty bare. There was a bed, four cubes that undoubtedly were chairs, a table and a bathroom. The white walls had no pictures. This was not a homey hotel.

"Look over here," the woman said. "This cube had a stripe. It's what you'd call a chest of drawers. Just swipe the stripe…" As she said it, the cube lengthened in width and height. There were four compartments and when she touched a singular stripe on one of them, it slid open with some form of clothing. Each drawer was completely full. This place didn't expect you to bring your own outfits.

"If you need to know the time, just simply say, 'time' and …" before Will's guide could finish, a pleasant female voice said, "It's 7:54 a.m."

She told him Kathy would be able to explain where he'd go to eat. Then she gave directions on how to get to his counselor's teaching area and abruptly left. Will sat at the corner of the bed, thinking that the good news was that there wouldn't be any distractions here. "No more time for thinking," he said, trying hard to pick himself up.

Will stood and headed out to meet Kathy. It took some trial and error to get there, and Will promised himself that if he got any free time, he'd figure out the maze that was the Crucible Compound. After all, it couldn't be worse than sitting in his jail cell of a bedroom.

Entering the learning area was definitely a distraction because it was patterned after a time that Will knew. It was full of colors and different shaped pieces of furniture. The shift in décor was such a transition that entering the room was a bit like taking a quick glance at the sun. It was overwhelming and required some time for his eyes to adjust.

While there was an old-school long couch on one side of the room, Will opted to sit in a chair with a table in the center. Because it wasn't a cube, the seat was relatively uncomfortable. But Will believed that by taking that spot, he was declaring his seriousness.

Kathy was already waiting for him. She arrived at the room by 7 a.m. to go over and over her teaching plan for the day.

"I hope you had a great Thanksgiving!" she said with more perkiness than Will wanted to hear.

While she often had difficulty reading emotions, Kathy could tell that Will didn't want to discuss that topic. The relationships between Exemplars and their last remainders could be tricky. The final members of a bloodline often felt guilty for somehow being the last person standing, and they weren't trained to be with people from vastly different generations. This often led to arms-length dealings. But Kathy believed that Will's and Deacon's relationship was – or at least should be – different. They knew each other intimately. At the same time, she was aware that Deacon was under intense pressure not to discuss Will's past.

For a moment, she wondered if that fact was causing tension. But, as was often the case with Kathy, when feelings were involved, she looked to avoid the discussion. Instead, she launched into the lesson.

"Our topic today is piloting drones," she said, maintaining an inhuman level of enthusiasm. Luckily, Will could get into this. Drones existed in his time and he'd had the opportunity to manipulate some high-tech remote controls in his day.

Of course, he wasn't prepared for the level of technology now in place. There were no longer remote controls. Instead, there was a neural lace patch affixed to the back of the head. There was also a strange set of eyewear. They looked like broken spectacles. Each side was affixed to his temple and they could be separately shifted up or down. One lens offered a view from the perspective of the drone, while the other provided information on the weather, altitude, speed and any other important piece of information he could imagine.

The neural patch allowed Will to simply think of what action he wanted the drone to execute and then see it happen. It was a weird sensation, especially because this generation of drone could do so much — from barrel rolling in the air to quickly picking up and dropping objects on the ground. While they sat in the comfort of the office, Will controlled a real drone outside. The view from above Denver was startling. With the exception of pockets of what he assumed were wealthier neighborhoods that had some of that brick-colored grass, much of the landscape was a dusty light brown primarily featuring lots of Ratzenbergers across its face. The footprint of the city was smaller and less densely populated than what he'd remembered. For the first time, Will got a deeper sense of how fundamentally different this world was compared to his.

What really caught his attention was a vast field of those white buildings with black turbines that he'd noticed when travelling by train from Eden. Kathy explained that they were carbon dioxide farms. Even decreasing populations wouldn't have been enough to prevent Armageddon, she explained. We had long since blown by any reasonable greenhouse gas emissions budget. Consistent and long-term efforts to suck the carbon dioxide out of the atmosphere were required through a process called direct air capture. The world was still years away from no longer needing millions of these machines churning across the globe to take CO_2 currently in the air and deposit it deep underground.

Kathy was a good teacher. She was methodical and logical in how she explained things. But she had two big failings. First, she tended to talk too fast. Second, Counselors were taught to always speak with words that were popular in their Exemplar's time. Kathy often forgot that rule. Language is an art that subtly transitions over time, but much like the music that Will listened to while riding in Mavis, if you give it too many years, it can become pretty strange.

Sometimes Will could understand a word by context. For instance, when he picked up how to land the drone quickly, Kathy would exclaim, "You have amazing *timeskill.*" He figured that meant he was a fast learner. But other times it wasn't so easy. For instance, when Will was trying to navigate between two buildings, he was left confused when Kathy blurted out "Avoid that *Esteban*! You can *findible* that space."

An *Esteban* was a mistake, Will learned. The term came from a virtual reality character in a popular game who never got anything right. And, *findible* meant splitting a space or area. Will tried to politely explain his confusion to Kathy when these moments emerged. It was fine to say an exclamation like *bywary* all the time, but these other linguistic mistakes slowed down his learning. In fact, when she said *Esteban* and *findible*, Will became so lost he had to quickly land the drone.

Nobody could be harder on Kathy than herself. When she made these types of miscues, she slapped her thigh hard and immediately walked into a corner.

She'd turn her back to Will and begin looking up at the ceiling. It was odd behavior, but Will promised himself he would avoid pointing out these moments as much as he could.

Despite the hiccups, the two worked well together, and Will finished the lesson pretty quickly. Because night flying was scheduled for a different day, Will was sent to dinner before dusk. He was assigned an eating pod. It was a small room with a comfortable chair and table. The wall featured something that resembled a virtual vending machine. Nearly all of the dishes were non-meat and came in a hot pocket — much like the meal he ate at his grandpa's before leaving for his first morning at the Crucible. Just like then, he was surprised by how great the food tasted. He ate two hot pockets and began to roam the tunnels of the compound.

After meandering for 30 minutes, he found himself on the west side of one of the taller buildings, looking at the sunset. Like those old-time prescription sunglasses that could shift from dark to clear depending on whether you were in or outdoors, the tinted glass surrounding the tunnels was now almost perfectly see through in the diminishing light. It was beautiful and calming.

"Enjoy that sunset while you can."

The voice was familiar. It was Charlie slowly walking up behind him.

"Because we're in the winter," he said. "We're on a time schedule similar to the one you know. But in the spring, we enter *heat time* and the clocks jumps forward three hours. Then, on the summer solstice, we go into *summer heat time* and the clocks move up another three hours. The solstice is now a big holiday because after that you're waking up in the middle of the night and going to bed before the late afternoon so that you avoid the hottest times. The summers are so harsh. *The Fervens* are these super heat waves that come up in the summers. Nobody leaves their homes for days during the daylight hours. They're like zombies coming out at night to breathe fresh air."

"So much is so different," Will said, still staring out toward the mountains. Only about a quarter of the sun was still peeking out.

"Yeah," Charlie continued. He was now standing next to Will. "The summers are rough. Rich people go on something called *The Cruise*. They buy or rent these big boats and follow the winter all around the globe. Must be nice…"

Charlie trailed off. Unlike Kathy, he really wanted to know how Will was doing.

"I'm sorry you had to hear about all that last night. It was so abrupt. I just wanted to help," he said.

"I know. It's tough. I love my grandpa so much. I'm just frustrated."

"You know how you asked last night about what it takes to win in the Crucible? Well, when it comes to the things you can control, I'd say the best way to go is to cut out anything that doesn't have to do with the competition. I know you have the ability to go far. Try not to be distracted. I love Big D, but if he's a distraction, it's probably for the best that you take this time to work on the task at hand."

"Makes sense," Will said. It was sound advice, but somehow it made him want to see Deacon more than before. "Still, I know he loves me and even if he isn't telling me everything, that love means something."

"He definitely loves you," Charlie responded. "And I know you need somebody to be there for you, even if he can't. Look, right now I'm not in a position to tell you anything more. In fact, we aren't supposed to even be talking because of everything I did for you in court. But while you are here, I intend to be there for you and help you all I can, for as long as it makes sense. You are not alone. Maybe you can see your grandpa at Christmas. But until then stay the course."

The two smiled at each other. *You are not alone.* Those words meant the world to Will. He wasn't with his grandpa and there was no Coop. To have someone to rely on gave him tremendous solace.

The sun was now completely behind the mountains and just a light pink hue remained. Charlie patted Will on the back, and they went their separate ways.

CHAPTER TWELVE

If his life were a film, Will figured he'd entered the montage portion. It's that familiar point in the movies when the music gets loud and the camera cuts to constant scenes of hard work that saves the viewer from the actual sweat-of-the-brow monotony that's truly needed to win at the end.

In the two weeks since leaving his grandfather's, doubts continued to surface about whether he could do this without the support that was key to propelling him in his first go-around. But Will worked hard to push that fear out of his mind. He'd follow Charlie's advice to avoid thinking about Deacon – or Coop for that matter – and, instead, get into the daily rhythm of the Crucible Compound. Most of the time was spent studying with Kathy for both the written and physical tests that would begin two days before Christmas.

One assumption people often made about Will was that he played baseball because he loved the game. It was true he enjoyed it more than other options like football, but his attraction to sport had less to do with the activity and everything to do with the process. Preparation and competition were Will's addictions. It cleared out the clutter in his life and gave him flawless focus. Present a task, and he would challenge himself to complete it. He loved that set-up because, in the end, he could tangibly measure his performance. There were no politics involved on a sports field or in a classroom – especially on multiple choice tests where Will was a master. Instead, there were hard numbers that reflected victory or failure.

For him, the first step in finding success in any game, including the Crucible, was understanding the underlying purpose of the competition. In simple terms, Will recognized the goal here was to win so his family's bloodline would survive.

But the intention behind tests always told him much more about what a culture was trying to accomplish. In Will's day, there was still the notion of the liberal arts education. The purpose was to produce well-rounded individuals. So, sure, there were career-oriented classes at Harvard, but at the same time you had English and philosophy and even music appreciation.

The world had changed – and not just in the ways he saw when flying a drone over Denver. Forget well-rounded, what was being tested here was how well the champion Exemplar could survive and contribute. There were classes on xeriscaping (a term for landscaping in dry environments), outdoor survival, water purification and even small-animal hunting. What fascinated Will most about many parts of the curriculum was how it spoke to that human quirk of always getting people ready for the challenges earlier generations faced. He remembered how, during World War I, armies still taught cavalry warfare in the face of new-fangled artillery and rapid-fire machine guns. They were preparing for wars of the past, rather than the dangers of the present. Geometry was taught in high schools to prepare people for working on farms long after most people lived in cities. That knowledge wasn't really useful when you didn't have to come up with measurements to create a field, but it's what had worked for people in the past.

The significant portion of the preparation spoke to fears from the pre-apocalypse era, which was the harshest period brought on by climate change. While learning those survival techniques might have been smart in 2025, he found that on the rare occasions he now left campus, the world seemed to be pretty stable. That said, Will and Kathy almost always stuck to what needed to be learned to win. But every once in a while, Kathy would recount some of the horrors of the pre-apocalypse. Farmable land was decreasing. People were starving. Hatred was increasing. Political corruption was rampant. Tribalism (another completely human trait) continued to build to the point where everyone expected nuclear Armageddon. What saved humanity? From what Will could make out, it was conflict fatigue – sheer exhaustion. Numbers were dwindling everywhere and people finally reached a critical mass of misery. A few brave leaders recognized it was simply time to find a new way.

During his time, Will often heard people spout about human exceptionalism. This was the idea that we were *the* superior animals on this planet, made special by opposable thumbs and a big brain. He often discarded this claim because it was usually made by somebody looking to convince others to act in a morally questionable way. But the recounting of how humankind pulled itself from the brink – sure there was a pre-apocalypse period, but, thankfully no actual full-blown apocalypse – suggested to him that, perhaps, he should give humanity a bit more due.

Of course, that calculation came with wondering whether he was part of humanity. On the rare occasions when Will couldn't help himself and subtly tried to shift a conversation toward uncovering some piece of his past, Kathy, with all her jittery energy and "bywary" exclamations, showed amazing skill at deftly sliding the subject back to the work at hand. Each day she was upping her game. She even slowed down her speech and stopped throwing in words from the present that Will didn't know.

After a while, Will gave up on trying to get information out of Kathy. Charlie's words about "staying the course" continually bounced around in his mind. Inspired, his new short-term goal was to *commit to the process*. If he could maintain a laser focus on the work rather than considering the possibilities of winning or losing, it simplified his task. Just work on mastering modern coding or understand planting edible crops in desert-like terrain. The results would then take care of themselves.

It was all a grind with a few notable exceptions. Each day, the four Exemplars would exercise together. The referees understood that the competition was an isolating experience and concluded that the pros outweighed the cons in having the Exemplars experience some limited interaction. There was always the fear that competitive aspects of the Crucible would lead to bad blood. In the past, there were instances of fights during exercise time. But in the Colorado District, at least, it generally worked, and this group got along smoothly.

Will was disappointed they were allotted only 45 minutes a day for exercise because working out was always both an important physical and psychological release for him. But technology in 2090 streamlined the activity. Machines called Eclines were now the standard for keeping in shape. They looked a bit like human-sized gyroscopes. A person was strapped in the contraption and moved through a series of maneuvers that required the user to resist or control the machine with counter-pressure. The result was a totally comprehensive strengthening and aerobic burn in just 35 minutes. The balance of the time featured five minutes of stretching on either side of the exercise. It was during this precious period that the Exemplars chatted.

Beyond that small window of human contact, Will's other great savior was Charlie. He was true to his word. He took numerous opportunities to find Will and talk to him privately. Often these conversations occurred where they first met in the tunnel looking out at the mountains. For the most part, Charlie tried to keep Will on target, making sure he was doing his studying and answering any questions that might have fallen through the cracks during Will's lessons with Kathy. He also tried to boost Will's chances by giving him some additional assistance on the margins.

In fact, Charlie tipped Will off to the fact that in the semi-final round there would be a personality test to determine an Exemplar's ability to interact with others. There was no studying for this and it would be a surprise to his opponents. "It's multiple choice. If you want to ace the test, just ask yourself 'What would a saint do, then pick the next best answer,'" he explained with a smile.

Charlie's hints created a moral quandary. Nothing he offered could give Will an outright victory, but he knew it wouldn't hurt. It was no different than stealing signs in baseball, Will rationalized. Sure, it wasn't technically fair, but finding competitive advantages – as long as there wasn't over-the-top cheating – was part of the game.

But even more than that, Will consistently felt like he needed Charlie's special support to offset the actions of Chief Marks. At the start of the Crucible, Will suspected Chief Marks didn't like him. While he hadn't brought it up with Charlie again since Thanksgiving, he was now sure of it. Any interaction with the chief referee was a bad one. For instance, Chief Marks did daily audits of all the Exemplar's training. Whenever Will gave an answer – good or bad – she would criticize it – and him.

"Mr. Herndon," she'd say dismissively. "I'm at a loss for how you were ever chosen as an Exemplar. Ninety-six percent, ha! The 100 percent original must not have been much."

If that wasn't enough, she would often pull Kathy out of lessons for long chunks of time, which was something the other Exemplars said never happened to them. Kathy always came back perplexed as to why she was pulled out, leaving Will with the undeniable conclusion that it was a way to throw Will off his game.

To compensate for those extra impediments, Will cut his sleep down at night so he could study. At least, that was the reason he gave himself. Deep down, he understood there was another reason for his lack of sleep. He feared his dreams. The beautiful blonde who had come to him the night before Thanksgiving was starting to show up on a nightly basis.

At first, he was happy to see her. But the more she invaded his dreams, the more he feared her. Some mornings, he'd even wake up in a sweat. Most of the dreams were the same. They were always around the fire. Sometimes she was laughing and sometimes she was pinning him down playfully. The dreams had given a few clues about her. She had tattoos on the lower part of her arms. Written in ornate script, one said "Love" and the other "Chaos".

What probably upset Will the most about the haunting images was that it was just another weight to divert him from remaining focused on the competition. Each time he saw the girl, it was like an echo from the past whispering in his ear, and it brought back his yearning to know the truth about what he couldn't remember. It was the ultimate distraction.

CHAPTER THIRTEEN

Two days before the start of the competition, Will ambled into the daily Exemplar exercises feeling prepared. The previous day, Charlie walked by him in a hallway and whispered, "coding, practice coding." He winked and skipped along as if nothing had happened.

If Charlie was trying to assist Will, Chief Marks continued to do her best – albeit a little more subtly – to undermine his chances. Kathy received the final schedule for the Crucible a full day after the other Counselors. It was difficult not to feel for her. The other three Counselors were experienced and knew all the ins and outs of this process. Kathy was smart and earnest, and enthusiastic almost to a fault, but she was learning on the job. She was specifically assigned to Will by Chief Marks, which was yet another reason why he felt no guilt that Charlie was helping.

As it turned out, the details of the rounds were as expected so Will didn't mind that Kathy was slow to get the logistics. The seeding round would start with a day of written testing followed by an activity-based competition two days later. Performances would be announced between the two events so Exemplars were aware of where they stood. The semi-final round pairings were then set and the same procedure would occur but flip-flopped (the practical assessment first and then the testing). Then two days later, the top pair would be matched in the final: the Gauntlet.

Sitting down to begin stretching with his Exemplar adversaries, he looked at the opposition and liked his chances. While they spent only a little time together each day, he'd gotten to know Trent and Amy reasonably well. In contrast,

Kevin kept pretty much to himself. This interaction left no doubt they were smart and talented and deserved to be representing their bloodlines. Will didn't have the support he'd been accustomed to, but because his limited memory represented nothing but success, he felt confident. As far as he could tell, he'd never tasted failure in his past life as long as he was thoroughly prepared.

"Hello, Junior," Amy said, already sitting on a mat stretching her legs. When the other three contestants discovered Will was just 19, they stuck him with the nickname. He'd wondered why his age had been such a big deal at his initial physical and, although he never got a full answer, he did learn that all the others were 21, which was the typically mandated age for Exemplars. The nickname wasn't as bad as being called "cafeteria" during freshman year of college, but the fact he didn't know why he was two years younger than the rest did frustrate him. He tried to shrug off the mystery and told himself he looked forward to his performance once again wiping out the unwelcomed name. But for now, he'd play along.

While he didn't really know Kevin too well, he liked Amy and Trent. Amy had shed the nervous behavior she exhibited on the first day. Will respected her straight-to-the-point approach. Although he'd always been awkward around girls, he didn't have any problem hanging with Amy. Maybe it was that they were Exemplars first and male and female second. He didn't know. As for Trent, it was impossible not to be impressed or attracted to his charisma. He had a knack for always saying the right thing and being cool and composed.

"Hey Amy, Trent, Kevin," Will said to his opposition. Trent was also sitting stretching his arms. Kevin's mat was farther away from the other two. He barely took notice when Will walked in. The three would talk conversationally about things like the weather and food, but the one point they agreed to follow was to never discuss the competition. It was a rule Amy was about to break.

"So," Amy began with a tentative edge to her voice, "what would you do if you lost the competition?"

Even Kevin perked up at Amy's words.

"Ground rules, Amy," Trent responded in an unbothered deep voice. "We don't talk about the Crucible."

"I know," Amy replied defiantly. "But this isn't about the mechanics or the preparation. It's about the after-effects."

Trent, who was such a natural leader, cocked his head in agreement and then looked at Kevin and Will, who both nodded.

For Will, it was a novel question; in fact, it was a thought he'd never even contemplated. Before thinking, he blurted out an elementary question that he couldn't believe he didn't know.

"What happens if you lose?"

Trent and Amy looked at each other and began to laugh.

"Junior, are you kidding me?" Trent asked in a friendly way. "You haven't even taken a moment to contemplate that you might not prevail here. Dare I say, I'm a little offended."

Trent never claimed he was flat out better than anyone else, so it would have been hard to call him arrogant. But his sense of self-confidence could be unintentionally condescending. For example, if an Exemplar said something Trent agreed with, he wouldn't say "I totally agree," but would offer, in a supremely self-assured tone, a one-word response: "correct". It was as if he always knew the answer and he was welcoming you into his club for gifted people.

As a result, even though it was difficult to embarrass Will, he could feel his cheeks getting hot and flushed.

"I was assured we weren't ground up to feed stock animals, so I didn't really worry about it," Will shot back, trying to diffuse his humiliation.

"Maybe you should," Amy responded rather ominously.

"Now Amy, that's not completely fair," Trent countered. "As an important point of fact, if you lose, you get to live your life. You are given a federal pension and are permitted to work. Actually, the only tangible sanction is that you're not allowed to procreate."

"But it's not what it means on paper," Amy said, leaning back onto her forearms to get a deeper stretch in her legs. "It's the societal ramifications. It's the stigma the losers must face. Truth be told, everyone always says they wish they knew now what they knew then. I *actually do know*. I'm not even sure I want to have kids in this world. Not sure I really like people enough."

Amy possessed the longest personal memory of the three. It was unclear what Kevin remembered. All he'd said was that he was born in 1885 and grumpily conceded that he lacked the same pedigree as the three of us. But Amy was born in 1977, daughter of Vietnamese refugees. A graduate of Northwestern University, she'd been a fantastic fencer, making it to the U.S. Olympics Trials in Epée. Married and divorced with one child, she lived to see the start of the pre-apocalypse period. Much of it was hazy – likely because it was probably so traumatic. She didn't know what happened to her son and her last remainder was a cousin who was so distant, they'd only met once since she returned.

"Come on, it's not that bad," Trent pushed back. "Look at Charlie Reed. He's a pillar of society."

"Yes, but he *won*." Amy would not relent. "Losers are like untouchables. They're pretty much shunned from the social order. Sure, I don't love people, but it's like being in purgatory. They even have a name for those who fail."

"Deliquio," Kevin entered the conversation for the first time.

The other three looked at him, waiting for him to continue, but that was all he was going to offer so Amy continued.

"Yep, deliquios. Three of us will be friendless, prohibited by law to procreate and just 21 – or 19 with Junior. That's why most deliquios just live at their Crucible Compound, where the suicide rates—"

"Okay," Trent interrupted firmly and Amy stopped. "We get it. But life is what you make of it – deliquio or not. I have no intention of ending up in this category. But for those who do, they should hold their head up high."

Will truly didn't think Trent was self-aware enough to understand that his comment presumed the other three would inevitably end up as deliquios. He was just hard-wired to assume it, Will thought.

"It's more than that," Amy said, pressing the issue. "They *sterilize* you if you lose. I mean they bring you back and then take away a fundamental right."

"Well, it is a choice," Trent said dismissively. "You can avoid sterilization and be overseen by a post-Crucible Counselor."

"It's like a parole officer!" Amy said, getting frustrated. "OHFs can't even talk about their DNA match scores for fear that regular people will think they're lesser people because they're not perfect copies of their former selves." She added air quotes around "regular people".

"If people hate deliquios so much, why do they accept the winner?" Will interrupted.

"Everyone loves a winner," Trent replied flatly.

"It's more complicated than that," Amy jumped in, now deeply annoyed. "After losing – and usually being sterilized – most deliquios sink into the shadows. So even though there are more of them than winners, few people ever even see one. Folks you never meet are the ones that are easily hated. The victorious Exemplar gets to live a life. Winners like Mr. Reed get a pass because they are in the world and receive enough attention in the media that people tend to be both interested and accepting of them."

Amy's observation left the group silent until Kathy entered the room. The Counselors rotated proctoring exercise hour, and it was her turn. Not surprisingly, she seemed a bit nervous.

"Uh guys, you're running five minutes behind. Can I ask that you commence your Ecline workouts?"

The four Exemplars quietly stood up and strapped themselves into their respective machines. The first time they boarded this wild ride they had all been hesitant. But now they'd learned the hang of all the sharp motions and spins that the Ecline offered. After only a few workouts, Will begrudgingly admitted that it was a great machine, and in his nearly three weeks of working the apparatus, he felt stronger and more limber.

He'd developed enough expertise that he didn't have to concentrate too much on what he was doing. It was becoming second nature. The telltale whirring sound of the Ecline machines began as each Exemplar started contorting in various ways. Will let his mind wander.

His grandpa was a deliquio, but he'd refused to hide in the shadows. He ran a building crew and lived in his own house. He had Charlie as a friend, but they were both OHFs, so that probably wasn't a surprise. Did he have other friends or was he shunned like Amy suggested? At 48, he'd had 27 years to contemplate his failure and size up the loneliness of his life. Increasingly, Will was looking forward to seeing Deacon for Christmas in just a few days' time.

The turning and tossing stopped, and the four slowly descended from their machines. Kevin sweated profusely and always had a towel close by. Trent was the exact opposite. There was not a drop of perspiration on his forehead. Will, who sweated somewhere in between the two, found Trent's lack of perspiration a marvel.

Will and Trent were different in many ways. While Trent was originally born in 1920 and spent his childhood in the City Park West neighborhood not too far from Will's Five Points home. The contrast in the demographics between the two neighborhoods couldn't have been more evident. City Park West in Trent's time was one of the grand Denver places to live (by the time Will came around, it wasn't nearly as fancy.) Trent grew up wealthy and was the starting quarterback at CU – Boulder. He graduated in 1941 and immediately started at

Stanford Law School. Sadly, his time there was short as he enlisted as a lieutenant in the U.S. Army not long after the bombing at Pearl Harbor.

Clearly, other than the sports background, so little of that backstory matched Will's, but he felt a connection to Trent for two reasons. The first was that Trent's memory also ended at a young age. And, the second was that in some ways, Trent reminded Will of his best friend Cooper Fielding. There was the same magnetism and charm – though he couldn't tell if Trent had nearly the same level of kindness and loyalty.

"Trent, do you wish you knew more about who you are?" Will asked as they began their post-workout stretching routine. "I mean, Amy knows her story into at least her 60s and I assume Kevin has a long memory horizon." Kevin nodded yes. "But we don't."

Trent took a moment to think about the question. He stretched down, effortlessly touched his toes and then stood erect.

"But I do know my whole story," he said matter of factly with no sense of the repercussions the statement would present.

The answer hit Will hard. He was sure Trent's personal historical knowledge was as limited as his. Trent made that admission early in their workouts. That fact comforted Will. Not possessing details about his past vexed Will more than anything in this competition and, now, he was instantaneously jealous. If only he could have the same answers, he could fully concentrate on the task at hand. Instead, despite efforts to the contrary, he wasted what he thought was considerable time on this very issue. He tried to compose himself quickly.

"But how?" Will asked.

"It happened almost by accident. I'd gone to visit my last remainder, Jenny, and while she was cooking dinner, I nosed around her front room. I wasn't looking for anything. I was just trying to pass the time and pulled out an old photo album. I mean I lived more than a century ago, what were the odds that I'd open right to a page with the telegram?"

He trailed off for a moment. Knowing his timeline, Amy audibly gasped.

"Was it from the U.S. Army?" Amy asked, already knowing the answer.

Trent nodded. "I was killed at the Battle of the Bulge, January 6, 1944. Apparently, I was awarded the Silver Star posthumously. I immediately reported this discovery to Chief Marks and she said not to worry. Learning past histories was not necessarily a failing offense. It depended, she said. And, in my case, it was considered minor. She alerted the other Counselors and that was that."

Amy was fascinated by this knowledge.

"Does it creep you out to know how you died?"

"Not at all. It's like having a surgery you don't recall. If I can't remember it, it doesn't matter. It wasn't congenital heart failure so it's not as if I carry any genes that may lead to an untimely death this time around. Not to mention, I clearly honored my bloodline. That bravery was probably part of the reason I'm here. Right, Junior?"

He winked at Will, who was frozen by all this and could feel the anger mounting inside. He wanted similar closure. Maybe he died young too. Could it have been a drive-by shooting? Or some disease? Did it really matter? He wanted to know.

Amy didn't wait for Will to answer.

"I agree. We're OHFs, so, existentially speaking, I can't even say it was really me. But I just wouldn't want to know the details. It's so chilling."

"But your DNA is the same, you are, in essence, the same person," Will emotionally interjected. "No offense Trent, but it doesn't seem right that you got to close that loop. Amy, fine, if you don't want to know your full picture, that's your choice. Not only that, but you also have so much history to work from. You have memories into your 60s! To deny me the right to know, is, well, it's completely unfair."

A hush fell over the group. Both Amy and Trent were sitting on their mats, looking at the ground. They were at a loss for words. Kevin, who seemed to enjoy the discord, was watching the exchange with a wry smile. He was hoping for more.

After another quiet second, Trent got up and started walking to the door. A disappointed Kevin did the same.

"I think our time here is done," Trent said.

Will and Amy remained on the ground lingering.

"Look, you know our original timelines overlap," Amy said quietly. "Your past is a bigger story than you might think. It's really not my place to say anymore, other than to promise you – and I'm really promising you – that you've got to let it go."

With that she quickly got up and hustled out of the room. Will was getting more heated by the moment. Why did she have the details of his life and he didn't? Knowing who he was – who he is – shouldn't be Amy's choice, or anybody's choice, but his. How dare they all hold back.

That night, he awoke suddenly in his sleep. He'd dreamed of the blonde woman again. Whether he won in the Crucible or ended up a deliquio, he vowed he would find out who she was and, more importantly, what happened to him.

CHAPTER FOURTEEN

Great athletes are masters of compartmentalizing. A family member is dying? You've been nursing the stomach flu for two weeks? Your best friend won't talk to you? None of that matters when you enter the field of play. True sporting heroes know that very discord can serve as a focusing agent. They channel all their anger and frustration with surgical concentration into achieving at their sports commitments.

Will may not have known everything about himself, but he was keenly aware that he was a great athlete. Despite efforts to the contrary, he was becoming obsessed with his past again. Still, he would cast it aside now and throw himself into the first round of the Crucible. In his final day before the written test, he redoubled his studying habits. *Code. Code. Code.* Charlie had given him that tip, and he was going all in. Unlike in his day, coding was a lot different in 2090. It was called "AI prompting" and was more about collaborating with artificial intelligence than embarking on laborious, line-by-line work. Will took some time to get the hang of it as he practiced over and over again, but he knew he could master it.

During his preparations the night before the first test, Will gave the AI an incorrect command. Tired, he let his mind wander and wondered to himself whether the reason he didn't recollect anything beyond 19 was because he'd made a critical misstep. Maybe he became the state's governor in the pre-apocalypse period and performed poorly. Nah, he'd have more memory to make it that far. He smacked his foot on the floor at the thought. "Remain focused, Herndon," he whispered to himself. Already accustomed to experiencing sleep deficit, thanks to his desire to avoid the blonde girl in his dreams, he stuck at it all night.

He was the first to arrive at the very same door he entered that initial day at the Crucible Compound. He jumped up and down and shook his head like he was about to go onto a field. He felt surprisingly awake as the adrenaline pumped wildly through his veins. Trent showed up next. He seemed unsure how to react to Will after the discussion in the exercise room. He was relieved when Will gave him a head nod. Kevin showed up next. As always, he was detached.

Charlie came out of the door. He looked around and asked where Amy was, but there was no answer. Just then, she ran up, apologizing for her tardiness. The four, along with Charlie, walked into the familiar old hockey rink, though the set up was a bit different. There was no longer a stage and no chairs for them to sit in. Instead, there were four eight-foot-tall white cylinders. Each was spaced about six feet from each other and had a door. Chief Marks stood in the room waiting for the Exemplars.

"These silos are your testing centers," Charlie explained. "They are soundproof, roomy and set up so that you can approach the test with all-embracing attention."

Chief Marks then interrupted: "You have three hours to complete the exam and you will get your scores immediately after all four Exemplars have completed their tasks." It unnerved Amy, who jumped just a little bit, at her voice. It was the most uncomfortable Will had seen Amy since the first day. "The tests will be graded on a percentage and the score will be combined with your performance in the practical portion of this round, which will take place tomorrow. If you complete your test early, please go into the hallway. Thank you."

The Exemplars entered their silos through silent sliding doors. Charlie wasn't lying about these contraptions. They were pretty ideal. The light could be altered depending on an individual's needs. They were also spacious and, as soon as Will sat down, a table and the chair, which was one of those cube contraptions, moved to what were the optimal distances. One of those handheld computers was situated on the desk.

Over the past few weeks, Will developed a mastery of the handheld. He slickly moved icons and documents around. The key was getting used to the weird sensation of the holograms having texture. Logically, he knew that these were laser-created light projections, but he marveled every time he reached for one, and they somehow delivered the feel of a real object.

In front of him was a countdown clock. There was one minute and twenty seconds until the test would begin. Will felt a quick panic. What if Charlie was wrong about the subject? Could he perform if he had to consider another topic? Before he could go down that self-destructive rabbit hole, the test began.

"Charlie is the man," he said under his breath. Coding was the topic and everything else – like his grandfather and his obsession with the past – left his mind as he began furiously commanding – and refining his commands – to the AI in order to develop a 3D printer algorithm for constructing a dishwasher. When that was done, he nailed the necessary elements for a program to follow weather fluctuations. The final assignment was a bit trickier. It was an AI prompting for a face recognition security system.

When you're confident on a test, time seems to fly by. Will put the final touches on his work and was surprised to see he had 19 minutes left. He could just sit there, but decided he wanted to stretch his legs. He got up and walked out of the silo.

His eyes took a second to recalibrate to the less precise light of the hockey arena. He saw six chairs lined up with Chief Marks, Charlie and the four Counselors now whispering to each other. Charlie threw him a knowing smile, while Kathy, who always looked just a little disheveled, offered him a sincere grin. Will turned to exit the door into the hallway.

The next moment was immediately awkward. Standing out in the hallway was Amy and she stuttered and gasped for air at the site of Will. The reaction upset Will, because, while he may have been angry at Amy, he never gave her any reason to be worried.

"Look, *Will*," Amy said, accenting his first name as if to say I'm taking you seriously and not calling you Junior. "I am sorry I upset you. Whatever I know, it's just...I guess I don't feel it's my place to break the rules and give you answers."

With the test over, all the adrenaline that had carried Will through was seeping away and he felt irritably exhausted. The compartmentalizing was over, he thought. They were off the playing field and he didn't need to hold back.

"You're looking at this the wrong way Amy," Will said with obvious exasperation. "What gives you the right *not* to tell me? Shouldn't we control our own destiny? I can't ..."

Will was clenching his teeth and squeezing his fists. He then unconsciously took a step toward Amy. The combination led to Amy cowering against the wall. At that very moment, the door swung open and Chief Marks saw the worst possible snapshot of the exchange.

"Mr. Herndon! What is going on here?" she shouted. There was venom in her words. Both Will and Amy straightened up, and Chief Marks regained her composure for a moment. Amy prided herself on being loyal, honest and, above all else, tough. She truly liked Will, but she did the calculus in her mind and knew what had to be said.

"Chief Marks, nothing happened here, but Will has a nasty obsession with his past, and as someone with an overlapping timeline, I don't feel comfortable in his presence at the moment."

"I'm sure you don't," Chief Marks said knowingly. "Thank you, Ms. Pham. Please go into the room and tell Mr. Reed that we may be delayed for a moment. Ask him to keep the other Exemplars in the room."

Despite Will's anger, Amy gave Will a look as if to say she was sorry. Sure, she wanted to win and this might put a competitor in a bad position. But she strongly believed in fair play and felt some remorse. She looked at Chief Marks and said, "Please don't –" but was cut off by the older woman. "That's enough, Ms. Pham."

Amy left the room and, much to Will's surprise, he didn't feel nervous. He felt defiant.

"Mr. Herndon. I wish, I just wish I could throw you out of this Crucible right now." Chief Marks was losing control, something Will had never witnessed. It always seemed to be bubbling under every conversation they had, but even when he could see glimpses of the anger, she would rein it in. Not this time.

"You don't deserve to be here!" She said with a fleck of spit flying from her mouth. "You want to know about your past? You think you have a right? Let me tell you this, you're as useless now as I *know you were then*. Does that help clear things up? Arrogant boy. Your current memory cheats you comprehensively. All you know is that you were some great baseball player. That you went to Harvard. Ha! Disloyal and disgusting is a better reflection of who you are. No court in the land will ever dissuade me otherwise. Now, listen closely. We'll see if your small mind can grasp this. Political forces may prevent me from kicking you out for this infraction and making you the deliquio you are bound to become. But I swear, if you go searching for your past any more – as much as I'd be delighted for you to know the truth about yourself – I will disqualify you. I don't care if I get voted out of office. It would be worth it. You've already dishonored an otherwise forgettable bloodline."

Chief Marks was breathing heavily, and Will's defiance had been blunted by the harsh nature of the woman's words. Will nodded. "I understand," he said, trying to remain strong but struggling as he processed the chief referee's words. "May I reenter?"

The chief nodded her head as her breathing began to slow. Will put his hand on the door and was about to open it, when Chief Marks spoke again.

"You know, Mr. Herndon, one of the great failures of youth is that you always assume everything is about you," she said, having regained the poise in her voice. "Understand, in this case, this isn't just about you."

Chief Marks followed Will into the room and walked back to her spot next to Charlie and the Counselors across from the other three Exemplars, who were lined up shoulder to shoulder.

"Sorry for the delay and thank you for your effort today," the chief said as if she hadn't just lost her cool moments before. She was a politician after all.

Will's heart was beating fast. Not because the scores were being released but because of what the chief had just told him. All along, he'd thought he was being denied information to protect him. But could it be that everyone – from his grandpa to Amy – were trying to protect others from him? He knew himself. Or he thought he knew who he was at his core. He *was* reliable and loyal. It was in his DNA, whether he was an OHF or the original article. He had to know it.

He was broken out of his deep thoughts by the sound of clapping. Trent slapped him on the shoulder and offered his hand to shake.

"I guess I should stop calling you Junior," he said with a dimpled smile. "But don't expect to be at the top of the board when this is over."

Will looked up and saw the projection of a board. It read:

Seeding Round: Written performance

Herndon, W 98%

Aberforth, T 96%

Pham, A 87%

McNabb, K 65%

CHAPTER FIFTEEN

The high-speed Maglev train sped silently through the tunnel toward the mountains. It had always struck Will as odd that while Denver was located on a relatively flat piece of land, it was best known for its connection to the mountains. He couldn't deny that they were beautiful and when he arrived at college he would talk about the view all the time. But he always saw them as a dividing line between rich and poor. In his time, skiing was not a sport a kid from his neighborhood would get the opportunity to enjoy. And although he was a native, he had only been up to the mountains twice – as far as he could remember – and both times he had stayed with Coop's family.

Cooper was an expert skier, but he often begged off trips in order to take extra batting practice. Even when it was winter, he'd go to the indoor cages, honing the mechanics of his swing. The two boys consistently pushed each other. The only difference was Coop had options. He had ski trips he could go on. For Will, achieving on the baseball field was everything.

As the train sped through the foothills toward higher elevation, Will was more conflicted than ever. After winning the first written test, exhaustion had gotten the better of him and, uncharacteristically, he went to bed early. That meant the blonde girl once again invaded his psyche. It was a siren song, pulling him closer to something he could never quite reach. Now, he was wondering about her. Was she laughing at him? With him? Or was it nothing to do with him?

Will began to consider the clarity of an OHF's memories again. It made sense that data on the chip wouldn't fade, but what about the echoes that both Deacon and Milo Swenson had talked about? Will figured the girl was an echo, but his dreams of her were every bit as well-defined as any other memory he accessed. Will was beginning to learn that the new memories he'd made since his return acted much like a normal person's recollections – they would fade over time. Why wouldn't echoes of the past do the same? After all they were organic rather than being digitally implanted.

All this left Will growing more indecisive about his past. Chief Marks' words resonated with him. She seemed to take *his* past personally, and, maybe, digging deeper into it would do others harm. He hadn't had the time or opportunity to investigate whether a now much older Coop was still around to give him guidance, and his grandpa was out of the picture for the moment. For now, he'd place his energies into the Crucible, he thought.

Maybe everything else could wait.

With that in mind, he moved up two seats to sit across a row from Amy. She was quietly staring out the window and didn't notice Will coming closer. She was watching a simulation similar to the one Will used on the Maglev. Outside of Amy's window snow draped every mountain and tree. A flurry was brewing that would surely cover the few clear spots left in the image.

"I'm sorry," Will said as soon as he was settled in his new seat.

Amy turned her head.

"Don't sweat it, Junior," she said. For once, that nickname felt inviting rather than taunting.

"I had no right to push you in any way. I was thoughtless and selfish."

"I've already forgiven you," Amy responded with a joking tone. "What else do you need? Total absolution?"

They looked at each other and shared a laugh. Amy was a no-nonsense person. She was spooked by Will's aggressiveness because, more than anything, it seemed out of character. She wondered whether the whole thing was to throw her off her game. But she'd ultimately taken responsibility for her relatively sub-par performance on the written test.

Things she knew about her own past did haunt her. Even in the memory she was allowed to have, she could distinctly recall people clawing for survival during the pre-apocalypse period. She was surprised she was permitted to remember things she thought would have been too traumatic. But the fact they were in her mind led to an undeniable conclusion: She must have survived many more unspeakable moments that had been edited from her mind. All this buoyed her confidence, making her believe that she must be tougher than she even knew.

"How'd your physical go?" Amy asked, shifting the subject. Before the practical exams, each Exemplar went to see Dr. Wilson to get clearance to compete.

"Fit as a fiddle," Will said with a wink. Because their timelines overlapped, Amy was one of the few people he felt comfortable with using metaphors that no longer existed. If Will were to say they were "floored" by a particularly surprising comment or he called somebody a "baller" nobody would get it other than Amy. They both sat quietly for a moment distracted by the passing landscape, watching the Era Simulator recall what it looked like in 1991. It showed an absolutely realistic mountain with skiers looking like ants slaloming down a number of different trails.

"They just revived this train line." Amy said, as if they were back to normal. "The original version opened in 2028 so skiers could easily go up to Breck, Copper, Vail – all the popular spots. I didn't get to the mountains often, but I remembered when it opened. It was such a big deal. Within 10 years, there wasn't enough snow to ski and the mountain resorts were dying. It became like ghost towns up here. Going to the mountains has only become cool again recently."

For the most part, Will avoided spending time on anything other than preparation for the Crucible. Sure, he'd pushed for information on his past, but otherwise had only picked up small threads about the big picture in the intervening years between when his memory ended and today.

He wondered how familiar the others were with the mountains. It would matter so much today. They were all told by Charlie that the practical competition would test three characteristics – teamwork, physical endurance and survival skills.

As the current "number one seed," Will was paired with last-place Kevin and would compete against Trent and Amy. The teams would be given basic supplies, a map and an old-school compass. Each pair was expected to find a predetermined camping site, and they were then required to set up shelter before returning the following day. Constantly monitored, each team would be graded by the chief referee on teamwork, accurate map reading, speed and ingenuity.

It was another perfect example of fighting the wrong war, Will thought. During the pre-apocalypse times, grasping these basic skills may have offered some value. But how necessary were these abilities now?

The 40-minute train ride dropped the group off at what was once the base of the Vail Ski Resort. It was eerie. Dilapidated buildings peppered the bottom of what, in Will's lifetime, was a vibrant bustling village. It was two days before Christmas, and the fading ghosts of happy revelers who once enjoyed this former winter wonderland felt like they were all around them.

"Teams, please follow me," Chief Marks said as she walked toward a series of rusted old gondolas, accompanied by Charlie and two other Crucible Compound employees carrying big boxes. At what felt like an arbitrary location, she stopped and the two men carrying the boxes placed them down 20 feet apart.

"Enclosed in these boxes are everything you need for this task – and more," she said. "You could not possibly be able to carry everything offered. As such, your first task is to determine, as a team, what is essential and what isn't. You will have a maximum of 25 minutes. When you are ready, alert Mr. Reed and he will give you your map and compass. Each pair will be required to reach a separate camp location. At dawn tomorrow, you will be expected to return. You shouldn't worry if you see drones flying overhead. That will allow *me* to grade your performances. Any questions? No? Good. Then let's begin."

The truth was Chief Marks didn't allow for any questions and, before Will could even react, Amy and Trent were already ripping open their box. Will looked at Kevin, who was strolling toward their supplies. Without saying a word to Will, Kevin opened the box and began inspecting and then pulling out supplies.

"Shouldn't we talk about what we need?" Will asked Kevin.

"Nope," Kevin said flatly. He continued to take materials out, placing each one he deemed important carefully into one of two backpacks.

Kevin was the forgotten Exemplar. He'd scored poorly on his DNA Match Percentage. He rarely spoke. And when he did, it was usually just a few words. Will never gave him too much thought. But now it was dawning on him just how difficult this test would be.

"This task is meant to reflect teamwork," Will said, trying to reason with Kevin. "I'm not sure you making all these decisions on your own helps us in that category."

Kevin stopped filling a water bottle for a moment and looked disdainfully at Will.

"I know the mountains. By the judge of you, you don't. So how about we say this teamwork is a leader/follower sort of thing."

Without missing a beat, he went back to work. Will knew better than to argue so he stood by awkwardly. He turned his head to see Chief Marks staring right at him. She offered a very disingenuous smile and then manipulated something on her handheld.

A moment later, Kevin said, "We're ready" and shoved a full backpack into Will's arms and waved at Charlie.

"Good luck, fellas," Charlie said to Will as he handed over the map and compass. Kevin reached out and took both. The forward move by Kevin surprised Charlie, who quickly took two steps back and turned away.

"I'll use the compass and you mark the map based on what I tell you. Got it?" Kevin was clearly asking a rhetorical question.

Kevin opened the compass and peered through a small hole in the apparatus and then began heading off toward the southeast corner of the mountain. Periodically, he would look at the map, point to a spot for Will to mark and then move on. The packs were heavy and Will's legs were burning after about two miles of walking what felt like straight up the mountain. There were still trees, but the terrain was rockier and the soil thinner than Will expected. Although it was nearly Christmas, the heat made it feel more like late spring. Whatever criticisms Will had for his teammate, Kevin was clearly country strong. He was sweating profusely, but he gave no sense of tiring a couple of hours into the hike.

The only signposts the two would see were rusted symbols of the ski trails that previously dotted the mountain. Every once in a while, they'd come across a funny one with a name like Hairbag Alley or Whistle Pig. Eventually, there was one final sign, nearly unreadable, that said, "Caution: Out of Bounds."

They continued on for another hour before Kevin brusquely declared: "We'll take a water break here." The two hadn't said more than a handful of words to each other for hours, but Will was grateful for the break.

As they sat, Kevin didn't take any notice of Will. Instead, he slowly sipped his water and studied the map.

"You're really good with a compass," Will said, trying to break the silence. Kevin didn't respond.

"Did you grow up using one?" Will persisted.

Kevin sighed. He realized that he couldn't avoid at least some conversation with his partner.

"Yes. Leadville. The highest town in Colorado. I spent a lot of time outdoors."

It was the most information Kevin had offered to date, and it piqued Will's curiosity.

"What did you do?"

"Son of a tavern owner; I became a surveyor. This isn't my area…but I spent many days out in this sort of place. When I was this age, 21, it was 1906. The world was a lot different then."

Kevin hadn't said a word to anybody – not even his Counselor – about his abusive parents, broken marriage or estranged kids. He laughed at the idea of wiping trauma from his mind, because his memories were a patchwork of horrible thoughts. The computer chip in his head was peppered with people calling him and his kinfolk the "good-for-nothing McNabbs." Still, up in the mountains, he finally felt comfortable and was willing to open up a little.

Will could sense this bit of softening so he pressed on.

"The span of time since we all lived is mind-boggling. The world seems so different to me. I can only imagine how you feel."

"No, you can't," Kevin responded with some conviction. It was a strange response, Will thought. His whole point was that he *couldn't* know how Kevin was responding with his bucketful of memories that, compared to the other Exemplars, were the furthest from the modern world.

"What do you mean?"

Kevin stood up and put his hands on his hips.

"What I mean is that I look at you and Aberforth and that girl Amy and I see you all striving, wanting to be here. I don't. Nobody asked me if I wanted to be brought back to life like some circus sideshow and compete for a family I didn't even like when I was around the first time. It's no honor to be the greatest McNabb. I'll tell you that. Let dead people stay dead."

Will was stunned. Life is so precious and the opportunity to live it a second time just seemed like a gift that any human would want. It wasn't immortality, but it was an extension none of the Exemplars would have expected.

"Does that mean you don't want to win?" Will asked with a good dose of trepidation. He was worried he'd push Kevin too far but he wanted to know.

"I don't care whether I win or lose. I know the odds are against me. I mean writing code? What the hell is that? Not sure why they reached so far back to resurrect my sorry mortal coil. Did you know that if this was five years ago, they wouldn't have been even able to bring me back? They just recently figured out how to take the minuscule amount of genetic material that was left of me and grow me back."

Kevin knew he was coming on strong, which was something Will had never seen. The small-but-burly 21-year-old paused for a moment to gain his composure.

"Look, all I'm saying is that it shouldn't be up to some last remainder and some Counselor to determine the fate of my soul. It's just ungodly."

After a moment of silence, Kevin decided he'd offered enough.

"Hey, you wanna use the compass for a while?" he asked, looking to ease the tension. "I'll show ya how it's done. We should make camp in another two hours, I reckon."

Kevin proceeded to explain the intricacies of the compass. The two did not talk about being Exemplars again.

CHAPTER SIXTEEN

Through the heat of the day, the pair pushed on, slowed down only by Kevin constantly checking Will's compass work. But with dusk coming, Kevin seemed pleased. They reached a clearing with a meadow and Kevin matter-of-factly said, "We're here."

Kevin continued to take charge, setting up camp. Even with the shift in temperatures, the evenings would still be cool. Using a flint and steel set (Kevin was surely the Exemplar who was most adept at using one of those), he set a fire. Then, explaining that while rain and snow were rare in these parts, it was worth being prepared, he erected a small structure from broken tree limbs and random wood. It looked like a poorly constructed tent, but was large enough for them to arrange their sleeping bags in opposite directions. Their interaction was more cordial than before their talk at the water break, but, nevertheless, they said little to each other.

They weren't perfect, but Will was happy about the teamwork they'd shown in the end. If they won, he'd certainly be the top seed and would likely either square off against Kevin or Amy, depending on their spread of victory. Knowing that Chief Marks was controlling the scoring, it would likely be close even if Will and Kevin outperformed the other team by a wide margin. Will hated the subjectivity of it all.

"Goodnight," Kevin said, tightening his sleeping bag. "It'll probably get a little cold so make sure you keep warm."

Will contemplated Kevin's dilemma. In his freshman year at college, he'd taken a philosophy class on death. One of the key takeaways was that a complete and meaningful life blunts the fear of death. "Death is nothing, but to live defeated and inglorious is to die daily," Napoleon said. Mark Twain cut to the chase: "The fear of death follows from the fear of life. A man who lives fully is prepared to die at any time."

One would expect that most Exemplars lived exceptional lives because it would stand to reason that most bloodlines had at least one achiever. Kathy had made that very point once as justification for the bloodline lottery. Trent, Amy and Will were all former great athletes who were equally good outside of sports. Heck, Trent was a war hero. When each of them awoke as OHFs, they had a full library of success and performance as foundations for the Crucible. For Kevin, perhaps there were only memories of disappointment and despair. Traumatic events might be taken from your memory, but a lifetime of failure? If it was woven into every experience, opening your eyes to do it all again couldn't be a very appealing proposition.

Then again, this was a classic second chance and everything came down to attitude. Kevin was gifted this amazing opportunity and it should be something that every Exemplar should appreciate. Maybe Kevin's past was an advantage, Will thought. After all, was Trent going to live up to his hero status? Could Will, himself, return to being a great athlete? The pressure to reach the levels that our former versions attained was daunting. If Kevin's life was what he suggested, he could easily outperform his past. In that context, Kevin faced less pressure to perform than the other Exemplars. Beyond that, if he was mistreated – or mistreated others – in the past, he could right those wrongs. It was a clean slate.

A soft breeze provided a tranquilizing effect. It was the coolest weather Will had experienced since his return, and he loved it. People thought he was crazy to choose the cold Northeast and Boston over the milder weather at Stanford. But he completely believed that battling through the snow and the wind's frigid bite was a sign of character. He closed his eyes with the memory of a winter day in Massachusetts.

The blonde woman looked down on Will once again. It was a familiar scene. The fire was blazing, the embers hopping and, in this variation, the beautiful lady was on top of him. But something was different. Instead of that usual laugh, she had fury in her eyes. She was yelling something, but Will couldn't tell what she was saying. She was initially leaning over Will pinning him down but she sat up, spit flying from her mouth as she continued her angry, but frustratingly muted, tirade. She slapped the fleshy part of her forearm where it said Chaos, and then stood up and began pacing. Will didn't know whether to run or to grab her. The smell of the fire began to grow stronger and acrid. It no longer had that fire-in-the-fireplace warmth. Will began to cough.

"Wake up!" Kevin yelled. "There's a forest fire!"

Smoke enveloped the meadow. It was the middle of the night, but there was an unnatural brightness in the sky that made the smoke look like morning fog.

"Stay here for one minute," Kevin said. "I promise, I'll be right back." He sprinted from their structure. All Will kept thinking was how weird it was that there was a forest fire in the middle of winter. But looking to be useful, he started filling up both backpacks.

Will heard rustling, but didn't see Kevin until he was just feet away. He was shaking his head. He was angry.

"This just can't be," he said. "I went to a point on the map that was supposed to be a marker. It wasn't there. But I did see this gully, which was here."

Kevin pointed to a spot on the map that appeared 10 to 15 miles from where they were supposed to be.

"Let me see the compass," he asked with his hand out.

Will fished through his bag and pulled it out. The smoke was growing heavier and the light brighter and brighter. But in the haze they couldn't see the fire. Kevin held it up and manipulated it for a moment. He smacked it, moved it around again, and then threw it on the ground. He then pushed Will so hard, he fell to the ground.

"What did you do to the compass?" Kevin formed those words as a question, but the intention was a statement of fact.

"I didn't do anything," replied Will, who was awkwardly trying to get up.

"You must have. I know for a fact that it was working when I was using it. Then I stupidly give it to you. A pity offering. Now it doesn't work, and I don't know how to get us out of here."

Will wanted to remind Kevin that the great surveyor from Leadville had checked his work throughout and should have recognized the mistake earlier. But arguing would do no good. Despite the danger in front of them, all Will could strangely think about was that for a man who didn't want to be here, Kevin seemed deeply concerned about his mortal future.

"Supposedly they're monitoring us with those drones," Kevin reasoned. "They probably know our location. But with this smoke we can't stay here. On the other hand, they won't be able to follow us if we leave." He thought for a moment and then added, "Fires burn faster and more intensely uphill. We should drop altitude quickly." Kevin wasn't certain, but he nodded his head as if to convince himself it was the best course of action.

The smoke was quite thick now. Uncertain of the source of the fire, it was going to be a guess which way to go. The spot where he'd checked for the marker was clearer, so he set out in that direction.

"If we can get far enough away from the fire and find a stream that's properly flowing, we might be able to wait this out," Kevin said, talking more to himself than to Will.

The blaze created additional light, but with the smoke it remained difficult not to trip. The breeze, which was comforting back at the campsite, now felt stronger and more menacing. For 30 minutes, Kevin and Will worked their way downhill. Will was optimistic. The lower we go, he thought, the closer we're likely to get to other people.

For a while the smoke thinned. It now appeared darker, and they could see bits of the night sky. All of this was good news to Kevin who had slowed the pace of their descent. Twenty more minutes passed and Will was starting to grow more confident. But then a rumbling sound started to build and from the dark a bright light blinded them both.

Maybe it had been the wind or maybe they just weren't paying close enough attention, but in what seemed like a matter of seconds, the fire was on three sides of them. What was worse was that while there hadn't been too many trees in most of the locations they'd traveled, they were now in some sort of nursery for re-growing the forest. More than at any time on the hike, they were in the perfect location for the fire to feed itself with kindling.

Neither Will nor Kevin needed to say a word to understand their only plan of action. Kevin took the lead as they leapt down the mountain with reckless abandon. The fire felt like its own person, chasing them. For a few minutes, the two men's agility seemed to be getting the better of the flames. It was now only menacing them from one side.

But just as Will realized this, he looked ahead and saw Kevin trip. With the sharp downward angle in which they were running, Kevin began to tumble along the rocky slope, picking up speed and increasing the distance between him and Will. To compensate, Will shed his backpack and increased his pace. He needed to keep Kevin in his view. If he lost sight of his teammate, he may never find him in the smoky gloom.

After about a hundred yards, Kevin stopped. A moment later, Will caught up to him. Steadying his breath, he listened for a heartbeat and checked to see if he was breathing. He was alive. With the fall, they'd covered a lot of ground, but the fire was still in sight. Will lacked all outdoor skills, and they were lost.

Keep moving to lower ground. That was the only strategy that buzzed in his mind, especially considering the fire was closing in on them from above. Kevin was short, but stocky. Will pulled the backpack off his partner, noticing cuts on his arms and legs, but no obvious breaks. Awkwardly, he lifted him up and flung him over his shoulder. If the backpack slowed him down before, this was vastly more difficult. The weight distribution was completely off, and after every handful of steps he needed to rearrange Kevin. Will kept hoping Kevin would wake up and be strong enough to walk. But for the next hour, his only companion was the fire, which sizzled and crackled at his heels.

Throughout his life, Will never gave up. When his college baseball team would run pole-to-poles, a sprint in the outfield from one foul pole to the other, teammates would be throwing up, but Will was always ready for one more. He fed off their struggles. It was an objective sign that he was more prepared. And, with the exception of Coop, nobody ever stuck with him. But he'd never been pushed like this. He couldn't feel his legs, and his shoulders and arms cramped every time he tried to shift Kevin's weight.

He staggered forward. He had little left to give. Then he heard a new sound. Along with the fire, there was a rushing sound. A creek, he thought. He stumbled toward it. Only his desire to get there kept him going. He saw the water and carefully shed Kevin from his shoulders. It wouldn't save either of them. He knew it. Will took a sip of water and lay down. Even he had his breaking point. He closed his eyes and laid down.

The next thing he sensed was shaking. He opened his eyes and immediately noticed it was brighter outside, but it was a different color than the fire.

"You're okay, Will."

Charlie was standing over him. He looked over to see another person attending to Kevin.

"Let's get you out of here. That fire is still raging and we don't have much time."

They loaded into what looked like a mini helicopter. The pilot deftly navigated it as Will closed his eyes again.

CHAPTER SEVENTEEN

The sound of rain against the roof. Will awoke to that comforting rhythmic percussion. Although he was disoriented, he could tell from the gray light that it was either near dawn or dusk.

"People here used to hope for a white Christmas, now they just want a wet Christmas."

It was the unmistakable voice of Will's grandpa.

"You're in our house, and you're fine. Your left shoulder has a slight sprain, I assume from carrying that other boy. You were also dehydrated. But, man, can you sleep. It's been about 36 hours. I argued that you might be more comfortable here for the moment."

Deacon hesitated in offering those last words. He knew the two hadn't been on speaking terms since they last saw each other at Thanksgiving. He'd thought long and hard about his decision to withhold information from Will. He really believed that it would be a distraction, and he wanted to make sure Will had the opportunities he deserved and didn't get the first time around. He'd also made a promise and hated the idea of ever breaking a commitment. He believed deeply in honor, and going back on his word made him less of a man. But looking at his grandson and knowing all he'd just gone through, Deacon was thoroughly reconsidering his priorities.

Will tried to collect his thoughts. His throat was dry.

"Kevin…" he said hoarsely.

"Amazingly, he's in better shape than you. Lots of cuts and bruises and a mild concussion, but he didn't have to carry anyone three miles straight downhill, did he? He complained about something to do with a compass, but he credited you with saving his life. He figured you could have left him for dead. Charlie is going to come by tomorrow to give you an update. But they pushed everything back a day so you and Kevin can get a little rest."

Will sat up. He was sore, especially in his left arm when he tried to rotate it. There was an initial burst of pain, but with each rotation he thought it felt a bit better

"Are we okay?" Deacon asked tenderly. He was more vulnerable than Will had ever seen him. It made him so easy to forgive.

"Sure grandpa. Look, I'm still trying to figure out so much and I'm just not sure what …"

"A 'yes' would have been just fine. Save your energy and let's eat." Deacon smiled and offered his hand to help his grandson up.

Gingerly, Will walked down the stairs. When he reached the landing, he saw a sumptuous Christmas meal all set out. At one of the two place settings, there was a colorful box. Deacon waved him to that seat.

"You've gotta hold the box with the palm of your hand and press the button on the top," Deacon explained. "That's how they do wrapping now."

Will followed the direction and the box folded upon itself underneath the gift. It was a framed picture of Will, his mom, brother and grandpa laughing. It wasn't one he recognized. He must have been about 13.

In his original time, Will remembered people his mom's age complaining that no one read print newspapers anymore. She had loved the tactile nature of turning pages and having something to hold as opposed to scrolling down some screen. At the time, Will didn't get it. Now he did. Pictures were all holograms nowadays. They were impressive in clarity and depth but lacked the true feel of glossy paper. Will squeezed the frame and smiled.

"Normally, you order gifts nowadays and the drones bring 'em to your door, but I made that frame myself," Deacon said proudly as he began heaping food onto Will's plate. "You wouldn't believe how hard it is to find a new frame for sale!"

The two ate silently. The rain and the clanking of cutlery on their plates served as the dinner's only soundtrack. For Will, it wasn't that he didn't want to talk, he just needed food. Every bite gave him a boost of energy and cleared his mind.

After eating, they retired to the living room. Deacon had a beer and Will was sipping grape soda.

"Grandpa, what's it like to be an OHF who didn't win?"

"You mean a deliquio? Charlie always calls me Big D. The man went all the way to the United States Supreme Court to get our family a second chance and give you the right to serve as an Exemplar. But I think he's like everyone else and can't help making fun of my 'status' with that nickname."

Deacon chuckled. He'd held so much back from Will – not by choice, but as calculated by necessity, he reminded himself. That said, his journey was a different story and he *could* tell it. He had to be more flexible for Will. Of course, he wanted to be careful. But he owed the boy that much – a truthful rendition.

"Willie, I won't – I can't – sugarcoat it. I don't have too many friends to speak of. I worked as the low man on my 3D printing crew for 15 years before I got the promotion that I should have gotten ten years earlier. Everyone I knew and loved was gone. My last remainder was a cousin, who I actually knew the first time around, but she only lived one year after I returned."

"Why is it so difficult?" Will knew that his question was too simple for such a serious topic, but he didn't want to slow down the story.

"For all our great human traits, people typically, and unfairly, look down on others if they have one of two fundamental traits: being different and being a loser. If you have both, you're in big trouble. Bad times humble us, but when things calm down, we often listen to our darker angels. The winners in the Crucible, they are different too, but they won. They proved they were the best – true Exemplars – and are loved for it. They are sort of exotic tokens. But that isn't me."

Deacon then did something that Will couldn't remember him doing. He slipped into an extended monologue. The man could spin a yarn but, even then, he was concise and short on words. However, it seemed that the years of relative solitude broke his emotional dam. There wasn't any crying, just heartfelt introspection. Will was glad to listen. He cared deeply about his grandfather and, more than that, it all seemed so pertinent to where Will was right now.

Most notably, Deacon recounted his time in the Crucible. He was in the first Crucible class for the District of Colorado. It wasn't a fine-tuned machine back then, and his Counselor had no experience. He prepared inadequately, performed poorly, and, yet, still made it to the finals. There was no excuse, he just ultimately lost.

The other two who failed in the competition became the first long-term residents of the Crucible Compound. He hadn't seen them once since then, but knew that one passed away of unknown causes just a couple of years later. Not one given to self-pity (and with no precedent for how OHFs would be treated), Deacon sought to make a life for himself. Before long, he saw prejudice. It was a type of treatment he was aware of as a Black man born in 1952. Now, as he had then, he took the same approach. Ignorance and stereotypes drive that sort of hatred, so his goal became to prove each person he met on an individual basis plain wrong through his actions.

Deacon knew that kind of strategy could only succeed in delivering incremental, personal change, but it was his way. In his life, it did lead to a slow trickle of respect. At the same time, he served as witness to decades of little overall improvement. Some groups, he lamented, just seem to always be pushed to the bottom. He tried not to think too much about it, but he did wear the mantle of guilt that his bloodline would be extinguished at the bottom – just like every deliquio's family. It was ironic that if an Exemplar lost, he or she would be the best that bloodline had to offer but would provide every ancestor the worst fate – extinction.

"Are we different in a bad way?" Will asked, breaking the momentum of Deacon's soliloquy.

"I subscribe to Descartes old saying, 'I think, therefore I am.' I'm not less or more than any other person, even if I was grown in a lab in Canada. I guess the bigger question is whether I *am* Deacon Lionel Herndon?"

For all of Will's yearning to know his past, maybe the answer to this reductive question was what he was actually seeking. If he filled those holes, maybe he would know. His grandfather grappled with this for than two decades. Maybe he could offer a shortcut to the answer.

"So? Do you think you are?"

"I don't know," Deacon said with a laugh. The conversation had gotten so serious, and he had spoken for way too long. He figured a little lightheartedness might be in order. Then, noticing that Will was downcast at the answer, he recognized he'd incorrectly read the moment.

"That's not completely true," he said, quickly moving to a serious tone.

Will straightened up.

"Like you, I was prohibited from knowing so much of my life while I was in the Crucible. But in the years that followed I filled in many of the pieces – good and bad. When I found out you'd be coming back, I have to admit I was nervous. I had memories that seemed so real in my mind, and then I had things I'd read about you, and me, and the family. They seemed like stories and not personal. But then I saw you."

Deacon stopped for a moment to hold onto his composure. He never cried and he wouldn't right now.

"But then I saw you," he repeated. "I felt the love you only feel for a child. I know I'm not your daddy, but close enough. You could say the memories that were planted in my head in that damn chip would be enough for those feelings, but I don't think so. No, sir. The love I have for you is deeper in my bones. All that is to say, I might have been regrown from old pieces of a dead man, but what's in my heart for you Willie ... if that isn't the essence of Deacon Lionel Herndon, then I don't know what is. So, to answer your question, I figure his soul is my soul and mine is his."

The two men embraced, and neither could hold back. They both cried. As much as he had been angry at his grandpa for holding out on him, Will felt exactly the same way. Neither may be the original version of themselves, but that spark that carried them through life the first time around was still there. The sobbing was reflexive, but after a moment both men came to their senses and were uncomfortable. Will took it on himself to break the mood.

"Grandpa, I hope you'll feel the same way after I lose," Will said, wiping his eyes. "Kevin and I must have lost big points for getting lost and almost dying."

"Yeah, how'd you break a compass?" Deacon responded, trying to also jog himself into a lighter mood. "Come on Willie, you're better than that!"

It was a question Will couldn't answer. But he now knew – win or lose – he'd have a home and, unlike most Exemplars, his last remainder was young, and he'd have someone no matter what.

Although Will had slept for a full day, it was late and he was surprisingly tired. They said their goodnights and Will had little trouble falling asleep. After the fire, he hadn't dreamed. Now the blonde girl was back to haunt him. She was angry again, pointing and yelling.

Will was thankful to wake up the next morning. He didn't want to be in bed and quickly hurried down the stairs to find a note from Deacon.

Willie – I had to go to work. Winter is the busy season. There are leftovers in the fridge. No matter what happens, I'm proud of you. Now, get some rest today and get back at it tomorrow! Love, Grandpa.

Remnants of the Christmas Day storm persisted, and Will looked out the window to see a light sprinkling of mist. It would be a cooler day, but he was looking forward to spending it sitting quietly inside. Will's left shoulder continued to hurt, making it a bit difficult to put together a plate of food. But he was enjoying the aloneness, until the doorbell rang.

Charlie stood at the threshold. He was clearly worried.

"How are you feeling kiddo?"

As he welcomed Charlie into the house, Will assured him he was fine. Charlie had a serious tone. It was pep talk time.

"Well that whole compass debacle put you in a bad place. You guys were 11 miles from where you should have been. If you'd gone to the right place, you would have been far away from the fire. Not that anyone expected that blaze. We lost sight of you on the drones. Luckily, we found you just in the nick of time. Anyway, I'm sure you realize you dropped in the standings. Big time," Charlie tried to catch himself. The pep talk was clearly starting poorly, but he needed to get the bad out of the way first. "Here's the good news: You may no longer be first, but you fell to third place, which means you'll face Amy in the next round. She's smart and tenacious, but so are you. Because of our past relationship, I must, of course, recuse myself in scoring your semi-final. But I'll be rooting for you."

Charlie couldn't read Will. Was he still focused? Could he get the job done?

"I will say what you did for Kevin was amazing," Charlie continued, wanting to pump Will up. "You saved his life! I know what you think of Chief Marks, but even she was impressed. She thinks all of us OHFs are just cheap clones. Even me. But you showed great humanity, Will. I must say I did help a little. I pointed out to her that your actions of valor deserved recognition. It was the difference between you falling all the way to fourth and sticking in third place."

"So be it," Will said. "It's just a position. I'll be ready for the next round."

Charlie smiled. It was the attitude he was hoping for – and expecting – from Will. He didn't fight all the way to the Supreme Court to bring back somebody without some fight in him. It was reassuring. Will was here to serve a purpose, and he was demonstrating he was just the person Charlie thought he'd be. He could only hope Will would continue to prove him right.

CHAPTER EIGHTEEN

Kathy Riley lacked control when it came to fidgeting. It was a tick, like saying "bywary" all the time, that started when she was young. For all intents and purposes, Kathy was an only child. She was 16 years old when her parents had her younger brother, Jason. Though it was never explicitly stated, Kathy always believed that they wanted another child because they'd concluded it was too much of a gamble to leave the responsibility of maintaining their bloodline to her.

It wasn't that Kathy was anything less than brilliant. Like Will, she'd attended Harvard. She was a virtuoso in every subject she ever took. But she was consistently nervous. Unless she was in a classroom, there was an uncertainty to everything she did. Dating, eating, whatever it was, she would waffle to the point of paralysis.

As academia was the one area in which she thrived, she'd considered becoming a college professor. But, from a young age, she'd been more drawn to the plight of the OHFs. By their sheer lack of numbers, they were outsiders, and Kathy, who was perennially misunderstood, loved an underdog. She figured if she was going to teach, it would be for people who were complicated and talented, just like her.

She knew the road to being a Counselor was difficult. It required the intellectual agility of a polymath and the soft touch of the most caring mother. The job demanded balancing a holistic understanding of their students with an ability to impart problem-solving skills. She earned a Ph.D. in the subject from the University of California-Berkeley, the top school for aspiring Counselors. It hadn't been easy. A popular job for losing Exemplars was to work with universities as test cases for Counselor hopefuls. Whenever Kathy was compelled to work with an OHF, she consistently faltered at interpersonal relations. In her defense, the deliquios were not the happiest bunch to begin with. They were typically the most well-adjusted of their kind, but even the most gracious losers in the Crucible could be surly. Despite being a top student at Harvard, Kathy's subpar people skills meant she just got by in her graduate work.

The upshot was Kathy's efforts to secure a Counselor job, which could be a worldwide endeavor, was generously sprinkled with failure. After months, she secured a position in a southeast corner of Sweden called Småland. Their cooler dispositions apparently allowed them to overlook her shortcomings. But Kathy ended up being her own worst enemy. Eventually, indecision over whether it was a good choice to move to a country she didn't know (despite the fact she'd taught herself fluent Swedish in just two months) was too much. Tail between her legs, she went home to Chicago before she even really began and readied herself to consider a straightforward teaching job.

Then there was a miracle. Chief Marks contacted her and said they had an immediate opening. There was a warmth to her invitation. The chief threw a metaphorical life preserver to Kathy, who was about to drown in a sea of her own self-doubt. For once, she accepted the position on the spot and the following day she was traveling to Denver.

When she arrived, Kathy found a very different Chief Marks. The warmth had evaporated.

"There will be no easy road for *you*, Ms. Riley," Chief Marks said. "I know your backstory, and I will test you immediately to see whether you have the mettle for this job."

She then handed her Will Herndon's file. It was odd because normally it was the job of the Counselor to work with a last remainder in choosing their Exemplar. That interview process was painstaking, and, if Kathy was being honest with herself, she was glad to bypass it. But she was well aware of Will Herndon's story and how his case travelled all the way through the court system. Further frazzling her was knowing the lawyer who had pled the case was the district's deputy referee, Charles Reed.

"You are strictly prohibited from receiving information or even talking to Mr. Charles Reed," Chief Marks told her when she gave Kathy the handheld with the Herndon dossier. "He will be involved in an oversight capacity with this Crucible but under no circumstances are you – or Mr. Herndon – allowed to fraternize with him. Do you understand?"

She hadn't said a word to Mr. Reed, but had seen him talk to Will on more than one occasion. She considered alerting Chief Marks, but decided otherwise for numerous reasons. The first was she didn't want to deal with the tongue-lashing lecture she'd receive for letting it happen. The second was that silence seemed the best act of rebellion she could muster against such a shrew of a boss. Besides, any guilt disappeared when she noticed Mr. Reed would also often talk to Trent Aberforth privately as well. The deputy referee was either very chatty or, if there was something more sinister going on, it was likely Will wasn't the only Exemplar receiving wisdom from Mr. Reed. And she also kept her mouth shut because she'd become thoroughly fond of Will.

Kathy was familiar with Gastree's Syndrome. Counselors, especially those working their first case, would develop a deep connection with their client. It wasn't so much a romantic attachment but rather a maternal or paternal one. The amount of euphoria some Counselors with Gastree's experienced if their Exemplar happened to win led them to quit the business altogether. They suddenly believed that they could never attain such heights again. For Counselors with failing Exemplars, there was depression and self-hate. Learning the symptoms of this syndrome and how to distance oneself from their Exemplar was practically a first-day lesson at Berkeley.

Even so, she was drawn to her charge. She knew what Will didn't know about his past and admired his determination. She'd read so many stories about how Exemplars, the best of the best, could be driven. Now she was seeing it personally, and it was inspiring. Learning came easy to Kathy. It wasn't necessarily hard for Will, but when he faced bumps in the road, he was thoroughly graceful about applying himself until it all clicked. Complicating matters was that he had no idea just how complicated his past was. It was a quandary for her: Did he deserve to know, or would it only complicate matters?

Considering she was turning a blind eye to Mr. Reed's conversations, her internal dialogue on the subject ultimately left her resolved to follow the rules on this one.

In any event, she was wracked with insecurity after Will's compass disaster. She couldn't understand how he'd fallen short. While no Counselor knew exactly what the tests would include, they were all given a curriculum for each Crucible. Survival skills were certainly included in the 83-page document, and when she heard that ability would be part of the first round's practical portion, she leapt a little inside because she thought she'd prepared Will comprehensively for that possibility. Indeed, a whole day was spent on compass work and, while Kathy had no personal outdoor experience, she was certain that he was an expert on the instrument by the time they were done. What had she done wrong? "The coding had gone so well, but I must have failed him," she thought, chastising herself.

When Will returned to the Crucible Compound two days after Christmas, he didn't look too bad even if his left shoulder still killed him. Kathy wanted to hug him as he entered their study office, but whispered under her breath "Gastree's, Gastree's."

"Bywary, Will, I'm so sorry about what happened in the mountains," she said. "You were so incredibly brave. But I have to ask, what happened with the compass?"

Will was glad to see Kathy. For all her strange actions and tentative movements, she was unreservedly on his team. It was what he needed more than anything.

"I know," Will said, sounding as surprised as Kathy. "I swear, Kathy, I followed everything you taught me. You did a great job. Not only that, but Kevin was checking my work."

This was why Kathy was so grateful for Will. Even in his darkest hour, he was reassuring her.

"Well, it's done, and the good news is this all happened in the seeding round," she offered in the hope her student would be as equally heartened by this fact as she was. "You're the third seed and we can do this."

To channel her nervous energy, Kathy would often offer acts like a high five or a thumbs up. The gestures she delivered weren't common in 2090, but she'd done her research on Will's time and learned them so that her positive reinforcement would seem familiar to him. In this instance, she offered a celebratory fist bump, another ritual she'd taught herself, and the two brushed aside the past and dove headlong into the future.

By this point, they'd covered every element of the curriculum. This was about revision. Avoiding the sections that had already been tested (there was rarely any duplication in the Crucible) cut out about 20 pages from Kathy's handbook. Will knew better than to share that Charlie had hinted the personality test would be part of the next round. He'd be happy to follow whatever course of action Kathy suggested.

Trent and Amy had softly joked during their exercise period about Kathy. The irony about the Exemplars was that, while they were one failure from being outcasts, more often than not, they had been shining successes in their past life. They weren't bullies, so to speak, but their original versions had so often achieved by following the rules. This meant they were conditioned to be uncertain about anyone weird or different – even though if they became deliquios, they'd be precisely that.

As the only baseball player in his neighborhood going down to the rich part of Denver to regularly play ball, Will understood what it meant to dress, talk and act differently. In his day, he'd worked hard to shore up those perceived inadequacies. But he respected Kathy for letting her freak flag fly. Whether she chose to be that way or couldn't help it, she'd also earned Will's respect for the primary thing that mattered to him: An undying work ethic.

Over the next week, in the run up to the semi-final round, they challenged each other to flinch when it came to putting in the time. Will wouldn't ask for a break, and Kathy wouldn't offer it. There would be no compass mishap again.

Winning in this event was no different than winning in sports. "Preparation then confidence," he told himself repeatedly. They went hand-in-hand. The more repetitions, the more second nature any endeavor becomes. Ultimately, you reach critical mass and the confidence builds.

"How are you feeling?" Kathy asked on the final day before the next round.

Will's left arm was still sore and he was tired, but he felt a wellspring of certainty about his chances.

"I've got this," he said with a smile.

"Bywary, I'm sure you do," Kathy said, giving a double thumbs up.

CHAPTER NINETEEN

D r. Wilson didn't like what he saw on the handheld. He'd used his stethoscope-looking device to simply touch Will's left shoulder. It didn't hurt. In fact, the cool of the metal surface felt pleasant against his throbbing arm. But there was no way to fool this technology. Dr. Wilson manipulated what looked like MRI images floating above his computer, pointing at one and then the other. He was making mental notes, before setting the handheld down and going to the wall.

"Phone Chief Marks. Can you please come in?"

It was the first time Will had seen the key referee since before the mountain fire. He readied himself for a sharp look and the snarky comment about his compass work. This would inevitably be used to cut Will down just before the second practical exam.

Will wasn't nervous – about either a mean comment or the exam – but he was well aware of the stakes. Locking in the seedings was one thing. He was in third place, which was effectively the same as being in second as point totals didn't carry over from round to round. But now each Exemplar was only one miscue away from being a deliquio. In the early going, Will never gave that prospect any thought. In fact, he had been the last of the Exemplars to even figure out what the consequences of failure meant. It just never dawned on him. Now, he was acutely conscious of the fact. Being a deliquio meant being an outcast.

Chief Marks brushed by Will as she entered the room. Rather than ridicule, she simply ignored him. She and the doctor studied the holograms, whispering too quietly for Will to hear. Dr. Wilson moved his left arm in a windmill fashion and shook his head. Chief Marks watched intently and shook her head as if to say, "no."

She then stood up tall, straightened her dress and walked over to Will.

"Mr. Herndon, while I don't believe such things concern you, we are governed by rules and regulations in the Crucible," Chief Marks started with the type of cut down Will always anticipated in her presence. "There is some flexibility in the way this code is applied. I do have discretion…"

She paused. It seemed like she was weighing her options, then she rolled her eyes as if to say she'd come to a conclusion she didn't like.

"Mr. Herndon, I must inform you that following Dr. Wilson's examination and, in consultation with me, the chief referee, you are not physically fit to compete in today's practical exam. If you were a *regular* person we'd administer pain medicine, which would easily prepare you for this task. But the rules of Crucible prohibit Exemplars from this sort of healing advantage. Now, this does not mean you get to *avoid* this test. But we will set a new timetable based on your *wellness* and act accordingly. You've dodged a bullet, young man."

She got up and started walking toward the door when four words from Will stopped her cold.

"I want to compete."

"What?"

Chief Marks never acted surprised. Ever. But this wasn't what she expected. To her, Will was weak, selfish and represented so much that was wrong with the human condition. When she first learned of his inclusion months before, she was certain, for so many reasons, he shouldn't be in the Crucible. His actions in saving Kevin McNabb on the mountain had softened her position ever so slightly, but even with that glimpse of valor, she'd remained steadfast in her position.

"Please repeat that, Mr. Herndon."

"With all due respect to Dr. Wilson, I don't believe I need special treatment. I don't feel great, but I will perform to the best of my abilities."

"Mr. Herndon, do you comprehend what hangs in the balance here?"

The chief had thrown so many hurdles in Will's way. Kathy Riley was hired to simply make his training more difficult. But she never thought Will himself would serve as the greatest obstacle. Either he simply wasn't smart, or she'd undervalued his sense of integrity.

"Chief Marks, there is no doubt that under any guidelines set forth by the Association of Crucible Physicians, Mr. Herndon has the right to ask for an extension," Dr. Wilson interrupted. "Still, his range of motion and strength levels are good enough that he could be fully functional."

"Yes, but it would be foolhardy," Chief Marks said looking at Will.

In Will's mind, not to compete would be the coward's choice. He'd played injured in sports and, for better or for worse, he was conditioned to take situations as they were presented and make the most of them. Seeing Chief Marks' surprise merely redoubled his desire. He would prove her wrong. Win or lose, he'd do it with honor.

"I'm ready to go," Will said with his best tone of finality.

"Fine," Chief Marks responded as if the wind had been knocked out of her. "Be outside ready to go in five minutes."

As instructed, Will was on a driverless electric bus five minutes later. It was odd that such a big vehicle was needed, because apart from Chief Marks and four support staff, the only other passengers were Will and Amy. Trent and Kevin would be competing elsewhere in a different practical challenge overseen by Charlie. Will understood that Charlie had to recuse himself from his competition, but, under the circumstances, he sure wished he was there.

Unlike the time he shared on the train with Amy before their last practical competition, Will didn't expect any small talk on this journey. It would be a respectful competition, but it just couldn't be friendly at this point. It was early morning. While it hadn't rained for a couple of days, the humidity had stuck around. It was uncharacteristic for the normally dry Colorado climate. The bus was heading south past the affluent neighborhood of Greenwood Village, one of the few areas in town that still had that real brick-red grass. This was Coop's 'hood. Will smiled as they drove by the turnoff where he'd gone so many times to his friend's house to take batting practice. What would he think of all this? Would he have accepted Will 2.0? Coop was an inclusive guy. When he made mistakes judging the content of a person's character, it was never because he was dazzled by superficial traits like wealth or success. It was quite the opposite. He always cared about the lost souls.

Will's emotions about what sort of support he needed to survive the Crucible ping-ponged so often. At first, he felt vulnerable that he didn't have Coop and his grandpa, who had been there for him throughout so much of his past memory. Charlie and Kathy couldn't replace them, but they'd given him enough confidence that he could do this on his own. It was reassuring that, while he missed Coop, he could survive without him.

The bus wound nine long miles to Highlands Ranch. Will knew the far south Denver suburb, having played baseball there in high school. But it looked so different. Instead of a series of subdivisions featuring a healthy serving of generic big homes, each with their own design name like "The Pinion" or "The Corinthian" model, the area looked more like a roadside stop in the middle of the Mojave Desert – or maybe the compound where Luke Skywalker originally lived on Tatooine. Other than a few dozen Ratzenbergers peppering the landscape, it was just a light brown rocky plain surrounded by scrub brush hills.

The bus stopped at an open field of arid dirt. Chief Marks and her support team got off the vehicle and immediately started unloading. Will and Amy, about eight rows apart in the back, both got up slowly and stretched. Will gave a sideways glance to Amy, who smiled back.

A little breeze helped offset the humidity that greeted the two Exemplars as they stepped off the bus. Chief Marks' team worked quickly, setting up a makeshift open operations tent about ten yards away from the bus. Two workers then placed goods at specific locations while another outlined a sort of boundary for a rather large square. Once that was done, they walked about 200 yards to another patch and did the same.

Chief Marks inspected the work and when she seemed satisfied, she summoned Will and Amy.

"Ms. Pham. Mr. Herndon. Today's practical examination will be focused on agriculture. You will be tested on your acumen in this discipline as well as your fine motor skills and brute strength."

After the statement, she looked at Will as if to say, "You fool. You're not up to the challenge."

"Your goal is to set up an operational site that can sustain the growth of crops. Underneath this tent are two sets of all the materials you could conceivably need in order to complete your task. Each of you have been given a plot of land and have 24 hours. I alone will judge your performance at the end of the allotted time. Now, please begin."

"Atmospheric water harvesting," Will inaudibly said to himself. He'd enjoyed Kathy's lectures on how, with the world facing a limited water supply and lots of marginally arable land, there were now really only two ways in which crops were grown. There was hydroponics, which required more water and gear than they could conceivably use out here, and then there was atmospheric water harvesting. He'd need to dig trenches, lay irrigation lines and then create a system to pull water from the atmosphere and feed the liquid to seeds planted in the trenches.

He began fishing through the materials. Chief Marks was right. Everything was there. He'd use the power shovel to create the trenches and then install the irrigation lines. After completing those tasks, he'd build an atmospheric water generator. It was vital he did the first two steps quickly, because to power the generator, he needed to set up solar paneling during the warmest part of the day so that the generator could have enough power to pull water from the air overnight.

Will grabbed the shovel and hurried out to his plot of rocky, dry land. He'd read about the hydraulic instrument that he was now holding and had a sense of how to use it. Relying on a jackhammer-like movement, its vibrating motion would cut through the hard ground like butter. Will methodically outlined how he wanted his rows to be aligned. It took a bit of time, but he was certain he could cut the trenches quickly.

After about an hour, he was ready to begin digging. He placed the shovel against the hard terrain and turned the instrument on. It started to vibrate smoothly. He lifted it high and then drove the shovel into the ground.

Pain shot through his left shoulder like he'd been hit by an exploding bullet. He dropped the shovel. Will was taught in baseball to never show pain. If you were hit in the back with a 95 mile-per-hour fastball when at bat, you simply jogged to first base no matter how badly it hurt. "Don't rub it," his teammates would tease from the dugout. But with no one around, and the pain excruciating, he dropped to the ground. He took a moment to regain his bearings, gritted his teeth and tried again. But the pain was unbearable, just like the first time.

What was he going to do? It was the vibrating that made it impossible for him to fully utilize the shovel. Will thought for a moment and then began fiddling with the controls. He needed to disable what made the tool such a wonder of technology. If he could turn it into an old-fashioned manual instrument, maybe he could get the trenches done.

Once he'd turned the vibration off, Will immediately recognized he was facing a good news-bad news proposition. On the positive side, he didn't feel any serious pain in his shoulder. He could lightly steady the shovel with his left arm and do all the heavy labor with his right. But that couldn't generate anything near the power of the vibrating action. There was no time to think. Will began flailing away at the dirt with reckless abandon. If he lacked the technological advances, he'd make up for it with pure heart.

He didn't pick up his head for hours, slowly chiseling out the necessary depth to plant the seeds. When he finished one row, he immediately went on to the next one. When he finished the second row, his right arm, which was carrying the slack from the limited value his left could provide, was numb and throbbing. He finally stopped for a moment and leaned on the shovel.

Panting, he looked into the distance and saw Amy had completed her five perfect rows. Not only that, but she'd also set up her solar panels and was tinkering with the atmospheric water generator. Already so tired, he looked at the set up for a moment, giving it little thought other than he knew he was behind. But it was just past midday, and he'd still have time to set everything up.

He began digging his third trench, sweat dripping into the cervices he was creating. Then about halfway through the next line, he stopped cold and looked at the sun. It was warm, but not unbearably hot. But that wasn't why he was staring into the sky.

"How stupid could I be!" he yelled out loud. He looked up again and internally did some calculations. Sure, he could finish the digging and set up the generator before sundown. But it wouldn't matter. By then there would be no sun for the solar panels to power the machine and pull water in order to complete the project. In fact, doing the math in his head, even if he were to set up the solar panels now and double back to finishing the trenches, it was too late.

Will dropped to his knees. Adrenaline had kept him going before, but now he'd hit a wall. He banged his fist against the hard ground. He was angry. If he'd had the magical shovel, he would have been fine. And if he hadn't been so arrogant to think he could do this with one arm, he'd have been competitive later. But deep down he knew neither of those were the real mistake. He'd simply not thought his plan through correctly. Everything would have gotten done if he'd only laid it out in the right order.

What do you do when you have no hope? Will wasn't going to just lose; he was going to lose epically. Amy would get an insurmountable lead before the written exam, and Will was done.

One element that Will really appreciated about baseball was that there was no set clock. You always had a chance to win as long as you didn't make your final out. Clearly, that principal couldn't be applied here as time was completely his enemy. But he could apply a philosophy he'd possessed on the baseball field: *keep going until it's over.*

He got up and went back to the trenches. At first, his plan was to claw back as many points as he could. He wouldn't be able to fully complete the project but maybe he'd pick up just enough points to give him a chance in the written portion. He'd have perfect trenches and he'd lay the irrigation lines just right. Chief Marks hated him, but there would be something substantial for him to show.

Keeping positive, he worked diligently into the late afternoon. Amy was already done, when Will began connecting the irrigation lines. There would be no water to run through them, but they'd be properly installed.

He looked up at the sun as it was setting. He was thankful for the breeze – even if the humidity kept it sticky.

And then it hit him.

There might be another way. He got up and sprinted to the tent, hoping there would be the right gear. He picked through one box after another until he found what he needed – poles and netting. He laughed to himself.

By then, it was dusk. Will faced difficulty pulling the necessary poles out to his plot, but he was feeling a second wind that would give him the energy he needed. He had a solution based on something Kathy had mentioned in passing during his irrigation lesson. Today, generators were the norm. They were cheap, reliable and easily powered with solar energy. But there used to be another option called fog nets. These mesh contraptions could pick up moisture in the air. They weren't as efficient and there were purity issues, but in the right conditions they could easily water his plot.

Maybe if it were a different time of year, they wouldn't work in Denver. But, for once, luck was on Will's side and the weather presented just the right combination of wind and humidity. He needed to do some guesswork as to the best way to set up the fog nets since Kathy hadn't provided full details. He picked a direction where the breeze would hit his nets just right, and he set up a funnel system that could get the water into the irrigation system. It was well after dark when he finished.

Cramping all over his body, he stumbled back to the tent. All he could do now was wait.

Nobody talked much during the night, and Amy slept quite soundly. She'd undoubtedly done things right. Chief Marks and her team had set up sturdier tents on the other side of the bus. They'd take turns staying up to make sure that neither Exemplar did anything unruly. Will barely slept. He listened for the wind and wondered whether the cooling temperatures and moist conditions would be enough.

Will was awake as the sun rose. It was a beautiful sight and made him grateful he was alive. The quiet moment was broken by the sound of the officials leaving their tent. Amy was still sleeping comfortably next to him. Will nudged her, and she slowly awoke.

"It's time for the reckoning," he said warmly.

Will sat in the tent as Chief Marks and Amy went to her plot. Normally, he'd be curious, straining his eyes to see whether he could figure out what was being said by body language. But this time, he didn't bother. He knew his fellow Exemplar's work would be, well, exemplary. Instead, he was worried just how well his improvised effort would hold up. The two walked back slowly, betraying nothing of what was said between them.

"Mr. Herndon," Chief Marks said as Amy, who looked satisfied, peeled off to the tent. Chief Marks began walking to Will's plot without him. He had to jog for a moment to catch up to her. They reached Will's square and Chief Marks began silently measuring. For his part, Will looked at the fog nets. They'd held up. He looked at the planted rows, and they were wet! He hadn't completely failed. Maybe he'd even pulled this one out.

Chief Marks looked at the nets and manipulated a few things on her handheld.

"Why didn't you use a generator?" she asked curtly.

Will was embarrassed and didn't want to get into it. "It's complicated," he said, trying to deflect the question. He knew immediately that was the wrong answer.

"Too complicated for me?" Chief Marks said completely offended. "Well, try me. I think I can handle what you think is *complicated.*"

"Sorry," Will said sincerely. "I struggled with the vibrating shovel, and by the time I figured I needed to put up the solar panels, it was too late."

"How did you know about fog nets? It's not a central point in the curriculum. In fact, it was an afterthought to include them in the available materials."

"I just tried to be prepared."

Will was looking at the ground. There was no pride or boastfulness to his explanation. Chief Marks could have torn him down, but she was aware just how physically demanding it must have been for Will to finish his assignment.

"Well, your saturation levels are not optimal and, at any other time of the year, those nets wouldn't have worked. You're very fortunate about the conditions," Chief Marks said coldly and then with a bit more heart added: "But you did complete the project. You lost to Ms. Pham but by a respectable margin. This means the written exam remains an important component."

Will still had a chance and that was all he needed to hear.

CHAPTER TWENTY

Will spent much of the one day between the practical and written tests resting. Kathy didn't argue too much after hearing the details of what happened in Highlands Ranch. All things considered, she was proud of how Will shifted to use the fog nets. It was a valiant effort, especially because they hadn't talked in-depth about that technique. He'd done so much on the fly and nearly pulled it off completely.

Amy earned a 96% and Will scored an 89%. The difference was a pretty big divide, but it was within the realm of possibilities that Will could still win. His big advantage was he knew the topic – Charlie had tipped him off it would be some sort of personality test. But all that truly meant was he wouldn't be forced to agonize over what would be on the exam. There was no real route to correct answers other than, as Charlie had put it, to "figure out whatever a saint would do and then pick the next best answer."

Silly advice, Will thought. He would go from the heart and either it was good enough or it wasn't. From the standpoint of the competition, how Amy answered the questions was equally as important. She was a great person, but she also had said often that she wasn't a big fan of people. Maybe, just maybe, that quirk in her personality would lead to less-than-winning results on the test.

In truth, Will thought the whole idea of a test to determine leadership and teamwork skills was ridiculous. As a kid, he'd been a Denver Broncos fan and would closely follow the annual draft, where teams took turns picking college players to add to their rosters. Along with assessing athletic ability, each player was given an exam called the Wonderlic Test up until 2022. It was broadly developed to evaluate general cognitive abilities, but it became a catchall for determining whether a player was not only smart but would also be a good teammate.

As a 12-year-old, Will became obsessed with the test. He went online to take practice questions and studied the exam's concepts and outcomes. He was attracted to its certainty. He could prove all the skills he wanted by crushing this test. Sure enough, within six months, he was getting top scores. The fact that he could even finish it – only two to five percent could achieve that feat – was impressive enough.

But as he got older and took on leadership roles, he found that what he learned to succeed on paper didn't overlap with what it took to thrive on the field. He determined that leadership was an ever-changing organic characteristic. Too many variables went into doing it right. Who were your teammates? What was the team chemistry like? Did they have a lot in common? Were you winning or losing? Empathizing with others, reading their actions and reacting appropriately were all untestable traits that couldn't be distilled down to a multiple-choice test.

Knowing all this, Will asked Kathy if he could use his time to rest. When it came to the test, he'd remember what Charlie said, but primarily he knew the best way to perform in this case was to look at, and answer, each question with a clear head.

It was the first time Will had ever asked for this kind of break, and it surprised Kathy. Nevertheless, she respected his work ethic so much. She also knew he was spent physically, so she didn't push back. She just held her breath. This test would be make-or-break for Will.

Although Trent and Kevin had received a different assignment for their practical exam, they were standing outside the usual door to the hockey rink just like Will and Amy. Will hadn't bothered to find out what the results were for the other semifinal. It really wasn't relevant to his task at hand. Everyone assumed that Trent would soundly defeat Kevin. But after spending time with Kevin in the outdoors, he wasn't as sure. The issue with Kevin wasn't whether he could prevail, it was whether he cared enough to do so. Trent wanted it. You could see it in his eyes.

Just like in the seeding round, the four Exemplars were led into the room and stood in front of the big white silos.

"Exemplars," Chief Marks said imperiously. "This is the written examination for your semifinal Crucible Round. This test will probe the inner reaches of your respective personalities. You can unclutter your minds of everything you've prepared because you will be asked to show your inner self. Your scores will reflect your propensity for teamwork, leadership and interpersonal success. Please enter your testing centers. The exam will begin in five minutes."

In Will's mind, this moment ended his advantage over Amy. He was able to bypass the angst of not knowing what to expect, while Amy was probably combing over every topic to prepare. Now she could relax. There was no way to prepare for this roulette wheel of a test. In three hours, all would be determined. It was crazy, Will thought. Answer some arbitrary questions, and if you happened to choose "B" instead of "A" one too many times, you'd be relegated to life as a social untouchable – a deliquio.

The test was nothing like the Wonderlic that Will had once loved and then hated. There were no SAT-type questions about antonyms or speed-reading. Instead, this exam was more of an ethics test.

Peter hires an architect named Mary to prepare architectural plans in connection with a new house he is building. Mary agrees to do the job for $350 per hour. Mary works hard for Peter, doing historical research on the type of building Peter wants, writing memos with preliminary information and drafting most of the blueprints. Midway through the relationship Peter tells Mary that her work is terrible and that he would be embarrassed to use it. Still, Peter pays

Mary at the agreed rate for the efforts. One month later, Peter insists that Mary give him all of her work. What documents should Mary give to Peter?

   A. Only the document drafts, but not the underlying research

   B. Only the underlying research, but not the document drafts

   C. None of the papers, because Peter fired Mary

   D. All of the papers, even though Peter fired Mary

"Who cares?" thought Will on reading the question. "Why isn't there an E. Punch Peter in the face?" But he innately knew an angry answer was the wrong one. He'd always had a sixth sense with multiple choice tests. Though it was probably what a saint would do, he answered D.

For the duration of the test, he muddled through social conundrums and questions of character and leadership. Unlike the first written test, he was rushing at the end to complete the exam. When he was done, there were only 36 seconds left. Even if he'd had more time, he wouldn't have rechecked his answers. After all, would his moral compass have changed that much since he gave an answer just minutes before?

Will rubbed his face with his hands. He could still feel pain in his left shoulder and his right arm was now equally sore from all the shovel work. The second day after an injury was always the worst. For a fleeting moment, he wondered if he could get on his grandfather's 3D printing crew. He could take the ribbing, but didn't want to be one of the deliquios sitting around moping. It wasn't his thing.

The handheld let off a warm and inviting chime to alert him that time was up. Will gingerly stood up to meet his fate.

Trent, Kevin, Amy and Will stood shoulder-to-shoulder. The term *moment of truth* came from the Spanish *el momento de la verdad*. It was used in bullfighting for the split second when a bullfighter was on the verge of killing the bull, and both bull and *toreador* knew it. If ever there was an appropriate time to say it was the moment of truth, this was it.

"Thank you all for your diligence and hard work throughout these first two rounds," Chief Marks said after quickly conferring with Charlie. The Counselors all sat solemnly with the exception of Kathy who was uncontrollably bouncing her right leg up and down. Kathy's nervous energy vibrated off her. It was as if there was a low hum always preceding her. Chief Marks shot her a look and an embarrassed Kathy tried to physically hold her leg down.

"The nature of the Crucible is it's a zero-sum game. Not everyone can advance and, I'm afraid, for two of you, this will be your time to exit the competition. You will be welcome to stay in the dormitories until the end of the final round in two days. After that, your Counselors will help you transition either into the permanent wing of the Crucible Compound or out into the world. I wish you the best wherever this second life opportunity takes you."

If his grandpa had been there and asked him if he was nervous, Will would have said no. But of course, that would have been a lie. He clenched his fist. With his aching muscles, even that act of tension hurt. But in a way, the physical pain blunted the emotional turmoil churning in his brain. It was a distraction.

"Here are the results of semi-final number one – Aberforth, Trent Quinn and McNabb, Kevin Richard," Chief Marks said as she pressed a hologram on her handheld and the results projected above the group.

Practical Examination
Aberforth, T 98%
McNabb, K ....82 %

Written Examination
Aberforth, T...............................91%
McNabb, K 74%

Final Totals
Aberforth, T **94.5%**
McNabb, K...............................78%

It took the Exemplars a moment to read the board. But before they'd fully processed it, Chief Marks, Charlie and the Counselors were already politely clapping. Trent smiled and offered his hand to Kevin. Will wasn't sure how Kevin would react, but he shook it.

"Now the results from semi-final number two – Herndon, William Michael and Pham, Amy Lan. The board cleared for a moment. Then Chief Marks pushed two different holograms and the scores emerged.

Practical Examination

Herndon, W 89%

Pham, A ....96 %

Written Examination

Herndon, W...............................97%

Pham, A......................................85%

Final Totals

Herndon, W...............................**93%**

Pham, A......................................90.5%

There are moments in every person's life when the world around them goes completely quiet. It doesn't matter if, in reality, the individual is surrounded by noise. The person can't hear a thing. Will experienced that sensation. He was only broken out of this trance by two things: A loud whooping sound from Kathy, and Amy nudging him to shake her hand.

Led by Trent who was closest to the door, the four Exemplars marched out of the room. In the hallway, they lingered for a moment. Trent shook everyone's hand again, but felt awkward by the situation. There were winners and losers, and he didn't want to be a part of that uncomfortable interaction. He wished everyone the best, including Will, to whom he offered good luck in the finals, and hurried off.

Kevin just stood there leaning against the wall. Will felt obligated to say something since he hadn't seen him since the mountain debacle.

"Thanks for being such a great guide," Will lamely offered. "I'm sorry about the compass."

"Doesn't matter," Kevin responded. He didn't seem too bothered by the results. "You saved my life and, in the process, you made me appreciate it more. I'm going to go back up to Leadville. I'm sure I'll hear the deliquio comments, but, no mind, there's a lot of nature up there. No marmot ever called me anything."

For the first time Will could remember, Kevin smiled, waved and walked off.

Will then turned to Amy. As soon as their eyes connected, she burst into tears and began to run off. Just then, Charlie entered the hallway and said, "Hey, Will!" They both then paused to watch Amy turn the corner.

As soon as she was gone, Charlie continued to speak.

"Congratulations, my boy. I wasn't sure if you were going to make it after that questionable performance in the practical. Man, you sort of sucked in that one."

Will was a bit taken back. Charlie was sometimes critical but never callous. Will recoiled, suddenly defensive. In spite of everything, he'd done what he needed to reach the final. He'd hoped to at least get a few points for that.

"Let's just be thankful I helped you through the written," he added with a whisper and a conspiratorial nudge. Will just nodded.

"Anyway, I need to talk to you about something a bit more serious," Charlie said, keeping his hushed tone. Will worried there was something wrong with his grandpa but said nothing and let Charlie finish.

"I know you menaced Amy looking for information about your past, and I don't blame you. Exemplars are so hamstrung by rules. It's like we're children who can't handle the hard facts. As you know, I've long fought for the rights of OHFs – none more so than you. I firmly believe you deserve to know all the facts. You're a man, right? After much internal struggle, I've decided I want to help. Let me complete your picture in the name of honesty and clarity. It's the only fair thing to do. And I'm going to do it for you. Can we meet in 20 minutes at Mustard's Last Stand? It's a restaurant just down the street. It's probably the only one that was around when you were first alive."

Will was definitely familiar with it. The offer was such a shock and without thinking he blurted out, "sure."

Charlie hustled off, leaving Will frozen. After all this time, he couldn't believe he would get answers. The question was whether he still wanted them.

CHAPTER TWENTY-ONE

Mustard's Last Stand was so very different from what Will remembered as a child. The small restaurant once featured outside space, but now everything was enclosed with signs boasting its cool dining room. And since beef and whatever other animal products they had once served were scarce nowadays, the hot dog and burger restaurant now primarily sold non-meat products.

Will immediately understood why Charlie chose the restaurant. It was within walking distance of the Crucible Compound, but was so rundown that nobody from the complex would likely go there. It was more than 100 years old and, looking around, Will wasn't sure if it had many years left.

So much had happened so quickly. He was no longer sure what information he really wanted. Did he actually want to know everything now? After all, he'd made the finals by focusing. Maybe he should stop Charlie before he told him. He'd still have the rest of his life to figure it all out. But his entire internal discussion was completely scrambled. Charlie was the one person who consistently looked out for Will's best interests. He was smart and thoughtful. If he believed it was time to unravel his mystery, then maybe it was time.

Charlie flew in through the door, quickly walking right by Will to a corner booth out of view of anybody at the front of the restaurant. Will followed and sat down.

"Thanks for coming, Will," Charlie said looking him in the eyes. He then took off his glasses and rubbed the bridge of his nose.

"I've been wrestling with so much for the past six weeks. You just don't know," he said.

Actually, Will thought, he was pretty familiar with dealing with a lot over the past six weeks.

"Well, let's start. You are aware that I was instrumental in getting you this opportunity. I knew your grandfather, and I could tell from the first day I met him what a good man he was. I fought all the way to the highest court in the land for you. But did you ever stop to think why you? Why should you get a second chance? Or why you're 19 and every other Exemplar in the Crucible is 21?" Did you ask yourself why your case got all the way to the Supreme Court?"

Of course, he had. A day hadn't gone by in which so many of those questions didn't haunt him. The one exception might have been the court case. He realized he hadn't really pressed on that odd fact. He knew it was an important puzzle piece, but maybe he had neglected pushing for more information about it because he was focused on other aspects of his past. Now, as Charlie began to lay out what weighed so heavily on Will's mind, he wanted all the answers. Every doubt he held about avoiding his past melted away.

"I have, and I'm ready to learn what's missing from my memory," Will said.

Charlie took a deep breath. He never told a story quickly, and this one really deserved a little time. He began with a history lesson. Like every country worldwide, the U.S. embraced the idea of the Crucible to assist in maintaining population equilibrium. But in order to allow for the creation of OHFs and the Crucible in this country, the states ratified the 29th Amendment, which was widely known as the Exemplar Amendment.

For the most part, it left the details of the Crucible criteria and construction to the states. But there were a few rules that everyone had to follow, he said. There would be a lottery rather than letting districts pick last remainders for the Crucible. And those lottery-winning families would only be given *one* chance at re-initiating its bloodline. There were no second chances. The other major rule is that anyone charged with a felony crime would be prohibited from being an Exemplar.

"I don't know any easy way to say it, Will," Charlie said, slowing down. "But you were a criminal of the highest order. The reason you don't know it is, well, it is traumatic. But here we go. I'm determined to give you the full story."

Will wanted Charlie to stop for just a moment so that he could regain his emotional balance. What in the world could he have done? But he was too paralyzed to utter a single word.

"Do you remember a blonde girl? Beautiful." Charlie said, breaking Will out of his stupor.

"Yes," Will responded immediately. Charlie had to be talking about the girl in his dreams. As Will had surmised, those images were indeed echoes of the past.

"Well, her name was Katrina Love and, boy, did you love her." The laughing, the rolling around – it all made sense to Will. He was well aware that he'd been terrible with the ladies, but this must have been his true love, he thought.

"But here's the problem, Will, so did your best friend Cooper Fielding. It was the classic love triangle. As girls went, it was understandable. Unfortunately, you were more emotional about it than you could handle. You and Cooper went on a camping trip near the South Platte River during winter break of your sophomore year and BANG!"

When Charlie said BANG, Will jumped. Charlie had been whispering until he said that word and it startled Will.

"You were tried for first degree murder in the death of Cooper Fielding, sentenced and executed by lethal injection nine months after your 20th birthday."

Charlie offered this hammer of a newsflash without any emotion. He looked into Will's eyes for some response. But Will's eyes glazed over. Earlier everything had gone blank in joy when he found out he'd qualified for the Gauntlet. Now his mind was going vacant for the completely opposite reason.

"I thought I should tell it to you like taking off a band-aid – quick and straight," Charlie added, again aiming for a reaction, but receiving none.

Coop's face flashed before Will. All his memories of his best friend were positive. Beyond yearning for deeper support from his grandpa, Coop was the one person he wished he had by his side. He knew nothing of a love triangle and couldn't recall a single fight between the two. Without thinking he began shaking his head as if to say, "no."

"I'm sad to tell you, it's all true," Charlie said responding to Will's gesture.

"Then why did you represent me in the first place?" Will couldn't wrap himself around nearly anything he'd been told, but that was the first question that came to mind.

"You know, public defenders are always asked that. I do believe that every person deserves due process under the law. That concept is enshrined in the Constitution as much as the Exemplar Amendment. At the time, I was fixated on what it meant for OHF rights in general. If you gave your bloodline the best chance at re-initiation, well, it didn't seem fair to force your ancestors to carry the burdens of your crimes. But..."

Charlie trailed off and looked down at the table.

"Look, I've gotten to know this Will Herndon," Charlie continued. "He is a man of high moral integrity. And, your original version did deny his role in the crime until the final day – even if the original evidence proved his criminal involvement. I love your grandpa so I fought to bring you back because I *was* convinced it was the right thing to do. An Exemplar reflects the best genes, and, despite it all, your original version represented that for your family. It wasn't fair. But I can't lie, I've had my own misgivings, and, if you win, I don't know. I don't know what it would say about society. In law, we talk about the slippery slope. You allow this and what's next? I worry I may have made a mistake. I needed to unburden myself. Please accept my apology."

Will acted dazed for what seemed like an eternity. Finally, whatever Charlie was hoping to get, he seemed satisfied and he spoke again.

"I hate putting pressure on you, but take it all in and do what you feel is right. I have no doubts you will act appropriately. Think about what this means to OHFs and society in general. Maybe just going away in some manner would be best."

Charlie let his words sink in before quietly saying, "Anyway, I need to go before anyone sees us here. Do what's right."

He walked off, leaving Will all alone. So much was banging around in Will's mind that he couldn't concentrate on any one thought.

Moments later, Will began to hear the sounds of the other patrons again. Some were laughing. It made him sick. He needed to be alone. He got up and sprinted out of the restaurant. His head down and his eyes fixed on the floor, Will ignored the other patrons, wanting only to escape Mustard's Last Stand without seeing or being seen.

Thankfully for Will, both he and Charlie had been so engrossed in the conversation and left so abruptly that neither noticed a hooded figure in an adjoining booth listening intently.

CHAPTER TWENTY-TWO

Will wasn't quite sure how he made it back to his room at the Crucible Compound. His head hurt so badly as he tried to force his mind to unlock what happened. At his core, he couldn't believe any of what he'd heard was true. Everything he remembered and knew about Coop and their relationship, compelled him to think otherwise. It didn't feel right.

Then again, the vision of Katrina Love kept bouncing in his mind. He undeniably possessed feelings for her. There was no way around that. But the gauze over those emotions made it feel like he was trying to comprehend a language he didn't understand.

Charlie was such a good friend to him and his grandpa. What it must have taken to wrestle with his conflicted feelings for so long, Will thought. His mind bounced all over the place. It was 2090, but to him – with the exception of the past six weeks – it was still 2025. Coop was his best friend. The more he tried to clarify everything, the more he felt like he was going crazy.

What was the right thing to do now? If he killed his best friend, how could he possibly deserve to be here. He began to get angry at his grandpa. How in the world could Deacon have rationalized that Will should come back after such an atrocity? His grandfather should have known him better than to think Will would take this news and feel comfortable continuing on. It was ludicrous and whatever he decided right there and then, he couldn't imagine ever talking to his grandpa again. But even that determination made him sick. Was he overreacting or was that type of cold-hearted decision some sort of proof that the cloning process limited an OHF's empathy? Or even worse: That he was malignant just like the original Will?

The darkness descending over Will's mind was like a great cloud obscuring the sun. It was now clear why everyone was trying to hide his hideous nature. How could Amy even talk to him, knowing what a monster he was? He looked at the family picture Deacon had given him at Christmas hanging on the wall. It all made sense why his mom had died early and his brother Royce couldn't face the world. It was his fault. How could he have done it to *them*, let alone Coop?

He fixated for a moment on Coop and his parents and family. Besides Will, all those who really knew him were surely dead by now. Why didn't they bring Coop back? Will's promise as a human being was microscopic compared to Coop's. Will was the better athlete, but Coop was the better person. He was sincerely kind to everyone and was an overachiever in all the best senses of the word.

But, of course, that was a foolish statement because he couldn't imagine that Coop's rich bloodline had ever come close to being severed.

"I'm so dumb," Will thought. "It's just more proof I shouldn't be here."

His eyes shifted to some additional cord left over from putting up the photo. Maybe he could use it for another purpose, a more useful purpose – at least as far as society was concerned. He took the wire in his hand. It was sturdy and long enough. He could easily use it for what he was thinking. For all the sins of his former self that he was carrying, it seemed a proper course to consider.

"Act appropriately" were Charlie's words. Will assumed this wasn't what he meant, but maybe it was nevertheless the truly appropriate act. His genes were corrupted. There was no reason to bring them back into this world – let alone procreate with them.

He held the cord tight in his hand and squeezed his eyes shut as tightly as he could. Nobody would ever understand his pain. Why not end it? He'd heard all the stories about deliquios taking their lives. He'd just be another forgotten statistic. He stood for nearly an hour weighing his future.

When it came to harming himself, perhaps the only obstacle preventing such a rash action was that he was so tired. He was exhausted physically and mentally and just couldn't debate with himself anymore. He sat on the bed and then laid down. He knew what he had to do. He promised himself he was up to it. But before he could act, he was asleep.

When he woke, it was dark. His body was relaxed and limp and, for just a second, Will wondered whether what Charlie told him was a dream. Not a realistic one like all those with Katrina Love, but one of those wispy types that quickly floats away.

He sat up and ran everything over in his head again. He was a pro at playing devil's advocate whenever he had an issue in his life. It was his problem-solving technique. He'd always tell Coop, "There isn't a problem unless you have a solution." What he meant was that instead of complaining, a person needed to focus on figuring out how to deal with the issue. To get there, he'd go about brainstorming every contrary idea or explanation he could think of until he came up with one that worked.

In this case, the obvious defense was that he – Will Herndon, the OHF – was *not* the same as Will Herndon 1.0. Since the instant he was conceived in a Canadian laboratory to this very moment, he had done nothing wrong. His knee jerk reaction on the mountain was to save Kevin. He'd had moments of anger, but this version of Will would never hurt anyone. He knew that as an article of faith. Yet, maybe somewhere in the darkest recesses of his being, there was some dormant monster waiting to be unleashed.

"No," he said out loud.

Will, who had held the cord throughout his nap, let it drop to the floor. He looked at the metallic rope and resolved that he wouldn't need it. Will was here now. Like Kevin, who'd lamented his return to the world but embraced survival when faced with his mortality, Will was compelled to do the same thing.

Instead, a different bold action was needed. He would drop out of the Crucible. Maybe he was different, but the core of his DNA was not. If victory meant giving his useless genes life again, he wanted no part of that. Even more so, he didn't want to give his grandpa that satisfaction. Maybe being a deliquio would be the penance he deserved. It would be a heavy load around his neck that he would carry for Coop.

Will felt good about the decision. He'd talk to Kathy in the morning. He wouldn't go into details. There was no reason for it. He was sure Chief Marks would be thrilled. There would be no spectacle of the Gauntlet, but Will didn't care. For the moment, the decision took a weight off his shoulders. It was late and maybe he could go back to sleep.

A knock on the door broke his deep concentration.

"Who is it?" he asked.

Another knock. Nobody ever knocked on his door in the compound before, and it was so late.

He got up and opened it.

Standing in the hallway was Amy. As soon as she saw an opening she ran into Will's room.

"What are you doing here?"

"Had to run in quickly. Fraternization between Exemplars isn't allowed. Although, I guess now that I'm a loser, what's the big deal."

The last time he'd seen Amy, she'd run off crying. But she now seemed deeply composed.

"You still haven't answered what you're doing here."

"Well, Junior, I think you need to be educated." Will could tell that Amy was trying to keep it light. She could grasp that Will was heartbroken and she wanted to pick him up.

Will was in no mood.

"I'm sorry you lost today. Quite honestly, I wish you'd won, but maybe I could help. I'm quitting the competition tomorrow, and I'll push for them to reinstate you."

He hadn't thought of this solution before, but there was an elegance to it. Before his crisis of conscience, Charlie helped navigate Will to success. He helped Will cheat. This act could right that wrong.

Amy mulled over Will's proposal for a few moments. It was tantalizing. She believed in her heart she could beat Trent, but quickly discarded such a choice.

"I know exactly why you're saying this, and it's just all wrong."

He stared at her, puzzled. With their time overlap, she had to know what he'd done. And knowing the truth, why would she want to dissuade him?

Amy explained that she'd turned the corner crying after she lost when she heard Charlie come out to talk to Will. Something in his voice told her to stop, and she overheard him say that he planned to tell Will everything. It struck her as very odd, and she was compelled to find out what exactly was going to be said. She snuck into Mustard's Last Stand and hid in a booth next to them. She heard everything.

"How's that possible?!? I didn't see you in ...." He stopped remembering his haste in escaping the restaurant unseen. "But you already knew all that, didn't you?" Will added, changing tact. He was embarrassed about what he'd done, even though Amy had admitted to being aware of his awful past.

"Well, yes and no," she responded quickly. "Will, Mr. Reed didn't tell you the whole story."

Will cocked his head. It was like he hadn't understood her.

"He lied?"

"No. I suppose everything Charlie said was 100 percent accurate."

"Then that's it, isn't it? If he spoke the truth, then that's it as far as I'm concerned. I don't deserve to be here. I don't want any part of this."

"No Will!" Amy was getting frustrated. But her tone stopped Will for a moment. "He didn't lie to you, but he was selective."

Will listened almost hypnotically as Amy methodically unfolded the full drama.

Coop's death and Will's subsequent trial was catnip for the media, she explained. At such a fractured time, anyone with a political position had an opinion on the greater meaning of the rich white boy being murdered by a working-class Black boy. The discussions dehumanized everyone involved and also put extreme pressure on lawyers to prosecute Will to the extent of the law.

Throughout, Will protested his innocence, but he'd been found in his sleeping bag with the gun, complete with Will's fingerprints, resting by his pillow. Coop's body was discovered about a mile from the campsite and the single fatal bullet to the back of his head matched the gun. After a guilty verdict, Will's execution had been the story of the year – if not the decade – in Colorado.

At this point, Will was ready to throw up. The details were too much for him to handle. He ran to the bathroom and unloaded into the toilet. Amy followed, soaking a towel and handing it to him. "Clean up, I'm not done yet."

"What else could you possibly tell me?" Will cried.

Amy looked around worried that somebody would break the door down and burst in there.

"The most important part: YOU DIDN'T DO IT."

Will sat up and looked at her. He was faint and struggling to concentrate. For a moment, Amy's focused face softened. She slipped into a small, but warm smile. The gesture was like a shot of adrenaline to his heart. Immediately, Will didn't just listen to what Amy was saying, but he actually heard it for the first time.

"Six years after your death a new forensic technology was developed. One cop out in Jefferson County never felt comfortable with your execution and figured he could use that technology to reopen the case. The gun had been in storage all that time. The media made a big deal out of the fact that the 'chain of custody' had never been broken. Anyway, the testing was definitive. The weapon had been in your hand but according to granular DNA testing you'd never put enough pressure on it to pull the trigger let alone hold the gun. It had been a set up."

Without thinking, Will responded with "Katrina Love."

Amy nodded, pleased by how quickly he pulled it all together.

"Nobody ever definitively determined the murderer, but the one name that kept coming up was Katrina Love. You refused to see her in jail, but you never fingered her. When you were subsequently exonerated in a court of law after your death, conspiracy theorists always pointed to her. But she was never charged. Her life was checkered, and she died of a drug overdose two years after you were cleared."

The new information put the dreams of Katrina into context. The facts were like tumblers in a lock rolling into place. Will Herndon was not the monster he feared he was.

He crumpled to the floor, head buried in his hands, sobbing. She put a hand on his shoulder.

"The sad thing is the Fielding family never believed in your innocence," Amy added. "But I can tell you they were alone in that estimation. The scientific evidence was so clear."

Will was torn by mixed emotions. He was pleased that he was innocent but mournful for Coop. Most of all, he was perplexed why Charlie hadn't told him everything. He needed to deal with each of them, but first things first.

"So should I stay in the Crucible?" he asked Amy tentatively.

"Of course! You earned it. I wouldn't take your sloppy seconds even if you begged me."

"But…"

"But nothing!"

"I got help along the way…in the competition," Will shyly admitted. Moments earlier he thought he was a criminal. Even though it wasn't true, he felt like he needed to compensate for those emotions. He was compelled to now be as truthful as possible. "The test today, I knew it was going to be precisely the type of examination we got. Charlie, um, Mr. Reed told me."

Amy laughed.

"Well, call us even then. Before the practical exam on the mountain, Mr. Reed gave Trent a whole bunch of hints. Whether you'd gone off course or not, there was no way you were going to beat us. And, beyond that, knowing the test's content didn't mean you had the answers. There was no way to prepare for that thing. Look, I'm a mean-hearted witch who doesn't like people. I was going to be a loser no matter what."

Will needed to fully disgorge himself. "I also knew the written exam for seeding the Exemplars was going to be on coding," he blurted out.

"And I still beat you in that round!" Amy shot back. "Is that it? Because if it is, you need to get over it. I'm tired of being your mother confessor. The bigger question you should be asking yourself is why didn't your precious Charlie tell you the whole story? He's your buddy, and then he's not."

It was a valid point and one that Will couldn't answer.

"Look I've got time on my hands. I'm in no rush to spend my second life as a deliquio. Let's come up with a plan," Amy offered.

CHAPTER TWENTY-THREE

The difficulty with any plan is the buy-in. Every participant must agree to it and be committed to its ultimate success. Amy and Will struggled on this front. Will was not convinced that Charlie necessarily acted maliciously. The list of things he'd done for him was long, Will reasoned. He gave his family a second chance, and he quietly helped him. More than anything, he instilled confidence in him along the way. Beyond that, he didn't lie to Will. He just didn't tell him the whole story.

Amy was perplexed by his analysis.

"He made you think you'd murdered your best friend! How can you come to any other conclusion?"

But Will kept pushing back. Charlie was his grandfather's friend for years. Maybe something was lost in translation? Maybe he was trying to explain more but, in the moment, he lost his way. In Will's heart, he wanted to give Charlie another chance to clarify the record. Surely, there was a reasonable explanation.

In contrast, Amy believed the goal should be to out Charlie.

"We need to tell Chief Marks because the best-case scenario is that he's broken a fundamental rule in the Crucible: You cannot divulge traumatic information. That alone tips the scales in Trent's favor in the Gauntlet, doesn't it? You now have all those inner demons dancing in you."

The two went back and forth for what seemed like hours. Will admitted to Amy that he didn't think Chief Marks liked him and she couldn't be trusted to make things right (if, in reality, there was anything wrong). Amy appreciated that perspective.

Eventually, she grew tired of pushing back. Will would talk to Charlie and try to get clarity. For her part, Amy, who was now free to do whatever she liked, would use her time to see if she could do some research on Charlie that might explain why he'd acted so strangely.

Light began to trickle through the blinds. It had been an all-night discussion. Amy yawned and rubbed her eyes. "I'm going to take a little nap, is that okay?"

Will ignored the question and responded with a question of his own.

"Why are you doing this?"

Amy shifted uncomfortably. Will meant it as a relatively superficial query, but he immediately realized it had touched a deeper nerve.

"When I lost, I actually felt a sense of relief," she said. "I know I cried, but that was the competitor in me. The truth is I hadn't been myself throughout this whole competition. I may have put on a good show, but I was nervous and more tentative than the strong person I knew I'd been the first time around. The more I thought about it, the more I knew I was acting out of character because, deep down, something didn't feel right."

Amy looked at the ground for a moment, inhaled and continued.

"One thing nobody knew about me is that my last remainder wasn't barred from having children. My family was still on the list of those who could continue their bloodlines. But she's barren and can't have children. So, that meant that, organically, the Pham line was meant to die. It also gave her the opportunity to apply for the Crucible. I thought a lot about that, and quite honestly, I wasn't sure I had a right to be here. But I knew your story. I knew how your life, your old life, had been unjustly taken away. There was nothing organic about that decision. Trust me, I wasn't rooting for you, and I wasn't trying to lose. But it happened. And then I heard your conversation with Mr. Reed. I felt compelled to help."

The old Will never had friends of the opposite sex. He was intimidated. He couldn't decide whether this time around he was more mature or whether he'd just met a particularly exceptional person who could help him overcome his anxieties.

For all of her bravado, Amy had so much more heart than she ever let on, Will thought. There was a moral foundation to her that impressed him deeply. But she was also strong-willed, and the exhaustion made her emotional. Trying to catch herself before she appeared more vulnerable, she added, "And, anyway, what else was I going to do? I'm a full-paid deliquio now. Maybe if you win, you can get me a job."

They laughed as Amy left Will's room. There was no time to sleep. He had his final day with Kathy, and he'd have to figure out how to get Charlie alone.

Kathy spent most of the night awake as well. She wanted to be certain her lesson plan was perfect. Will had overcome so many obstacles, and she needed to present the best version of herself on the final day for him – and for her. Working with winning Exemplars was a badge of honor in her business.

As much as the Crucible was a reflection of population control and public policy, to the vast majority of people it was like a sporting event. The last test, the Gauntlet, was open to the public and took place in a big arena. It was a spectacle that was broadcast around the world. There were people who kept track of Counselor wins and losses. Some Counselors were even poached by other districts if they showed a consistent record of success.

It was hard for Kathy to admit to herself, but she'd been scarred by her difficulty getting a Counselor post. And the way Chief Marks had treated her also hurt. No, she would navigate Will all the way to the finish line, and they'd win.

Kathy noticed as Will entered their workspace a little slower than normal.

"Bywary, is everything okay?"

"Yeah, just a little tired."

One topic that Will and Amy debated the night before was whether to bring Kathy in on the Charlie developments. Will explained that Kathy was deeply loyal, a forceful advocate for him and an excellent teacher. But Amy countered that none of that mattered if she didn't have the juice. To put it another way, even if she confronted Charlie or Chief Marks, what could she do? This made sense to Will, and he dropped the idea of including her.

Kathy discarded any concerns about Will's demeanor because she was so excited to share her lesson on the Gauntlet. The first two rounds were unique each time the Colorado District Crucible was convened. But the Gauntlet was always the same. Held at the old and decaying Ball Arena, which was a popular sporting arena back in Will's time, the Gauntlet was like a high-tech maze. Speed and agility were important, but so was technical skill, she explained. The course was littered with robots, known as Centurions, whose job was to detain competitors.

The exact configuration of the Gauntlet changed for each Crucible, but in every case, Exemplars would travel up three levels that reached from the ground to the rafters and back down again. For their part, the competitors were expected to decommission the robots. The winner was determined by the fastest time to finish the course along with bonus points for shutting down Centurions. Kathy offered a rough schematic of the course, which resembled a three-dimensional chess board. She explained he should expect a big crowd and every spectator would be able to follow everything he did and said in the Gauntlet as if they were standing right next to him.

Rooms in the Gauntlet contained different types of robots. Kathy was quick to point out that these cyborg-looking beasts – there were six variations – were specially programmed not to hurt the Exemplar, but to hold them down for a pre-determined amount of time. They would then release the person in their clutches, allowing them to continue on the journey. It was nearly impossible to achieve a clean run without being thwarted by a robot in the Gauntlet. But more than two miscues and you were likely a loser.

The balance of the day was spent explaining each type of robot Will would face, how to evade them and, equally important, how to decommission each of them. Both Exemplars would be given a choice of tools that would be useful on different Centurions. But, invariably, Exemplars would have fewer instruments than were needed to overcome all the bots. That meant one of two things needed to happen: either the weaponless Exemplar would have to retreat and find another route to the exit or that person would have to improvise.

It was a productive session, but after seven hours straight, Will had reached a saturation point. He was proud he'd stayed focused on the lesson for that long. His mind hadn't wandered to Charlie until right at the end. But once he shifted, he struggled to think about anything else.

"Kathy, I think I'm ready," Will said. "Can we call it a day?"

"Well, I do have one more thing," she said with a mischievous tone. "When *you* finish the Gauntlet first..." She snickered because, while she was always supportive, she rarely made cocky statements. "You will be taken to the Quiet Room, a sealed space completely cut off from the surroundings. It's to give you a moment of solitude from the crowd and a chance to finally breathe while waiting for Trent to finish. At that point you will finally be out of the eye – and earshot – of everyone. You can party!" She laughed again.

No good athlete ever fixates on winning. They throw all their energies into the process and, if they are so lucky to come out on top, it is just a by-product of the hard work. Will knew this, but didn't want to diminish Kathy's optimistic approach.

"Sounds great," he said wearily. "I'll do my best."

"Oh, and one final fact," Kathy added as she didn't want to forget anything. "When you come out of the Gauntlet, your last remainder will be there. I think that's less for the Exemplar and more to add drama for the crowd."

Kathy could tell Will was distracted. He'd only asked to end early once before and the results were great, so she figured there was no reason to press on.

She stopped talking and began clearing her handheld. With Will's mind now firmly away from the Gauntlet, he wanted some perspective from Kathy on the big picture before tracking down Charlie.

"Kathy, do you think it's the right policy to keep large pieces of an OHF's original life from them?"

That caught her off-guard. Will was usually all business. There was rarely a philosophical conversation and he'd pushed a little early on about his past. But this was the type of touchy-feely discussion where Kathy faltered. How to answer? Her mind started racing, and her heart began beating fast.

Will sat patiently. Kathy was so smart, he thought, and he wanted her input.

"I understand the rationale," Kathy said tentatively. "Your job is to represent a bloodline. Each bloodline is different, but to the extent that all humans react adversely to trauma, cutting that element out of the competition levels the playing field, so to speak."

"But that speaks to the broader purpose of the Crucible rather than the responsibility to the Exemplars who are competing," Will countered. "Aren't we human too?"

"Absolutely. Keep in mind that there are no rules preventing you from learning all the details of your past after the competition. It's a classic balancing act between societal needs and individual rights."

"But what if an Exemplar is defined by trauma? Is it fair to either that person or the other competitors to take away a huge part of his or her essence? Doesn't that create an unbalanced playing field after all?"

This line of questioning was starting to make Kathy very uncomfortable. She was intensely aware that Will *was* defined by his most traumatic experience. At the same time, she knew that his memory span reflected a different life. Up until the death of Cooper Fielding, he was one of life's all-stars, and that was what his mind reflected. Could he have discovered some of the details of his prior life?

Or was he probing? He was just a little more than a day from being able to learn all the sordid details of his downfall, and he had to hold on.

"I see your point," Kathy said, trying to keep him focused. "But we aren't the legislators who make these hard choices. We're just the ants trying to do our jobs."

It was an unsatisfactory answer, and they both knew it. An uneasy silence filled the room. Will decided he had pushed his Counselor enough. He was asking questions like playing poker with a stacked hand and could tell the whole exchange was unnerving Kathy.

"Well, tomorrow it'll be over," Will offered blandly. "Thank you for all your skill and effort, Kathy. I'm grateful."

Kathy gave a twitchy smile. The words meant more to her than Will could have known.

"The pleasure is all mine. You're a good person Will Herndon. Whatever you learn or hear, hold tight to that truth. It is self-evident."

Will thought about giving her a hug, but figured it would be uncomfortable and opted against it. He gave a warm wave and walked out the door.

The goal now was to find Charlie.

Will knew the Crucible Compound pretty well by now. He'd go on walks after dinner when it was quiet. Work environments always seemed more enjoyable with fewer people around. At those after-hour moments, there was a calm vibe to the old university campus.

It took him only a few minutes to snake through the hallways and find Charlie's office. This area was typically off-limits to Exemplars. Referees and Counselors had full run of the facilities, but like so many other aspects, the OHFs in competition faced strict rules. Walking up to the door, Will wondered whether Charlie would even be there. The Gauntlet was tomorrow, and he was unsure there'd be any reason for Charlie to be around. He was a lawyer, after all, and presumably had his own offices elsewhere.

Will's answer came surprisingly fast as Charlie opened his door before the Exemplar even knocked.

"Will!" Charlie said with some excitement. "It's so good to see you. Come on in."

Charlie's office was unlike any room he'd seen at the Compound. Charlie was originally a very late Baby Boomer and the décor consisted of a slew of artifacts from that era, among them a Howdy Doody doll, a Grateful Dead poster, a lava lamp and an old TV.

"Do you like my office?" Charlie said, sitting down and squeezing an ancient stress ball.

"It's certainly unique. You like to live in the past."

"Not the past. It's my history. Like you, I remember my first life as if it was yesterday. Now, I've had more than a decade to build new memories, but this period is part of my personal fabric. So, what can I do for you?"

"I want to discuss our conversation yesterday."

"Yes," Charlie said. His anticipation seemed to be building, but Will couldn't tell what for.

"Why did you tell me I killed Cooper Fielding?"

That question was categorically *not* what Charlie was expecting, and Will could see his mood shift ever so slightly.

"What do you mean?"

"I know I was cleared of any charges."

"Where did you hear that?"

"Does it matter? Is it not true? You left out that fact. Seems that was pretty important, no?"

Charlie took off his glasses and squeezed the bridge of his nose.

"I never lied to you, but I also didn't tell you everything because I didn't want to complicate the discussion."

Charlie stood up for dramatic effect.

"I think I told you that I worked as a senior prosecutor in Jefferson County before I moved out East?"

Will nodded. He didn't remember, but there was no reason to protest.

"I was working for the district attorney when Cooper was killed. The whole thing was handled atrociously. I can't lie, there were people out to get you and there was enough to pin it on you. I fought so hard for the case to be properly handled. But I wasn't the attorney assigned to it. I was near the end of my career but went out with a bang. I actually left for Boston in protest after it was said and done. Years later, I was thrilled you were exonerated of pulling the trigger, but I also mourned the fact that it was six years too late."

"So why tell me anything different?"

"Well, here's where it gets complicated. We all knew from the start that Katrina Love did it, but the evidence wasn't quite strong enough to convict her. The Fielding family was so powerful in this city, and they were out for blood. They needed someone to be responsible. What they seized upon was there was equal evidence you were complicit in the crime. If we'd charged her for the murder, you would have been charged as an accessory to it. Interviews and evidence all pointed to the conclusion that you'd been thoroughly involved. I think that's why the prosecutors were comfortable charging you. There was enough of a case there to find you guilty of something, so they had no misgivings pinning it all on you."

The emotional seesaw whipped Will in the wrong direction yet again. "So why not tell me?" he asked faintly.

"Because there may very well be liability issues. You've probably heard of double jeopardy. Clearly you couldn't be found guilty of first-degree murder again. Heck, you died for that charge already. But is it a legal possibility that you, Will the OHF, could be tried for the *different* crime of accessory to murder? It's a legitimate legal question, and it was one I didn't want to open. While I might not think you should be the winning Exemplar, I didn't want to leave you in the precarious situation of facing criminal charges all over again."

Charlie let Will consider that point and then jumped back in.

"Look, if you just step away from this competition, I think we can let this all fade away. Take this as a second chance to rewrite Will Herndon's story. The attention you'd get if you won would make it just too difficult for me to sit on the additional information I have. Help me protect you. I know how physically beat up you've been from the mountain and then the agricultural challenge. We can say you were too hurt to rise for the bell. No harm, no foul."

Will thought best not to answer. He wanted some time to figure out his next step.

"So do we have a deal?" Charlie asked.

"I need some time," Will said. But figuring he didn't want to leave Charlie antsy, he added cryptically, "I don't want to revisit the pain I had to face the first time around."

Charlie smiled. "Also, think of your grandpa. It was so tough on your family the first time. Don't do it to Big D."

Will walked out. He needed to find Amy.

CHAPTER TWENTY-FOUR

Will paced for hours in his room until he finally heard a knock at his door. Amy quickly slid in, clutching a handheld, which struck Will as very odd. Exemplars were basically barred from using technology without the supervision of their Counselors. The fear of either learning irrelevant, but distracting, information or investigating holes in an individual's memory were the reasons given. When Will went off campus, Deacon had to sign a document saying he would not furnish his grandson with any form of computer.

"How'd you get that?" Will asked, forgetting for a moment that he had more important issues to discuss.

"I sweet-talked my Counselor," she replied, setting up the computer. "I pointed out that I was no longer in the Crucible, and I needed to start preparing for my 'new life'. It wasn't that difficult. But I can't begin to tell you what it can do! Remember the Internet? Forget about it; these things now have everything."

Amy began to explain how the Internet had been replaced by the Transom, which was a far more powerful peer-to-peer network. There was greater security and speed than the net, which collapsed on itself just as the pre-apocalypse period began. In practice, it wasn't much different than the Web, but its infrastructure made it such an upgrade.

"For normal users, there are limitations, but, whoops, this baby is a computer assigned and cleared for a Counselor for the Crucible in the Colorado District. Because Counselors play such a big role in identifying Exemplars, they have access to so much stuff. It's fantastic!"

Will was impressed and wanted to discuss it more, but they didn't have much time, so he immediately jumped into explaining his earlier conversation with Charlie. Unlike the first time Charlie dropped the bombshell on him, Will was far more cautious about accepting what he'd heard. He believed it was plausible, but it would take more to convince him.

With that update, Amy took over. She had bombshells of her own.

"I did a deep dive into Charles Reed's background," she said, barely able to contain her excitement. "It was difficult because his name is common, but I cross-referenced birth records with those of his family to identify some important history. Let's put it this way Will, I don't think your buddy *Charlie* has taken such an interest in this Crucible by accident. And, I don't think it has anything to do with you."

Amy started manipulating icons. She worked the handheld effortlessly. After a minute, she made a big expanding motion with her arm and a series of large documents sprung up as if they were actual pieces of paper. Amy cleared her throat and began to walk Will through them.

"In 1920, a girl by the name of Jessica Middleton was born in Pueblo, Colorado," Amy began her step-by-step explanation. "By what I can tell her family was middle class. But I suspect they were strivers and wanted more. I don't know if Jessica was a wild child or just fell in love with the wrong guy, but when she was 16, she got pregnant, which did not go over well with her parents who immediately disowned her. She found her way to Denver and struggled to make ends meet. That said, she must have been determined to have her baby, because on September 24, 1936, she gave birth to a girl she named Mary Middleton. I have little doubt she wanted to care for her newborn and even tried for a bit, but she didn't have the means to do so. All of which brings us to the kicker."

Amy pointed at a letter from the Colorado Department of Human Services dated May 3, 1937. It was a thank you letter to a Peter and Constance Aberforth for their willingness to serve as foster parents to baby Mary Middleton.

After giving Will a moment to soak it in, Amy asked, "I probably don't need to tell you who Mary Middleton's son was."

Will panned between the documents for a half-second.

"Charlie Reed."

"Yep," Amy said. "Records are a bit spotty, but the Aberforths only needed to foster young Mary for about two years before her mom got on her feet. Mary ended up marrying well. Her husband was named Phillip Reed and was from Colorado Springs. Their only child, Charles Emerson Reed, was born June 19, 1964. You see, Charlie and Trent's family have a connection that's about 150 years old. This isn't about bloodlines, but it's about a family bond. Without the Aberforths, Charlie may have never been born."

"Why doesn't anybody know about this?" Will said, staring at the various documents.

"Why would they?" Amy responded. "It's not the sort of research that would be done when choosing an Exemplar as it didn't really have anything to do with bloodlines. Also, unlike your history, it wasn't high-profile. Mr. Reed had no pressure to publicly recuse himself even though his mother was fostered by Trent's family for two years. Unless you were looking for it, I'm not sure anybody would find it. You know, Trent may have even known Mr. Reed's mom. Isn't that weird?"

It just all seemed too strange. Will defaulted to his devil's advocate habit.

"Even if this is true, how can we be sure he even knows about that connection? I mean, you said it, it was just two years. And, let's say he was aware, why would he want me involved? I mean, he fought all the way to the Supreme Court to get me into the Crucible."

"If he thought he could control you and shape the contest, he could manipulate the finalists," Amy countered. "And, when that happened, no doubt, he seemed certain he could get you to drop out at just the right moment. After everything he did to bring you back and win your trust ... why would you ever question him? It's one really patient con, but it would protect him from any questions when the Aberforth family won."

Will thought about everything that was required to pull off such an elaborate scheme. Looking at the documents, the connection was unquestionable. It just seemed too far-fetched. Still, there was enough smoke to ask the next question.

"Should we tell Chief Marks?"

"Well, I'm afraid to say, that leads me to my second big newsflash," Amy said as she wiped the holograms clear and began manipulating again. "This one was a lot easier to find."

A story appeared with the headline: *Chief Marks cleared to officiate Crucible: Connection to Herndon Determined 'Tenuous'*

Will kept reading. Chief Alexandra Marks was Cooper Fielding's cousin. Marks, whose record, the article noted, was "spotless," claimed Coop was a distant relative who was born and had died before her birth. A federal panel, led by U.S. Crucible Administrator Milo Swenson, agreed.

"Dude, nobody was rooting for you!" Amy said, trying to lighten the moment.

"Or for you either," Will shot back and then quickly added, "So what should I do? Do I quit?"

The two began to debate that thorny decision. Will pointed out that if he dropped out, Charlie wouldn't care about the past, and he'd at least avoid the potential of new criminal charges. He also thought that, under the circumstances, his chances of winning were probably a real longshot.

Amy offered the alternative position. Charlie could be bluffing. Will may not have helped Katrina Love at all. Or, even, if he did, the idea of charging an OHF for a crime his antecedent committed seemed nuts. And, anyway, what did Will have to lose? As events went in this competition, the final ordeal was the most objective. Get across the finish line first and disable the most robots and you win. Plus, while Chief Marks might hate Will, there were no over-the-top signs that she tampered with the competition to disadvantage him. Rooting for his failure was a lot different from making it happen.

Will thought about how Chief Marks assigned him to an unproven Kathy, tried to disrupt his lessons and berated him. Still, he had to admit that if she'd wanted to truly sabotage his chances, she could have done a lot more.

"All of this is great, but we're avoiding the bigger point here," Will said after nearly an hour of talk. "What if I truly helped Katrina Love kill Coop? Maybe I should drop out on principle."

Amy slapped a table.

"Will! Whatever happened back in 2025, it wasn't you," she yelled. "We are each our own person. We share genes with some other version who happened to live in the past and we have chips in our heads that reflect the bulk of *their* memories. But you cannot take responsibility for that person's actions, just as much as you can't take credit for their achievements."

"But we're *clones* of those people. If they did wrong, aren't we doomed to repeat their mistakes?"

"Why? You have the same free will as Will Herndon 1.0. In fact, I'd argue that even if *that* Will made an awful, indefensible mistake more than six decades ago, you're far better positioned to never do anything even remotely horrible because you have something to learn from."

It was a forceful argument, but Will's feelings and connection to Coop were real to him. If he'd played a role in his death, he couldn't re-engineer himself to not feel anguish if it proved to be true.

"Whatever we decide, I think we need serious help," Will said. "Can that handheld get me in touch with some people?"

"Absolutely," Amy smiled.

Will took the computer to call the one person who he needed if he was going to be ready for a fight.

CHAPTER TWENTY-FIVE

It was 9:30 p.m. when Deacon walked into Will's room. His grandfather appeared tired. Deacon wouldn't admit to it, but he hadn't been sleeping well. He'd been worried about Will ever since the mountain fire that nearly took his life. A call to meet immediately didn't help matters. He jumped in Mavis, asking the car to "accelerate" on more than one occasion.

When his grandpa entered, Will immediately ran to the door to give him a big hug. It was the largest show of affection he'd delivered to Deacon, who immediately sank into the embrace. Will then introduced him to Amy, who was standing in the corner. She didn't come from a warm family so the hug seemed weird to her. As for Deacon, since his return as an OHF, he was normally guarded with strangers. But Will's hug had disarmed him and he gave Amy a heartfelt handshake.

As soon as Deacon sat down, Will unloaded everything. He explained how Charlie told him he'd murdered Coop, but later shifted his story to say he was an accomplice to his best friend's killing. Both times, he pressured Will to drop out of the Crucible. He told his grandpa how Amy's expert research uncovered two very important revelations. The first was that Charlie's mom was a foster child to the Aberforth family – the same bloodline he was competing against in the Gauntlet the next day. The second was that Chief Marks was related to Coop.

When Will finished, Deacon sat for a moment looking back and forth between Amy and Will. He wasn't quite sure what to say.

"Well, I knew about Alexandra Marks; that was in the news," Deacon said. He was trying to scour his mind for signs that Charlie was playing him for all these years. His friends were few, but he trusted Charlie, who seemed so intent on OHF rights and giving the Herndons the opportunities they so justly deserved in the Crucible.

Will could tell Deacon was at a loss for further words and filled the space.

"The first question we have to answer is whether I compete tomorrow in the Gauntlet. Charlie appears to be threatening to bring charges on me if I do. Obviously, I'm no lawyer, but I can't deny Charlie's a good one, and even if he has a ridiculous claim, I'm not sure I want to put myself – and you, grandpa – through this."

The idea of quitting enraged Deacon. Will had already risked his life in this competition. He didn't care about whether their bloodline continued, but giving him a second chance as a winning Exemplar – rather than squeezing out a meager existence as a deliquio – was what Deacon was aiming for. It was the real reason he ever agreed with Charlie to mount a court case to bring Will back as the rightful family Exemplar.

"Don't give up," Deacon said with steely determination. "Will, both the first time around and since I've been an OHF, I've looked at every document, affidavit, piece of evidence and detective report that exists. I could have told you Katrina Love killed Coop the day it happened. She was one crazy girl, and I never understood why you defended her constantly. But there was nothing – and I mean nothing – to tie you to the crime other than that ridiculously placed gun. Even more, your mind is probably scrubbed of the memory, but I looked into your eyes in jail…"

Deacon trailed off and tears started to run down his face. He was crying, but it was less like weeping and more like an involuntary reaction that he couldn't control. The memory was so painful, and it always surprised him that it wasn't deemed too traumatic to be cleared from his mind. He paused, collected his emotions and started again.

"I looked into your eyes in jail, and I've never been more certain of anything. Willie, you and Coop had gone to bed and Katrina surprised Coop. They went out into the woods and had a fight. After she'd done the deed, she cleaned the gun, got you to touch it while you were sleeping and then dropped it by your sleeping bag and left. That's what happened."

There was such conviction in Deacon's voice. He was sure. Both his memories from the past and all the research he'd done since returning made him resolute about this point. At the same time, he agreed with Will's earlier comment that Charlie was an expert lawyer. He'd been in the courtroom at the trial and appellate proceedings to bring Will back. The argument that a long-since exonerated Will was the Herndons' true Exemplar and should have been given the right to save his family's bloodline over Deacon was flawless. He knew how persuasive and clever Charlie could be. He also was aware of how well he could frame the facts to suit his cause. Doubt was creeping in.

"Lord knows I want you to fight. I mean it when I say it," Deacon added. "But I get your fears. Anybody who knows the legal system can tell you they'd rather have a great lawyer even if the facts don't support their case than have a poor one with the truth on their side."

"We need to make him a bad lawyer," Amy interjected for the first time. "We've got to impeach his character."

"How do we do that?" Will asked.

"Let's assume the worst. Let's say that he wants to make sure Trent wins at all costs. He's probably still hoping you won't show, but if you do, he'll be prepared to use a phrase we'll all know: He'll go postal. We need to catch him and confront him."

"We've got to have the smoking gun that he claims to have on me," Will said, following Amy's train of thought closely.

"Absolutely. If we can prove his wrongdoing, it'll overshadow any weak claim he might have. He'll be so busy trying to save himself," Amy said before shifting her tone. "Will, this guy may try anything. If we go with this, you'd better be ready for all eventualities. And, one other thing: we'll have to involve your Counselor."

Amy laid out the plan. It was simple, but required quite a bit of luck. And most of all, it demanded one variable Will couldn't promise he could deliver.

He had to be the first Exemplar to exit the Gauntlet.

Like every Exemplar, Will was given a special device to contact his Counselor at any hour of the day. Still, he was surprised by how quickly Kathy arrived at his room after pressing the button. It was the first time he'd called her after hours. Luckily, Deacon and Amy had left just in time as this was a discussion Will needed to have alone with Kathy.

"I came as quickly as I could," Kathy said out of breath. "I live just across the street. You never know when you're going to need to be on campus."

Will felt a little guilty pulling Kathy into this. He was also fearful that she wouldn't get involved – or even worse – report him and Amy.

"I'm so sorry to bother you Kathy," Will said, trying to ease into the more difficult conversation.

"Not a problem, do you want to go over Centurion weaknesses one last time?"

"No, I have something a bit more serious to discuss."

Will went all in. He told her every detail about Charlie and Chief Marks. Having discussed the topic in full at least twice in the past eight hours, he was a master at succinctly laying out the facts. It only took a few minutes.

Like Deacon, Kathy was dumbfounded by the revelations. In a way, it all made sense. In her heart, she knew Chief Marks hoped she'd fail as Will's Counselor. It was a classic example of "which of these is not like the others?" Her Counselor colleagues were all respected veterans, and she was the one who struggled to get a job. She'd also seen Trent and Charlie whispering on more than one occasion. With hindsight, it all made sense. Nevertheless, the news made her sad. It confirmed she was a joke to Chief Marks.

And, more importantly, Will was in danger.

While she wasn't involved in choosing Will, she had read the detailed dossier on his life. Never shy to exercise due diligence, she'd also delved into the records of Cooper Fielding's death. She confirmed what Deacon had already said: There was nothing to support Charles Reed's claims. Though, she was quick to add that if he was in Jefferson County at that time, it was possible something was missing from the official record.

Counselors were not lawyers, but part of their training was to understand the law as it pertained to OHFs. It was common for Exemplars to ask about their status in the world. She was doubtful Charlie could get new charges to stick. But she would have also bet against him getting the Herndon family a second shot at the Crucible. Worldwide, it was an unprecedented occurrence. In fact, tomorrow's Gauntlet was the first sold out event of its kind in Colorado in six years. People were flying in from around the globe to see it because of Will.

She fidgeted like never before, her legs bouncing so uncontrollably she stood up and began jumping up and down as if it would shake the surplus of energy out of her body.

It made Will nervous. It was bad enough she now had all the awful details of what was behind the curtain, but he was going to have to ask her to help pull back that very curtain.

Rather than back into it, Will went straight in.

"I need your help," he said to a bouncing Kathy. "I have a plan. It could fail, but if everything goes right, it could take Charlie down and clear my name."

Kathy stopped hopping. She had wanted to be a Counselor for so long, and she'd loved every minute of working with Will. It confirmed every inclination in her body that told her that this was her calling. At the same time, what was this job if it wasn't to assist Will to the fullest of her abilities? If the cause was just, and the Exemplar needed her, shouldn't she serve? Of course, this was all an elaborate rationalization because, like any job, there was a code of conduct. This one had a set of protocols prohibiting malfeasance, and that list surely didn't allow doing an end-around on the chief referee. But Chief Marks could be complicit and, anyway, Kathy's hiring alone proved that even if she wasn't actively looking to thwart Will, she was certainly there to set up obstacles.

"Tell me my job, and I'll do it."

Kathy was 100 percent in.

CHAPTER TWENTY-SIX

Beads of sweat began to develop on Amy's back as she and Kathy first set eyes on the Denver Municipal Arena in the early dawn light. It wasn't the heat; the building was making her uncomfortable. In her day, it was still known as the Pepsi Center and then Ball Arena, and it housed some of her last memories from her previous life.

Unlike the other three Exemplars who were in the competition, Amy was the one who'd experienced the pre-apocalypse. History books say it started in 2038, but like most worldwide events, in the beginning, it did not impact every corner of the globe equally. For a handful of years, Africa and then parts of Asia and the Middle East were primarily hit. It wasn't that other areas weren't feeling the crushing effects of never-before-seen temperatures, but it was that they had the resources to combat them.

Migration away from heartache is as old as civilization. If a region is uninhabitable because of war, famine or genocide, people do whatever they can to find a way out of there. But what happens when a whole continent becomes nearly impossible to live in? The European Union, which long considered itself a sanctuary for justice and liberty, agreed to close borders. At the same time, wealthy people in southern European countries used their money and influence to head north and west where the temperatures were a bit milder and they were farther away from those trying to break down the EU borders. This had a destabilizing effect on the economy, and nations that previously prided themselves on being inclusive and open-minded engaged in cold-blooded genocide on those who were seeking safety in this heat storm.

America watched from afar. As has long been the case in its history, they thought their distance from massive human exodus gave them a buffer from the worst of this catastrophe. Of course, the southern borders were bulked up (something that was already happening for other reasons before this calamity). By 2040, problems in the U.S. began from within. In Georgia, the governor shut down its border with Florida, which had lost 30 percent of its land to flooding. Much like elsewhere, Floridians looked to move to avoid jeopardy.

The United States boasts a long history of allowing free movement across the country. The court system determined that Americans had this right through the U.S. Constitution's privileges and immunities clause. But the interpretation of that document can shift wildly depending on the nine members of that court. Not long after Georgia's governor began preventing Floridians from entering his state, the highest court came down with its landmark ruling in *Shuster v. Georgia*. In a 5-4 decision, the court acknowledged the right to move freely across the country, but gave states an out. If a state believed that "the safety, security and well-being" of its current citizens were at stake, it could close borders for as long as it took to "ensure amity" within its borders.

In the West, this led states adjacent to Arizona to immediately close their borders. Hundreds of thousands of locals were dying there. Temperatures had reached 150 degrees on some days and, while wealthier pockets in the state had built tunnels to stubbornly avoid going outside (people elsewhere mockingly called them "the mole people"), the bigger problem was that companies stopped bringing in necessary food and other key life-sustaining supplies. Some survivalists created innovative ways to grow food, but only the most resilient stood a chance.

The rest looked to flee. It was at the Ball Arena, in 2043, where Amy saw Arizona refugees who had braved everything to escape. While Colorado and Arizona barely share a border, it was one of the few states, at first, that allowed limited migration where the Four Corner states – Arizona, Utah, Colorado and

New Mexico – meet. For anyone with a heart it was an unsettling site to see state troopers in Utah and New Mexico, guns raised, watching as a steady stream crossed between those two states from Arizona into Colorado. But, after a while, even Colorado became hard-hearted. Internment camps were set up, and residents were limited in the number of rations they received. At the same time, they restricted the refugees' mobility to very confined spaces.

The arena served as the home for one of those camps, and, for Amy, looking at it more than four decades later made her shiver. In Amy's perfect memory of the past, people were living on cots and death was an everyday occurrence. With so many refugees trying to survive in such close quarters, disease was rampant.

At the time, it seemed natural for Amy to volunteer to help at this camp. America allowed her family to come to the U.S. from Vietnam, and she felt it was her duty to at least offer some comfort to those seeking the same opportunity. She was always a tough soul, but what she saw in that arena – the level of desperation and fear – broke her heart. The idea of bringing "your huddled masses yearning to breathe free," as the base of the Statue of Liberty famously said, was truly dead, she thought.

While she didn't personally have memories of how America and the rest of the world pulled itself out of the nose dive into oblivion, she assumed that we were saved by two factors. The first was humanity's ability to think its way out of problems. Creations like the Ratzenbergers and new food development techniques surely played a role. But, like in so many other moments in our history, the pure toll of lives lost shook us out of our selfishness and into realizing that our time is limited and we are just stewards for a future generation.

On a personal note, like any Exemplar, Amy puzzled on the fact that her time at the Ball Arena was effectively her last memory. Although she was a spirited 66 years old at the time, she concluded that she didn't live much longer. In this life, she was encouraged by her Counselor to save further questions until after the Crucible. It seemed that if there was one characteristic that bonded every

Exemplar together, it was their ability to be disciplined about casting aside their past to focus on the present. She wondered if it was a trait that bloodlines looked for when selecting their champion.

Now that the competition was over for her, she hadn't decided if she even needed to know more about the past. A bigger question for her as she walked next to a fidgeting Kathy toward one of the unguarded doors at the arena, was why was she willing to go so far for Will? She barely knew him. Except for their physical training and a few other interactions, she'd only watched him from a close distance. But she was so aware of his backstory and she couldn't help feeling like she had a connection. His grit and determination separated him from Trent's uncomfortable sense of certain success. Beyond that, she always loved an underdog, and strongly believed she could inject a little justice with her efforts. And, selfishly, it kept her in the game for a bit longer.

The two women were there early enough that only a skeleton staff was guarding the arena. As a Counselor, Kathy's biometrics could get her in through any door, but Amy was another story. Kathy was aware that each door was accompanied by sensors. If the Counselor was to open a door, and more than one set of feet crossed the threshold, then a Crucible employee would be down there immediately.

Kathy touched a door handle at a loading dock located down a ramp below the arena's main floor. The door clicked ajar, and she pulled open what was more of a sliding gate than a traditional door. Amy stood slightly up the ramp and took a deep breath. She'd need to jump high enough as she crossed past the door, otherwise it would create problems when Kathy walked through.

She began to sprint. She was athletic and, by chance, had done the long jump in high school. She picked up speed. The angle of the ramp would give her some leverage as she jumped. Unfortunately, just as she took off her feet got tangled. She didn't fall on her face but she also didn't nearly get as much vertical leap as she'd hoped.

Amy landed on the other side and immediately made eye contact with Kathy. They both shrugged. Neither was certain whether she'd gotten high enough. Kathy couldn't enter elsewhere because laying her biometric prints on two doors would set off major alarm bells. The other alternative was for Kathy to try to take a running leap, but that would only work if Amy had already been registered as entering.

All this uncertainty had Kathy shaking. She was not a cloak-and-dagger person and whatever stress she was previously holding was now being ratcheted up to unsustainable levels. Amy could recognize that everything was now quickly in jeopardy.

"Just come across," she whispered to Kathy, who was slowly taking two steps back. "It'll be okay."

Amy locked eyes with Kathy and delivered her warmest smile. It was just enough and Kathy walked in. They'd know in a matter of moments whether a problem existed. Luckily, it was dark in the bowels of the arena, so Amy headed immediately to a corner, quietly following Kathy, who knew where they had to go.

"Excuse me," said a man's voice from behind just about six steps after they began their journey. Kathy froze and started shaking her head.

"Yeesss," she said in a strange tone that Amy, who was out of sight in the corner, was sure would give them away.

"Counselor Riley?" the man said again with a bit more warmth

Kathy swung around. It was Michael, a Crucible employee – one of the very few she'd actually spoken with regularly.

"Michael!" she said. This time it was awkward because she said it too loud.

"Counselor Riley," Michael continued. "We noticed you'd come in but our scan was sort of weird. It was like one-and-a-half people just came in."

Kathy was still shaking, but even if she was nervous, her whip-smart intellect hadn't slowed.

"Michael, you know me," she said. For the first time, she was getting the rhythm of the speech correct. "I'm such a fool, always tripping. I fell as I was coming in, maybe that's what gave you a false read? I'm alone. Just here to check things out before my Exemplar gets a shot at winning this thing."

Kathy smiled, but it was a shaky one. Michael looked her up and down.

"No problem," Michael said. "I wish you and your Exemplar the best of luck."

Kathy's twitches and idiosyncrasies were generally a barrier to success in her life. But for once, it was her savior. Michael was familiar enough with Kathy that her weird behavior was perceived to simply be the way she always acted – he couldn't know this was the one time she actually had a reason for behaving so strangely.

Now emboldened, Kathy was right on point when the two got to the Quiet Room. Kathy's job was to lure away the guard at this location so Amy could go in to implant a surveillance camera. This time, Kathy acted as a superior to the Crucible guard. She first asked to look in the Quiet Room. Kathy didn't have the clearance to open this door so she commanded the guard to do it. He complied and walked in first. This gave Kathy the opportunity to put a small sticker-looking patch against the lock as she followed him in.

After five minutes of looking over the small all-white room, Kathy then insisted that she was concerned with the pathway down to the Quiet Room. She wanted to make sure her Exemplar could reach the space after he won without any interference from the crowd.

They walked off, and Amy ran to the Quiet Room. Instead of touching the handle, she took out a small tool and slid it under the door. Like a mini-grappling hook, it grabbed onto the other side and, since the patch Kathy placed on the door had prevented it from relocking, she pulled it open.

Inside, she stepped on a white block and stuck what looked like a little push pin into the wall. It was a nano-camera. She then pulled out a mini-handheld that opened up to show a three-dimensional view of the room. Hearing Kathy talk a bit too loud in the distance, she peeled the patch off the door, watched it close and heard it click. She then ran in the opposite direction of the voices.

Three minutes later, Amy saw Kathy walking by alone, clearly proud of herself.

"Great job!" Amy whispered.

"Thanks," Kathy responded, bobbing her shoulders a little.

Kathy would stick around and place a few other pin-sized cameras around the Gauntlet in order to record all the preparations before the event. None of them would put it past Charlie to stack the deck in Trent's favor more than he'd already done. As a Counselor of an Exemplar finalist, Kathy would have no difficulty roaming the arena. Amy was to find a quiet spot to hide until the public started to come into the arena for the event.

So far, the plan was working.

CHAPTER TWENTY-SEVEN

The Gauntlet was a magnificent feat of engineering. It loomed large. A colossal skeletal structure of transparent plexiglass and polished metal, shooting three stories into the arena's domed ceiling. Its twelve hulking Centurions were visible through its clear, shimmering walls.

Although it was fully renovated in 2074, the Ball Arena was a throwback to a different era of concrete and old-school plastic seats. Nevertheless, it was configured far differently than when Will went to Denver Nuggets games there with his grandpa. The Gauntlet needed more floor space so seats were pushed farther back and were more vertical, reaching all the way to the top of the building where the third floor of the Gauntlet was located. The tech was cool. Regardless of where viewers were located, they could press a button and view a 3D rendition of the maze in crystal perfect resolution. In addition, every word and sound in the Gauntlet was transmitted to a one-millimeter sticky speaker that could be placed just inside the ear to enhance the spectator's experience and pleasure.

Chief Marks watched as a dark light was cast on the outer shell of the Gauntlet. It made the inner contents impenetrable to the human eye, allowing for the fans to be amazed when the course was revealed moments before the Exemplars entered. In actuality, Chief Marks was paying little attention to the set up she'd seen so many times before. It was the job of the deputy referee to go over the finer elements of the Gauntlet. Instead, she had bigger problems.

She reminded herself that as soon as the Crucible was over, she needed to fire Kathy Riley. The other three Counselors were sitting in the suite high atop the arena, looking down on the Gauntlet. But Kathy was nowhere to be found. Even worse, Will Herndon was late, which was Kathy's responsibility.

Charlie was down on the arena floor, pacing. Things were looking up for him, but he remained cautious. The final would start in 30 minutes and, now that the Gauntlet was darkened, the gates were opening. A wave of humanity began flowing in. It was obvious from the slow speed in which they were entering that a long line of ticket holders was waiting outside. Within a few minutes, the buzz in the arena was palpable. Will was the boy who'd faced injustice in the eyes of so many people, and they were excited to watch him in the flesh.

Whether he could make the most of his second chance had become an international debate and, as a result, this Gauntlet was surrounded by a Super Bowl frenzy. Colors were assigned to each of the two competitors – Will was blue and Trent was red. Each ticket holder got a plug-in for their clothes that allowed them to flaunt on their shirts a neon version of the color that represented the Exemplar they were rooting for to win. At an additional fee, they could project messages like "Go, Will, go!" or "I'm for Trent!" Will had a lot of support, but it would be a mixed crowd. While the throng had a decidedly blue tinge to it, there was a strong red contingent, too.

All that said, there was an unspoken rule that everyone followed. Whether a person chose red or blue during the competition, everyone was expected to turn their shirt to the color of the first Exemplar to complete the maze. It was tradition as accepted as fireworks on the Fourth of July. (Although nowadays, fireworks were simulated and watched on handhelds as nobody wanted to be outdoors in the middle of summer.)

From the referee's box, Chief Marks relentlessly asked for updates from Charlie. Each time she called he promised that everything was set. He'd personally checked the motherboard of every Centurion and the table just in front of the entrance featured all the potential tools the Exemplars could choose before entering the maze. Trent Aberforth was on the floor and was stretching. The only problem was Mr. Herndon was not in place, he told his boss.

With 15 minutes remaining, Charlie's confidence began to well up. Everything he'd done had been tough work. Originally, getting Will a second chance was done with pure intentions, but when he realized Will could be the perfectly controllable Exemplar to help the Aberforths protect their bloodline status, he encouraged Jenny Aberforth, the family's last remainder, to begin applying for a spot in the Crucible.

Charlie lacked control over whether the Aberforths would win the lottery, but he did have a reasonable say in slowing down or speeding up Will's appeals. He timed it perfectly, and when the Aberforths were accepted, he was easily able to align the two Exemplars into the same Crucible.

With 11 minutes until the start, not a single seat appeared empty. The arena was filled with a collage of blue and red.

"Mr. Reed, Mr. Reed!"

Charlie jumped when he heard his name called. He spun around to see Kathy at the far end of the arena, beckoning to him. He looked up at the projected hologram clock, now counting down from 10:52. She was surely going to explain that Will wasn't going to be available, he surmised. Charlie smiled and left his post at the tools table to jog over.

"Ms. Riley, is everything okay?" he asked, trying to put on his most serious voice.

"Yes? Why?" she replied, feigning surprise with a little-too-bubbly tone. "I just needed to thank you, Mr. Reed. The transition into my first Counselor position has been a tough one. ByWary, Chief Marks hasn't taken a great liking to me. I know we're not supposed to speak, but watching you do your job so well as deputy referee ... I can't thank you enough for being such an inspiration."

Charlie stood confused for a moment. There was now a little more than nine minutes on the clock before the start of the Gauntlet, and Chief Marks was yelling in his ear.

"Thank you, Ms. Riley," Charlie said. "But I presume Mr. Herndon will not be joining us? His injuries have proved too much for this event?"

"Excuse me?" Kathy said slowly, watching Will sneak behind Charlie to take his position without having to confront the deputy referee. "Mr. Herndon is standing next to Mr. Aberforth at the tools' table. Byware, I should be up in the referee's box! I've got to go. Thanks!"

Kathy bounded off and Charlie crinkled his nose in anger. There would be hell to pay for both Kathy and Will, he thought.

"Do I see Mr. Herndon?" Chief Marks yelled into Charlie's nano earpiece. "Get going!"

Charlie ran back to the front of the Gauntlet. He needed to make sure he didn't reveal his red-hot anger. Everyone in the stadium was watching and listening.

"Mr. Herndon, thank you for joining us." Charlie said with no sincerity.

In the final remaining minutes, the two Exemplars chose their three allotted instruments. Will went with an electromagnetic pulse wand, pocket wire cutters and a vibrating knife. Trent also opted for the electromagnetic pulse device, but picked a roll of quick-cutting insulated electrical tape and a mini-blow torch kit.

The two Exemplars connected the tools to the utility belts each was given to wear around their waist. Moments after getting everything in place, a loud chime sounded. The aimless chatter of the audience went silent. The alarm stopped and the unmistakable voice of Chief Marks filled the arena. Despite the Super Bowl vibe, the U.S. government tried on the margins to avoid making people feel like they were at the Roman Coliseum. Sure, the spectators were given the ability to follow along through technological means, and many wore colored-enhanced garbs, but it was meant to be bare bones. To that end, there weren't fancy announcers or elaborate graphics on jumbotrons. This was the reason the chief referee introduced such a drama-soaked event.

Ladies and Gentlemen, Welcome to the Gauntlet. This event features our two finalists from the 33rd edition of the Colorado District's Crucible – Mr. Trent Quinn Aberforth and Mr. William Michael Herndon.

The crowd burst into applause. A spotlight shined on the two men, and Trent took the moment of attention as an opportunity. He reached out his hand to Will. They shook, and Trent added a pat on Will's shoulder, confidently offering a "good luck, Junior."

There was not a nervous bone in Trent's body. He had supreme confidence that his path would unfold just as he intended. Charlie had helped throughout the event, but he was the one who'd performed and, even if Charlie wasn't involved, he knew in his heart he would have been standing in front of the Gauntlet at this very moment anyway, ready to triumph.

The rules of the Gauntlet are as follows. Each Exemplar will choose their own path and seek to be the first to navigate themselves to the finish line. The difference in time, combined with bonus points for disabling Centurions, will determine the winner. And now I give you ... The GAUNTLET

The dark light turned off and the massive transparent maze could now be seen with the Centurion robots moving around in various rooms throughout the structure. A collective *ooooh* filled the audience followed by applause. Fevered competing chants filled the arena. For a fleeting second, Will thought about how the Crucible was meant to be an important piece of policy. Despite its role in trying to save humanity, people couldn't help but turn it into a sporting pageant.

He winced, then cleared his mind. The two Exemplars stared at the massive edifice. The walls were clear but from their angle, everything looked a bit hazy. They could see Centurions moving around, but it wouldn't help them navigate the maze any faster. Both got in a ready position, staring at the large opening in front them.

"Gentlemen, best of luck," Charlie said. "You will hear another chime and then you will be free to enter the Gauntlet."

Ding Ding.

They were off. The first hallway was long, and appeared to go the distance of the Gauntlet. Trent sprinted right, while Will went left. There were no entry points as Will ran down the corridor. Still, at the far end, he saw a ladder and began to climb.

He reached the second floor, entering a wide-open room with a Centurion on the far end. He surveyed what was around him and saw one exit straight ahead. He then trained his eyes on the robot.

"Aranea," he said to himself. The creature's eight spindly legs crept across the floor with rhythmic thuds that caused tremors through the plexiglass. The Aranea's array of green eyes glowed with an unsettling, predatory intelligence. Will remembered three important facts about this beast: The first was it could shoot a synthetic web. That was its delaying tactic. The second was before it shot, its eyes would flash, giving him a moment's advantage to evade the web. The third was that he needed to get to the back of the Centurion because its head did not swivel. If he could get behind the beast and then climb up its torso, he could decommission it.

Will eased his way into a corner farthest from the door. He wanted to draw the Aranea away from the opening so that he'd have room to get behind it. Will noticed that when he moved slowly, so did the spider. If he acted quickly, the Centurion would do the same. Knowing this defect, Will shuffled his feet as deliberately as possible, while focusing on its eyes.

When he was about two yards in front of the corner, he made his move: a fast and intentional lunge to the right and then a jump to the left, all in one quick motion. The Aranea's green eyes flashed at the move to the right and shot in that direction, but Will had already gone left.

As soon as he hit the ground, he ran directly at the robot. Its legs were moving as it tried to identify where he was. It would be dangerous, but Will took all his momentum and slid on the plexiglass floor under the spider's legs, coming to a stop on the other side of the beast. Without pausing a moment, he grabbed one of the legs and started to climb. The Aranea swung around hysterically, but Will held tight, climbing to the back of its head. He pulled out his small electromagnetic instrument, touched it to the base of the Centurion's metal skull and pressed a button.

The shifting and shaking robot immediately slumped motionless to the ground. The roar of the crowd was a distant tide against the plexiglass. It was a muffled, formless sound that Will barely registered over the frantic beat of his own pulse and the metallic thud of the Aranea's legs. He had no time to celebrate. He jumped down and ran for the one exit. Again, it was a hallway that cut right and led to another ladder up. On the third floor, he jumped off the ladder into a small landing that had an opening to the right and another straight ahead. Without even thinking, he went to the right.

He entered a room smaller than the first one he'd encountered. There was an exit directly opposite him. Seated just to the left of it was a white robot with two green eyes. As soon as he saw Will, he stood up. It was seven feet tall, with a large white body and impossibly bulky hands. On the opposite side of the exit were large blocks and, instead of advancing on Will, it turned toward the blocks.

It was the Alcander Centurion. Its goal was to place the three blocks in front of the doorway, making it impossible to pass. Again, on instinct, Will ran directly for the door. If he could get through before the blocks were in place, he could keep moving.

The Alcander had his back to the doorway, so Will was confident as he picked up speed. But just before he reached the threshold, the robot threw out its left arm, clotheslining Will across the chest. Will flew in the air and hit the ground. Surprisingly, the Alcander's plastic-looking arm was made of a soft material, which blunted the pain of being hit. Still, the wind was knocked out of him. As he tried to get to his feet, he felt himself being picked up and dropped into a corner. Will, who was still trying desperately to regain his breath, sat helplessly as he watched the Alcander move a first block into place. There was still a chance, Will thought, but he was struggling to get up. Then a second block was dropped in front of the door. Time was running out.

Will shook his head, remembering the Centurion's weakness. His first move should have been to disable the robot as the Alcander was generally slow moving except when protecting the portal. Will waited until the Centurion moved away from the door to pick up a third and final block. The Exemplar then moved against the wall until he was behind the robot. The white shell would protect the machine from an electromagnetic pulse so he took the knife in one hand and the wire cutters in the other.

The Alcander bent down to pick up the last block, and Will jumped on its shoulders. In one smooth motion, he pried the back of its head plate open and snipped a bunch of wires that made up its neural cortex. The robot collapsed onto the block.

Will looked up and realized he'd wasted too much time. The first two blocks now sealed the vast majority of the doorway. There was a small opening at the top that the Alcander was looking to fill, but he wasn't sure there was enough room for him to sneak through. Instead, he made a quick determination. He'd gotten points for disabling the robot, he wouldn't waste additional time trying to squeeze through the small gap. He returned to the hallway and hurried to the other room he'd opted not to enter when he reached the third floor.

Much to his surprise, it was empty with a ladder right in the center of the chamber. There was clearly action below as he could hear the crowd offering a series of *ooohs* and screams. He began to descend into a room that appeared far more dangerous than he anticipated.

CHAPTER TWENTY-EIGHT

W

ill looked down from a ladder that did not reach all the way to the ground. Below him was a Basilius Centurion, which, according to Kathy, was the most formidable robot in the Gauntlet – and the hardest to disable.

Under normal circumstances, he'd be worried, but he gasped at the sight. The Basilius wasn't behaving as Will expected. It had long pincher claws, which were supposed to grab and move Exemplars away from exits in a room. Instead, it was swinging them with damaging speed. It was flailing so much that Will didn't initially see that Trent was caught in one of the claws and was being flicked back and forth like a piece of yarn by a cat. He appeared to be unconscious, or maybe worse. Centurions were meant to be barriers to movement, not violent machines. Adding to the odd scene was the fact that the Basilius had red eyes rather than the typical green. There must be some sort of malfunction, Will thought.

Though he was hanging over the scene, Will hadn't been identified by the Centurion yet. The robot's back was to Will. There were also two doors behind the scene of the robot mercilessly thrashing his competing Exemplar from side to side.

Will was pretty sure he could drop from the ladder and quickly leave the room, the Basilius and Trent. To complete the plan he, Amy, Deacon and Kathy had put in motion, Will needed to exit the Gauntlet first. But at what cost? He'd been accused as an accessory to a murder in his past life. He refused to leave any doubt of his intentions this time around.

A large portion of the crowd was now yelling, "move on, move on."

Will wasn't listening. He hopped to the ground and yelled "HEY" loudly.

The Basilius released Trent and turned its attention to Will. It lunged with its massive pinchers, snapping with seemingly impossible speed, aimed directly for Will's chest. Will waited until the last possible moment, flinging himself to the side. The Centurion couldn't stop its momentum and it ran into one of the plexiglass walls, cracking it and getting its arm partially caught.

Using the time it was taking the Basilius to free itself, he ran to Trent. He was breathing. Will considered trying to drag him out of the room, but he quickly recognized that he'd have to disable the Basilius. There wasn't enough time to pull Trent to safety. Besides, his instruments couldn't do the trick. Its armor was too thick for an electromagnetic pulse. The same problem existed with the knife. And, even if he got through the base of the beast, there were no wires to cut. He'd have to use the shutdown code he'd memorized with Kathy the day before.

Will grabbed Trent's mini-blow torch just as the Basilius pried its claw free. The Centurion was just a robot and not a sentient being, but Will was certain that it was now angrier than it was before. Its gyroscopic wheeled feet began to spin as the Centurion swept its head around looking for Will.

The Basilius had a long neck and a wide body. The only way to shut it down would be to get onto its back and then hold on for dear life while blowing a hole in the right place and inputting the exact code. "Suicide mission," Will whispered to himself after going over what needed to be done. Distraction was his only hope. Trying to use the same tactic he successfully applied in the first room, he slowed his movements. With a normal Centurion, the tactic typically worked. But this was a different beast.

After rotating its wheels, the Basilius barreled forward at Will, who had moved away from Trent to protect him from becoming collateral damage. The bot was so fast, but Will dove instinctually out of the way. Again, speed was the enemy for the big robot and it crashed into another wall, temporarily stunning it. Will used the moment to jump onto its back, climbing up its dragon-like neck. He crawled up to the head, pulled out his knife – and plunged it into one of Centurion's red eyes. The beast shook its neck, throwing Will back onto the Basilius' metallic body. He grabbed hard and avoided being completely thrown off. The robot tried frantically to pull the vibrating knife out of its eye, but the powerful pinchers were not so skilled at such fine surgery. Ignoring the Basilius' efforts, which had the crowd screaming wildly, he began cutting through the metal skin with Trent's blow torch.

The bright light of the fire made his eyes water, but he refused to stop working. Once he'd burned a large enough hole, he used his wire cutters to pull back the molten metal. He'd hit just the right spot because beneath it was a touchscreen. He started to type in the code when the Basilius lurched. To hold on, Will grabbed a side of the new hole he'd opened.

The jagged edge cut his left hand, and he screamed in pain – but didn't let go.

He would have likely been bucked off the Centurion, if not for the fact that the beast had surprisingly stopped. Will steadied himself wondering what had pacified the monster. It had pulled the knife out of its eye and with its one good eye caught a glimpse of Trent who was starting to come to, but was still disoriented. The Basilius spun its gyroscopic wheels. It would run directly into Trent, who wouldn't be able to evade it.

Will typed frantically with his one good hand. The code was complicated, and he was sweating. Just as he inputted the last elements, the Basilius sped forward throwing Will to the ground. He braced himself for the groans of the crowd.

Instead, he heard applause. He looked up to see the disabled Basilius. It began its charge at Trent, but Will had completed the code just in time. It rolled a few feet harmlessly and then stopped. Will's hand was gushing blood so he ripped a piece of his long-sleeve shirt and created a bandage around his hand. He then ran over to Trent.

"Are you okay?" Will asked.

Trent had fully regained consciousness. He looked up at Will and then to the Basilius.

"I don't believe it was supposed to attack me," he said almost absent-mindedly.

"No, I don't think so. Can you get up?"

"Yep. My head's hurting, but I'm still in this," Trent said and without another word he ran out of one of the doors. Trent's fans in the crowd let out screams of elation.

"No good deed goes unpunished," Will mumbled and headed to the other door.

Then again, maybe he was being rewarded. He was in a hallway again with a ladder at the end, which took him back down to the base level. Will didn't have an exact sense of where he was, but he figured he had to be close to the far end of the maze. His hand was throbbing and it took all the discipline he could muster to not survey how much damage the Basilius had wrought. But he was sure he could feel blood dripping through his makeshift bandage.

At the bottom of the ladder was a large room with a Centurion. It was Tiberius. It looked like a metal man with an over-large strong right arm. Its job was to throw balls at the Exemplar. They were soft plush balls, but the bot was capable of throwing with such velocity and in such great quantities that it was an adversary that Kathy warned not to underestimate. The Tiberius rotated its arm as if it was warming up and then a ball magically appeared in his hand and he threw it at Will, who did something that no Exemplar ever did – he caught the ball. He could hear the crowd go *eewww*. It was a reflexive reaction. He then threw the ball back at the Centurion with his good hand, hitting it in the head. Will still had a cannon for an arm and it shook the Tiberius' balance.

It looked to steady itself, so Will made a break for the one door on the other side of the Centurion. Will took about four steps when a series of balls knocked him off his feet. He tried to get up but balls were pelting his head. Will decided to stay low and began to crawl, taking shot after shot. They hurt, but worse, they pushed Will away from the door. Nevertheless, Will wasn't giving up, even though he could see his blood smeared across the plexiglass floor as he forced his way to the opening.

As soon as he was through the door, the balls stopped. For the second time in the Gauntlet, he was knocked out of breath. He stumbled to his feet and saw an opening at the end of the hallway where two corners met. As hobbled as he was, he saw daylight and sprinted full speed through the space.

The roar of the crowd was deafening. Throughout his time in the Gauntlet, he never fully noticed the noise. But it now washed over him.

He looked out at the vertical seats ascending into the rafters that surrounded the Gauntlet. Will saw a sea of blue. It was his color and it was in his honor. There was a warmth to the bright neon that helped displace the pain in his hand. This show of respect was one of two indicators that he was the first to finish.

The other sign was the look on Charlie's face: Pure anger. While the number of robots he and Trent decommissioned would ultimately play a role in deciding the win, he knew he'd completed the first task in his plan.

He saw his grandfather standing behind Charlie. As the last remainder, he'd been brought down to share the moment with Will. Despite what should have been an obviously joyful occasion, Deacon stood stone-faced. He was aware that things were just getting started. He subtly brushed his forehead with his right pinkie to let Will know that everything else was in place. He then hugged his grandson and whispered in his ear.

"I'm so proud of you. Now finish this."

CHAPTER TWENTY-NINE

Will couldn't feel the fingers in his right hand. Charlie was holding that arm so tightly that blood flow was limited. Between the throbbing of his cut left hand and Charlie's tight grip, the Exemplar was getting woozy. Charlie pulled him along and Will shuffled his feet, trying to keep up with the pace. Charlie had long legs – he'd been a marathon runner – and he wanted to get to where he was going.

The two entered the bowels of the arena and walked through a series of tunnels before getting to a room that looked out of place. Unlike the ancient concrete that made up most of the old Ball Arena, this was a white Millinex-constructed room with a single Crucible Compound employee standing in front of it.

"Hi Terry," Charlie said. "I'm bringing Mr. Herndon to the Quiet Room. I know it's a bit unorthodox, but I'm going in with him. You know, this is a big day for me too."

Terry didn't offer any objection as the two entered. The door closed. Even before anybody said a word, Will could tell the acoustics were different in there. The space featured a strange hush to it.

"No one can hear anything in here," Charlie said. That protection liberated him as he began to allow his fury to unfold. "I could snap your neck and nobody would hear you scream."

Charlie paused for a moment. As much as he hated Will for dashing so much effort and wanted to end him for good, he was at war with himself, fighting to stay calm.

"Will Herndon," Charlie said mildly. "You're a great disappointment to me."

"I'm not sure what you mean," Will responded in a voice begging Charlie to lose his cool. Will understood the calm lawyer-like version of Charlie wouldn't do right now.

Charlie took the bait, grabbing Will's shoulders again and shaking him. He threw Will against the wall and turned to face the door.

Will feigned puzzlement. "What did you expect me to do?"

Charlie swung back around, angered further by Will's apparent innocence.

"Nobody read your psychological profile more than I did," the deputy referee said in a measured voice. "Over and over again. I planted Katrina Love in your chip. I was sure that when I told you all about Cooper, her demonic image in your dreams would make you fold. Even when you pushed back, I was positive you'd pull out to prevent your grandfather from going through the awful spectacle of you on trial."

Will wanted to keep the pressure on Charlie. He had to keep manipulating the conversation.

"You know how my DNA Match Percentage was 96%?" Will teased. "It must have been that 4% that isn't in me that let you down."

Charlie grimaced, and Will continued.

"Why did you do all this? I know that your mother was fostered by the Aberforths. But come on. All of this just to keep their bloodlines alive?"

Charlie should have been surprised that Will possessed that key information, but he didn't pay attention to that fact. He was too consumed with Will's total lack of understanding of his motive.

"That tells me you're just as contemptible as everyone else," Charlie growled with anger. "Bloodline, bloodlines. What the Aberforths did for my mom and my grandmother is greater than what any blood relative ever did in the history of the Reeds. I told you when we first met how exceptional my bloodline was, but they were all jerks. My mother was fostered by total strangers. No relations to speak of. That's pure kindness. Blood isn't the most powerful determinant of anything. What Trent's parents did compelled me to do whatever I could to repay that debt."

"But why me?"

"You were controllable! I got you to splinter from Deacon so easily by dropping the fact that he'd been an Exemplar. Then you were just smart enough to take hints early in the contest. But I also needed to make sure you didn't get the number one seeding, so I sabotaged your compass. That meant Trent would have the easy road in the semi-finals. With Amy's social quotient scores so low, I was sure you'd beat her at the written personality test. You almost let me down in the practical agriculture exam, but there was no way to know about the fire. It wasn't easy. Still, I got you here. I told Trent to avoid the middle room on the second floor. If he hadn't been such a hero that Basilius I reprogrammed so carefully would have ripped you from limb to limb for your defiant arrogance."

Charlie sniffed. He needed to regroup. He was brilliant enough to still snatch victory from this terrible day, he thought.

"What are we going to do? What are we going to do?"

"I assume you're going to go to court and bring me up on charges in Coop's death?"

It was the one question Will still needed answered. He pushed his lips tight together in anticipation. Was Charlie distracted enough to tell him the truth?

"Silly, silly boy. That was all a ruse. I had nothing on you that we all didn't already know about Cooper Fielding's death. You were as innocent as that boy."

Will clenched his bloody fist in joy. No matter what else Charlie Reed threw at him, it didn't matter.

"But I'll still get my way," Charlie said haughtily as he started to get a bit giddy. "The reason I got your family a second chance was that I have such a perfect reputation. Considering I brought you here, nobody will question me when I challenge the results of this Crucible. Heck, you used Trent's blow torch kit – that alone can be a disqualifying maneuver. Before you know it, I'll not only get you kicked out of the event, and sentenced to a life as a deliquio, but I'll also have Trent installed as the winner. I am a great lawyer after all."

Just then, the door behind Charlie's back swung open and the two heard a familiar voice.

"Mr. Reed, you're now going to need a better lawyer than you," Chief Marks said.

Charlie's jaw dropped. How could this be? They were in the Quiet Room. Nobody could hear anything in here. It had to be a bluff.

"Chief Marks, I don't know what you think you heard," Charlie said.

The chief smiled and pointed to the far-right corner.

"It was highly unorthodox, but Ms. Riley installed a nano-camera and speaker in the room. Under any other circumstances, it would be a fire-able offense, perhaps a felony. But clearly, at much danger to her position, she knew what she was doing."

Charlie attempted to pivot.

"Well then, I suspect you misconstrued the meaning of this conversation," Charlie snorted.

"I don't believe I did," Chief Marks shot back in her signature staccato tone.

She opened her hand. In it was a small box. Chief Marks touched it, and the device opened up. Laying flat in her hand was a mini-handheld. She began to manipulate icons until she found what she was looking for and pressed the hologram.

Charlie' eyes widened.

"Where did you get this?" he asked.

"Counselor Kathy Reed with the assistance of Exemplar Amy Pham created a surveillance perimeter," Will interjected. He was grandstanding. It was something he wouldn't normally do, but he needed Charlie to know he didn't get the best of him. "As you can see from this footage, we have proof you tampered with the Basilius. I wish I'd known it before I went into the Gauntlet."

Chief Marks watched the footage a second time. The close-up images clearly showed the deputy referee reprogramming the Centurion. Charlie began quivering.

"Mr. Reed, I will ask you to remain on the premises of the Crucible Compound tonight as we determine further action in this case. There will have to be an inquiry."

"But, but…" Charlie trailed off as two Crucible employees led him off. Without skipping a beat, Chief Marks turned to Will.

"Now Mr. Herndon, please come with me."

"What for?" Will asked nervously.

"I need to take you back down to the floor. You've just won the Crucible…for the time being."

CHAPTER THIRTY

For the paying customers at the Gauntlet, the event was a spectacular success. Trent decommissioned one more robot than Will, but Will had crossed the finish line with more than enough time to overcome Trent's advantage. Some questioned what happened with the Basilius, but Chief Marks' PR machine swept it away, calling it "a regrettable malfunction that did not impact the integrity of the competition." The noble profession of journalism was already being degraded in the public eye during Will's day. Regrettably, its efforts to regain trust in the intervening years had generally failed. As a result, nobody pushed too hard.

But that didn't mean everything was over. As was the case with every U.S. Crucible, the results needed to be certified by a regional director. In this case, Chief Marks was a savvy enough politician to know that the cover up is always worse than the original crime. She immediately reported everything she knew to her superiors (carefully leaving out a few of her subtle, but unprovable, anti-Will actions during the competition). The average person wouldn't be any wiser. Still, this would be no normal certification.

A day after the Crucible, Milo Swenson rode the Maglev from Eden to personally oversee the proceedings, which were thankfully, he thought, not open to the public. He'd held the role of U.S. Administrator for 22 years and nothing like this had ever happened. No, he wouldn't leave this adjudication to a regional judge. Whatever the outcome, he'd be the one to sort it out. "This was cursed from day one," Milo thought as he pulled into Union Station. He liked Will at their first meeting, but he had great misgivings about his second chance. It wasn't that he didn't believe the Herndons deserved it. Every bloodline should have its true Exemplar and, when Will was exonerated of Cooper Fielding's murder, he should have been the one. But shifting rules always made him uncomfortable. He liked predictability, and once the Herndons were given this chance, who knew what would happen next.

Still, Charlie Reed had done such a good job of exposing the political machinations that had suppressed Will's candidacy the first time around and led to Deacon being chosen as their family's representative. It was appalling. *Innocent until proven guilty* was a cliché. But even after Will was *proven innocent*, the Fielding family couldn't let go. Arrogance of the wealthy, Milo thought. Because you've had success doesn't mean you're always right. They just couldn't accept what had become such strong family lore, and Charlie proved that they'd initially pulled strings to keep Will buried and give his grandfather Deacon, who was a good but lesser option, the Exemplar designation. That was enough in the Supreme Court's eyes to get the Herndons their unprecedented additional shot.

Milo arrived at the Crucible Compound still unsure how to handle all of this. He put on his white robe and entered the certification room. In Will's time, courthouses projected seriousness through their high ceilings and dark, rich woods. But the fates of the guilty – and the innocent – were instead now decided in small, predictably white, rooms.

"All rise," the bailiff said as Milo entered the room. "The Honorable Administrator for the Combined U.S. Crucibles Milo Swenson is in the court. This proceeding is now in session."

Milo's job wasn't to send anyone to jail. It was to decide whether this Crucible would be certified. Still, because it was the Crucible's administrative court, he did have jurisdiction over both Chief Marks and Charlie, so there was some leeway to punish.

Everyone in the little room knew this. Located in a semi-circle in front of Milo, who was perched above them in a traditional (albeit white) judge's bench, were Chief Marks, Charlie, Will, Kathy and Amy. There were no lawyers. Each would speak for themselves.

"I see neither Mr. Aberforth nor Mr. McNabb here. Why is that?"

"Your honor, you'll notice on your handheld the affidavits from both Mr. Aberforth and Mr. McNabb," Chief Marks answered. "Neither intend to contest the results of Crucible. As you know from the evidence I've provided, Mr. Aberforth is a spoiled candidate. The actions of Mr. Reed made that apparent. While the winner, Mr. Herndon, also has the taint of Mr. Reed's activities, Mr. Aberforth decided that it would be wrong for him to question the results. He has chosen to take up residence at the Crucible Compound and asks not to have his decision questioned."

Will was a bit surprised. Trent had been supremely confident every step of the way. There wasn't a moment of self-doubt. All Will could figure was that such a grand sense of self was a bit like a house of cards. If a guy like Trent was eventually given irrefutable proof that he wasn't all that he thought he was, every belief about himself would tumble. In spite of it all, he felt sorry for Trent.

"As for Mr. McNabb," Chief Marks continued. "He's provided the minimum of correspondence. He's returned to the Leadville, Colorado, area. When told about all these details, he shrugged and actually laughed. His only comment was that he would support Mr. Herndon. I believe his exact words were, "That man saved my life. The rest doesn't matter.""

Milo took a moment to examine a few images on his handheld and then looked up at Amy.

"Ms. Pham, beyond Mr. McNabb, who has relinquished his rights in his proceeding, you possessed the cleanest hands throughout the Crucible. What is your position?"

"I'm in support of Mr. Herndon, your honor."

Milo put his elbows on the table in front of him and ran his hands through his lightly graying hair. His job would have been easy if just one of the other Exemplars simply contested the results. The standard of review was clear – any verifiable tampering triggered either a replay of the Crucible or, at the judge's discretion, naming an alternative winner. With Kevin and Trent both showing complete disinterest in a replay, Amy could easily be chosen the winner. She'd been advantaged somewhat by Charlie's advice to Trent before the mountain test, but Milo could see past that fact because she indirectly gained from the information. In the administrator's mind, Amy had a reasonably clear shot.

"Ms. Pham, you realize that if you protest this Crucible, it could be deeply advantageous to you?" Milo said, trying to clear the path for a reconsideration.

"I'm fully aware. But the truth of the matter is I don't believe the results would be any different without all those shenanigans, and I'm at peace accepting the outcome."

"I never," Milo said. It was an uncharacteristic outburst for an unparalleled moment. Nobody had ever been willing to take the mantle of a deliquio before if that person could avoid it. Her actions were deeply disorienting for Milo, but he figured it wasn't his job to decide her motives.

"Fine. This leaves me in an awkward situation," an exasperated Milo said. "With no Exemplar to challenge the results, the standard of review now shifts. If an Exemplar questions the results, even mild misconduct can trigger a decision of no certification. But since I don't have an Exemplar who is willing to fight, I must now judge the facts of this Crucible based on a different set of considerations: The best interest of the community, country and worldwide Crucible."

He looked at each of the participants. Nobody in the room was completely innocent here. Even Kathy, who was shaking in her seat, had meddled with the Quiet Room, breaking rules.

"Now, this leaves me with an impossible decision," Milo continued. "If these proceedings are made public, Mr. Reed would surely go to prison. I suspect Chief Marks would be voted out of office. Ms. Riley would lose her job, and, with all the public outcry, I can't imagine Mr. Herndon would be allowed to continue as a victorious Exemplar. A very difficult situation, I'd say."

"Chief Marks, what's your perspective on all this?"

Chief Marks, who always had perfect posture, stood up for added effect.

"Your honor, I've been an elected representative in the Crucible for four terms. I've overseen approximately a dozen of these events. Like you, I've never experienced any like this, and I can say this has not been my finest hour. I admit I judged William Herndon. I was not a part of any past efforts to prevent his candidacy as an Exemplar, but I'd be a liar if I didn't say that I shared the sentiments of my family. My constant thought was that he was a blight on an otherwise insignificant bloodline. But I have watched him throughout these trials."

She stopped for a moment. Everyone in the room could tell this level of self-reflection was out of character for Chief Marks. That fact amplified the impact of her words.

"Whatever happened in 2025. This man. This William Herndon is honorable. He is brave and tenacious. He faced obstacles both in his tampered memory and, physically, in the Crucible that are unparalleled in my career. His victory deserves to be certified."

Silence filled the small room. Chief Marks sat back down assuming her perfect posture again.

"I see," Milo said slowly, visibly trying to buy time as he thought. "If the standard is the best interest of the community, country and Crucible, then I intend to certify this Crucible. The details here are wretched. There's no doubt about it, but the damage that this mess could have beyond this district is far greater."

Will was relieved more than he was elated. He'd taken chances to uncover Charlie's action. More than anything, he didn't want to see either Amy or Kathy get in trouble. He hoped this decision would assure they'd get a pass.

"Okay," Milo said in a loud voice. "This finding doesn't mean I haven't forgotten about you, Mr. Reed."

"Your honor, I will not dispute your determination," Charlie groveled. "But, as you said, we have a standard to uphold and any additional adjudication on this matter would be catastrophic to the integrity of the Crucible. Let's look at the bigger picture."

"That may be true, Mr. Reed, but I don't really care." Milo wanted to scare Charlie, and it worked as Charlie let out an audible squeak.

"Mr. Reed, you know that there is no statute of limitations when it comes to Crucible? You could still be charged with crimes for your actions in this Crucible years from now – even if I don't do anything today."

"Yes sir," Charlie responded in an unnaturally high-pitched tone.

"I'm not going to send you to jail, but for you to avoid it, I will be requiring your next biggest nightmare. You will have to give up your license to practice law. If I ever see or hear of you serving as an attorney in a courtroom, you better get ready for prison. You will also leave Denver. I suggest you return to the Northeast, the home of your first version in his later years. Go back and leave these people alone. I don't want to hear you speaking on OHF issues again. They deserve a better spokesperson than you. Now and forever. Finally, and most importantly, I rescind the right you won in The Crucible when you were an Exemplar. You *will not* continue the Reed bloodline. You've forfeited that opportunity now and forever."

"But…" Charlie still had some fight in him.

"BUT NOTHING," Milo yelled. He wanted Charlie to realize he'd played his final cards. He'd lost. The tone of the judge's voice did the trick.

"Yes sir," he said submissively. "I will adhere to your terms."

"Good. There will be no further punishment for Chief Marks or Ms. Riley. I might question some of your judgment, but nothing rises to an actionable offense."

He then turned his attention to Amy and Will.

"Ms. Pham. I can't figure out whether you're a fool or the most honorable person in this room. I'm an optimist so I choose the latter. I wish you all the best this world has to offer. I know it won't be easy with your new status. As for you Mr. Herndon, there is no denying that you gave both the Crucible and the Gauntlet the full meaning of their names. You made mistakes, but under the circumstances, they are forgivable. Please make the most of this opportunity."

Milo cleared his throat. It wasn't the most elegant outcome, but it would work.

"Then we're done here," he said. "I hereby certify William Michael Herndon as victor of the Second Crucible of 2090, 33rd for the District of Colorado."

Milo stood and hurried out of the room. He never wanted to hear about any of this again.

Will looked at Amy, who gave him a reassuring head nod. Kathy came to him and went for a high five. Will didn't want to do it, but also didn't want to let Kathy down so he connected. By the time he'd completed the gesture. Chief Marks had already walked out, but Charlie was still sitting in his chair. Kathy and Amy filtered out after a brief chat, leaving Will and Charlie as the last two in the room. There would be one more dramatic confrontation.

"You were right about bloodlines," Will said.

Charles looked up absently. "Huh?"

"If there's one thing I've learned in this 2090 world, it's that we've all been conditioned to think bloodlines are everything. But the real relationships that bind don't necessarily depend on blood."

"Great," Charlie said sarcastically. "Glad you see it my way."

He looked up for a moment and shifted to a more earnest tone.

"You may not get it, but I believe in honor," Charlie said, pleading his case. "What I was doing was the honorable thing."

"For whom?"

"For my mom and my grandmother. For the Aberforths. For the people I loved and had proved themselves in my universe."

"But by any means? The risk – and the damage to others – just wasn't greater than the reward."

Charlie laughed.

"Will, you're so naïve. It's easy to say that now that I've failed. But if I'd succeeded it would have all been worth it. And now what? Everything that makes me who I am is gone. I can't have children. I can't be a lawyer. I can't be in the public square to advocate for OHFs! You've done us all a disservice."

It was hard not to feel sorry for Charlie. His ego was his freefall, and Will was certain that his new life would, indeed, be a fate worse than prison. But, on the balance, the results certainly were just.

"Believe what you need to believe, Charlie. I just don't have to do the same. Best of luck in the Northeast."

Will walked away. He would never give Charlie Reed another thought, he told himself. He entered the hallway outside the room where Deacon was waiting. Will's grandpa had already chatted with Amy and Kathy and knew there had been a positive outcome. But the news didn't tell him how Will had reacted to it all. When Deacon saw a broad smile on Will's face, it told his grandfather all he needed to know. They hugged.

"Let's go home," Deacon said, fighting back tears yet again.

CHAPTER THIRTY-ONE

Holograms filled Deacon Herndon's living room. There were artificial streamers and a sign that said *Happy 21ˢᵗ Birthday Will!* It had been about 19 months since the Crucible ended and the rhythm of a normal life was just starting to kick in.

For weeks following the hearing with Milo Swenson, Will didn't do much other than make sure his memory chip was altered. He'd remember Katrina Love, but she'd no longer haunt his dreams. He wasn't allowed to add additional memories – traumatic or otherwise. It surprised him, but he was fine with that. He'd learn more about his mom and Royce, but there was no rush.

His whole first life and his complete existence as an OHF had been driven by a very specific goal. Now, he would chart a different course. He couldn't help but ask himself what he was supposed to do? He pondered it over and over again. Baseball was no longer a viable profession. But ultimately, he concluded that he didn't need to be guided by ambition, and he didn't always need to have a plan. He knew he had this great right to procreate, but he'd definitely give himself time on that front.

One of the Crucible's flaws was it never accounted for whether the winning Exemplar wanted to marry and have kids. He probably would as he was proud of his bloodline. And, more than anything, considering he couldn't be there for his mom or his brother his first time around, having his own family would give him an opportunity to be there for someone else. Of course, he needed to get better with girls. Despite his friendship with Amy, his generally uncomfortable demeanor in this area remained a characteristic he shared with Will 1.0. One thing was for certain: He was positive he would *not* go for a girl like Katrina Love ever again.

Beyond that, he figured he'd go back to school. While it didn't necessarily feel fair to him, the federal pension for winning Exemplars was larger than those of the losers. He'd have enough cash to return to Harvard, which still existed, and he would eventually finish his degree. For the immediate future, though, he'd decided to live with his grandfather and begin working on Deacon's 3D printing crew. Maybe, it would inspire him to come up with a better housing design than the Ratzenberger.

He'd meant what he'd said to Charlie in the courtroom: The greatest ties are not necessarily bloodlines. Amy wasn't close to her last remainder, so Will took the opportunity to offer her a room in Deacon's house. She had helped Kathy create the perfect surveillance system at the Gauntlet. She had no rational reason to uplift Will, ever. Yet, she was indispensable in saving him. If that wasn't family, then what was?

Amy used the opportunity for free accommodations to plough her money into returning to school. In her first life, she'd worked in investment banking. Now she planned on getting a law degree. As a deliquio, she didn't expect to be welcomed, but with Charlie gone, there was room for a first-class advocate to champion the cause of OHFs. She was going to be that person. She'd refused to get sterilized and dutifully saw her post-Crucible Counselor weekly. It wasn't that she wanted to have kids, but she hated the thought of having any rights taken from her. When she finished school, she planned to start a court battle against sterilization.

More than Will, she had a sense of purpose. Amy made it clear to Will that, unlike Charlie, she was the right person to fight for their people's rights.

"Why?" Will asked.

"No offense, but you *won* in the Crucible. To fully understand the Crucible experience, you've got to *lose*. Do the math, Junior: 75% of all OHFs are deliquios!"

They both laughed.

Will wasn't sure about that, but he was certain that Amy would fight like no other for what she believed.

Now, on his birthday, it would be a small group – just Amy, Deacon and Kathy.

After Will won in such dramatic fashion, Kathy became a minor celebrity and could have found a job elsewhere. Despite that option, she accepted Chief Marks' offer to stay in Denver. Kathy felt the chief was starting to warm to her. When Kathy was younger, her dad always told her to make way for the small victories as a path to feel better when she faced big failures. In the past, her collection of minor wins had done little to prop her up. But she also remembered something else her father once said: Success breeds content. After Will's win, she finally knew what he meant. Denver was quickly becoming her home.

Kathy, of course, was the most enthusiastic about Will's birthday. She wore a pointed birthday hat that might have been popular at a kid's party back in the 2020s, but was an odd artifact now (and completely out of place for a 21-year-old's party). Still, Will was so happy to spend time with his former Counselor. He didn't see Kathy too often, so they talked about the upcoming Crucible and how Kathy was learning some language and gestures from the 1950s, which was at the center of her new Exemplar's timeline.

Following their talk, Will sat on a cube-turned-comfy seat, enjoying its perfect shape. Kathy had to leave and said goodbye. He wasn't bothered in the least that his party had been a low-key celebration. He thought about just how much he needed people in both of his lives. Coop and Deacon were indispensable in his original success, and now Amy and Kathy had done so much for him this time. If he'd learned anything, it was that success was *never* a solo act. People who achieve often forget this, and he would not make this mistake in his second life. Since he'd won in the Crucible, not a day had gone by in which he hadn't taken a moment to give thanks for both the people who had stood by him and for being alive…again.

Will sat comfortably, while Amy and Deacon joked as they cleaned dishes in the kitchen. It was shaping up to be the perfect day, when Will was startled by the doorbell ringing. "Who could it be?" he wondered as he got up to answer it.

Will opened the door and froze. Chief Marks stood in front of him holding a box.

"I don't want to interrupt your party, but I was hoping to have a moment of your time," she said.

Will was stunned. He hadn't seen her since the hearing. He wasn't angry that she was there, just confused.

"Why are you here?" Will asked, ignoring Chief Marks' request.

"Well, it's your 21st birthday. Ms. Riley reminded me, and I thought I should give you a gift."

Chief Marks handed Will the box.

He opened it slowly, unsure whether this was some sort of gag or, even worse, a test. Will pulled back a piece of cardboard. When he saw its contents, he inspected it for a couple of seconds before identifying it. At that moment, he couldn't hold back his emotions. He began to cry.

It was Cooper Fielding's catcher's glove.

Chief Marks winced at the emotion, but she understood.

"I asked myself for months after your Crucible, why didn't you come to me with the pertinent information on Charlie," Marks said, pretending that Will was not sobbing. "I thought I was tough. I knew I'd made the Crucible harder for you with Ms. Riley and some actions on the margins. But, like most, I'm a product of my upbringing and, in my mind, considering what I thought you *were*, I really believed I was being more than fair. It took some time, but, in the end, I rate myself a perceptive enough person to know when I was wrong. I'm proud of my bloodline, but I'm not proud of how I handled your situation. I now know Cooper would have been proud of you. I thought it only fitting that you keep a piece of him to remember what I resolutely believe to be true."

Tears continued to stream down Will's face. The gesture meant a lot to him and, without thinking, he hugged Chief Marks. The chief was stunned. She didn't like physical contact of any kind. But she smiled, patted him on the back and let him finish when he was ready. After he let go, she shook his hand.

"Best of luck, Mr. Herndon. Truly," she said. Then, she abruptly turned and walked away. Chief Marks never lingered. Just like the way she talked, her actions were pointed and then she was done. Will stood at the entrance to the house watching her depart when he felt someone push him out of the doorway and onto the porch.

It was Amy. She looked out and saw Chief Marks walking away. She was shocked but wanted to act cool at the sight of the unexpected visitor.

"What did she want?" Amy dispassionately asked.

Will put Coop's glove on his hand and smacked it. "She wanted to say sorry."

Noticing the tears in Will's eyes, she looked to shift the subject. She still hated too much emotion.

"Did you ever stop to think that you've now outlived your former self?"

The observation caught Will off guard. Surprisingly, he hadn't considered that fact.

"You can now live your own life, my friend. Free from the past."

It was enticing to think that he was starting a new life, but Will couldn't decouple a feeling that he would always be shaped by his former self. He may not have lived that existence. But he believed it was surely a part of him that would continue to shape him this time around.

"Even better news for you," Amy said, looking to lighten things even more. "Now that you're 21, I can't call you Junior anymore!"

They both roared with laughter.

Deacon walked onto the porch with a smile on his face. He was proud that his grandson had won in the Crucible. He told anybody who would listen just as much. Though he didn't say it aloud, he was even prouder about Will's judge of character. Amy and Kathy were the right people to surround him, and Will intuitively knew it. Deacon was so glad that Amy was living with them. She was quirky and made him laugh.

Standing on the porch, Deacon waved his left hand at Will. On it was an old baseball glove with a baseball in the center of its pocket.

"Would you like to finish off your birthday by playing some catch, Willie?"

"Sure, grandpa, just this once. I'm not sure I'm into baseball anymore," he responded with a smirk.

Will and his grandfather jumped in Mavis and took a five-minute drive to the town's sprawling City Park. Much of it was now covered with artificial green grass, but there were still some trees and a bit of the natural brick red grass-AGE. The sun was beginning to set, and the scene offered Will a vague recollection of his youth.

Will, who always had flawless form, tossed the ball to his grandfather with perfect accuracy. He was absent-mindedly enjoying the moment and the lack of pressure and responsibility in weather that was undeniably hot but not completely unbearable. As for Deacon, who was never as good at baseball, he labored to get his throws to his grandson. Even with that difficulty, he was deep in thought.

Ever since the Gauntlet, Deacon had wondered how Charlie could have fooled him. Nothing made him question himself like that mistake. He tried to conjure up reason after reason, excuse after excuse, for giving that man his trust. But no answer was satisfactory. In the end, he figured the most plausible explanation was his love for Will had blinded him from any signs that should have led him to steer clear of Charlie.

But as he stood there, enjoying the quiet moment through a simple game of catch with his grandson, he decided to let it go. He no longer cared. After two lives of so much disappointment, things had finally worked out for the Herndon family.

ABOUT THE AUTHOR

Josh Chetwynd is an award-winning journalist and author. He has also worked in climate communications. He has previously written seven books, including one *New York Times* bestseller (*How the Hot Dog Found Its Bun: Accidental Discoveries and Unexpected Inspirations That Shape What We Eat and Drink*) and an NPR best book of the year (*The Secret History of Balls: The Stories Behind the Things We Love to Catch, Whack, Throw, Kick, Bounce and Bat*). This is his first novel.

www.ingramcontent.com/pod-product-compliance
Lightning Source LLC
Chambersburg PA
CBHW070745180626
46818CB00007B/2993